Books by
Royal G. Bouschor II

Deadly Crossing
The Gimlet Plan
Hot Ice
The Makers Wolf

THE MAKER'S WOLF

THE PERILOUS ROAD TO REDEMPTION

ROYAL BOUSCHOR

authorHOUSE®

AuthorHouse™
1663 Liberty Drive
Bloomington, IN 47403
www.authorhouse.com
Phone: 1 (800) 839-8640

Published by AuthorHouse 04/05/2019

ISBN: 978-1-7283-0575-2 (sc)
ISBN: 978-1-7283-0577-6 (hc)
ISBN: 978-1-7283-0576-9 (e)

Library of Congress Control Number: 2019903531

Print information available on the last page.

This book is printed on acid-free paper.

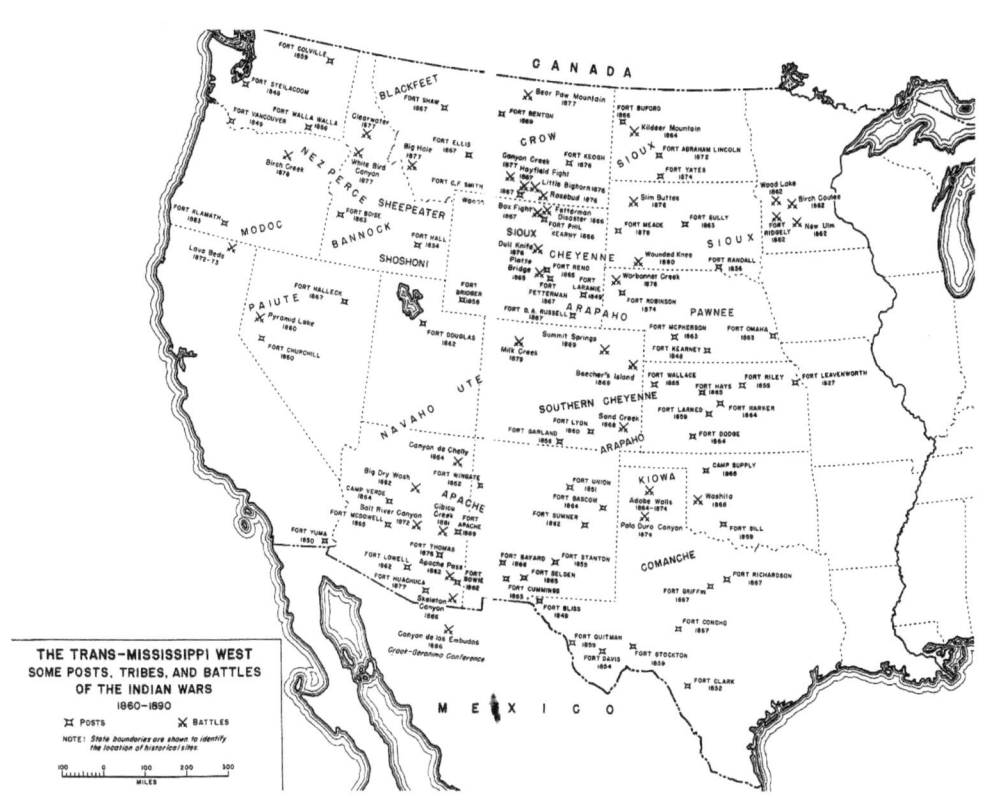

THE TRANS-MISSISSIPPI WEST
SOME POSTS, TRIBES, AND BATTLES
OF THE INDIAN WARS
1860-1890

⊠ POSTS   ✕ BATTLES

NOTE: State boundaries are shown to identify
the location of historical sites.

100   0   100   200   300
|⊥⊥⊥⊥⊥⊥|⊥⊥⊥⊥⊥|
            MILES

The river barge rocked against the pier on the cables that were connected to its river side. It was hot in the bottom of the barge and the air was heavy. The sides were eight feet high, and little air moved in the ten by twenty foot space. It was a humid July night and the wet hull of the barge didn't help.

The wharf side of the barge was lined with lanterns in front of the giggling ladies and working girls who loved this sport. They sat on benches and their "dandies" stood behind them and made bets on the fight.

The riverboat had lanterns all along its side and overhang, and lit up the barge in a grand fashion.

This was Wolfgang's twenty-seventh encounter. Blade fighting was not illegal, but it was frowned on. It was a deadly sport with one of the participants generally being so injured that it was fatal. Wolf had his scars to attest to the brutality of the sport.

What made him successful was his sheer power. He began lifting weights made up of a pole with two buckets attached with a rope that contained rocks when he was six or seven years old. He started off skinny and was bound and determined to do something about it so he wouldn't be picked on.

When Wolf moved his ten-inch modified Bowie knife, it was moved with power and speed, and that had sustained him.

The blade was razor sharp and he had a short lanyard that he could screw into the top of the heel of the knife, and loop it around his wrist and tighten it with a metal bead. If he dropped the knife or had it knocked out of his hand it was back in his grip, with a easy flip God how he loved the action and the adrenaline rush. Being placed in a deadly fray with another man with various skills as a knife fighter was an incredible experience.

★ ★ ★

He wasn't paying any attention to the hawkers, and bet men or the squeals of the ladies on the wharf and the riverboat. He didn't even hear them. He was all business watching the man he was going to fight that night. He was labeled as "The Black Knight." This fight was a highpoint in New Orleans. Wolf felt this was going to be a fight to the end.

Wolfgang "Wolf" Beaumont got his name by the insistence of his strong mother who was of German decent. His plantation-owner French father gave into her strength as she felt her German heritage should be carried in the name.

The "Black Knight" was a former slave who had made himself famous upriver with his prowess with a knife and had come south to make his fortune. His handlers worked him hard and babied him between fights by throwing whores at him as fast as he could handle them. Many of the women were injured in the process.

He strutted back and forth in the barge. He was barefoot and wore only a loincloth and liked to expose himself to the ladies in the front row. He would pull the pouch of his loincloth aside and let his huge horn hang out for all to see in hopes he might find a taker.

He was a tall and lanky raw-boned man well over six feet tall, several inches over Wolf, and had arms that looked to be four feet long.

Wolf looked the man over and saw there were very few body wounds. This was probably the result of his long arms keeping his opponents at bay. Wolf noticed an interesting thing that both hands had scars that looked like knife scars, which probably meant the big ex-slave was ambidextrous and would be a tough opponent.

The fight promoters were busy collecting bets and ticket fees from the riverboat crowd and his assistants were busy selling tickets to wharf side viewers.

The two fighters would each receive a share of the proceeds from ticket sales. Dead or alive.

From the fray of the movement of the viewers, Wolf could tell betting was heavy and he hoped his team was well placed. The odds were almost even as the betters viewed the big black man. He was obviously a dangerous man. Deadly dangerous.

Wolf hoped the barefoot man would slip on the wet flooring but he seemed surefooted and Wolf thought the bottom of the man's feet were probably as rough and tough as a rhino's foot. Wolf wore rubber-soled boots to all of his encounters to maximize his foot traction. This gave him a definite advantage in the rain.

When the big man pulled out his knife in his left hand it was a strange knife. It was pushing the twelve-inch limit but it was less than an inch square and honed to a needle-sharp point. A thrusting dagger.

The big man waived his dagger in all directions as he approached Wolf, trying to make a block difficult. Wolf had seen that approach before and knew to wait for the move.

★ ★ ★

Blades clashed and the men moved in all directions. A brush of the shaft brought a sting to Wolf's arm that confused him as he was not hit with the point. The big man grinned at the first strike.

The men moved very fast in their encounters and Wolf had inflicted several wounds in the man's knife hand, but that didn't seem to bother the ex-slave in the slightest.

Wolf had received several of the stinging cuts when the man

made a dramatic thrust that Wolf slashed away almost severing the man's knife hand.

The big man grabbed his dagger in his right hand and stared at his left. He knew he would bleed out, and dashed at Wolf for a fatal thrust.

As the blade neared him Wolf slapped it to his right, with a clash, moving to his left but felt a sting on his chest, much like the others. He then slashed to the man's right hand almost severing the hand but there was no knife in it. He then backhanded a cutting stroke as he lunged into the ex-slave taking him across the neck. He could feel his blade hit the man's cervical spine in the back of his neck as it passed through.

Wolf stepped back as the big man stared at him and collapsed on his back.

It was then Wolf noticed the man's dagger sunk into his chest on the right side.

He pulled the dagger out and saw it had penetrated about six inches.

It was then that he looked at the strange blade and saw it was square and hollow ground on all four sides to razor sharp edges. It was a true killing instrument.

He flicked it overboard as wooden ladders were dropping into the barge.

It was only then he heard the screams and cheers from the wagering and onlookers.

Two men from his team rushed up to him all smiles and slapped him on his bare back.

"Get me out of here. I'm hurt."

Smiles faded when they saw Wolf's hand pressed against his chest.

They helped him up the ladder and pushed their way through the cheering crowd toward his two carriages where men were holding the horses and waiting their arrival.

Wolf didn't stop or stay for the usual congratulation and drinking and only waived at the pressing crowd of revelers.

When they were underway wolf said, "Make it fast boys. I've got a bad leak here as he removed his hand to reveal the small puncture wound.

"Damn. We real did well tonight, Wolf. Better than ever before."

"Not interested in that right now. Fill me in later. Now I just want to get home fast."

One of the men opened the front hatch of the carriage and yelled at the driver, "Make speed, Jeremy, and go to the rear of the tavern block."

"Get Doc Beaufort immediately. You'll probably find him waiting at the Madam's place."

They would be using the rear door to Wolf's apartment over the tavern.

★ ★ ★

He was on his bed and two of the girls were sponging off his body and stripping off his boots and pants when Doc Beaufort came in and said, "How bad are you tonight, Wolf? God knows why you still insist on doing this crazy damn thing. You're gonna get yourself killed one of these days. You know that, don't you?"

Doc sat down alongside the bed and quickly glanced over Wolf's body. "Not too bad, my man, but you have a bunch of cuts that will need sewing up."

"Not the cuts I'm worried about Doc. It's this," he said as he removed his hand from his chest.

"Mother of God. What the hell is that?"

"Puncture wound, Doc. In the lung I'd guess about five to six inches. Blade got hung up in the ribcage," he said as he exhaled and a spray of red foam shot out onto Doc's white shirt.

"Damn, that's a bad one, Wolf. Keep it covered," and called over to one of Wolf's team.

"Wash your hands real good, Bert and get over here. I'll tell you what to do."

Wolf took another pull on the whiskey bottle and coughed. Red sputum traced his lips.

"Doc, give me some of that opiate stuff you have. I'm going to need it, I'm afraid"

"Hurry up, Bert. Hold your hand tight against his chest. When he breathes in and open when he breathes out. Keep the pad over it when he breathes out."

"How much liquor did you drink tonight, Wolf?" Doc asked as he got a small brown bottle and a big spoon out of his doctor's bag.

"Just two pulls on the bottle, Doc."

"Okay, swish this around in your mouth for awhile. It will kick in faster. Then swallow."

The girl washing his wounds with alcohol told the other girl. "Go get Angie right now."

Angie was Wolf's true love. She worked in the brothel that he was half owner of next door. Madam Gee's maintained the highest quality of all the brothels in the territory, and catered to the very best clientele. The girls were beautiful and Wolf made sure each got a fair share of their earnings and kept the tips they received. The girls were some of the wealthiest people in New Orleans.

Because of the fear of them being robbed, Wolf collected a bag from each girl on Mondays. Each bag contained the cash they wanted to deposit in the bank along with their bankbook. Wolf and two of his men would bank the funds for them each Monday and return the bag and their updated bankbooks to them.

The girls were very happy. Madam Gee, a petite and beautiful Chinese lady said, "Happy whores are the key to success. The men know they're happy and then the men are happy and treat them with respect."

Angie was a gorgeous Puerto Rican who carried that beautiful combination of French, African, and Indian genes that made her a standout. She was a true Cajun Queen.

She also was richer than many of the business and professional clients she serviced.

"I'm going to stop these other bleeders you have, Wolf. You don't need to be bleeding any more than necessary.

The lung is still kicking out more blood so we'll hold off on that for awhile. Breathe deep! Cough when you can. Get that juice out of your lungs. It acts like pneumonia, you know, but worse. Prop him up more Gracie. Don't let him lie down."

Angie burst into the room with horror written all over her face.

"Wolf, my love. How're you doing?"

"I've got a bad leak, love. You make sure you get squared away with the boys on how we did tonight, ok?"

"Don't worry about that, Wolf. I'll take care of it. Just get the hell better. Give up that damn game."

"I think you're right love."

"Look, Wolf. You're a rich man. You don't need to be doing any damn crazy things."

"You're right, love. I think I'll give it up."

"Halleluiah," Doc shouted.

Wolf started to cough and couldn't stop. The room was silent except for the hacking that was producing quantities of red sputum.

"Hang in there, my love. Hang in there. Fight like you've never fought before. We're all here counting on you."

Wolf fell silent as the blood was washed from his face and neck.

Angie was crying and holding his hand.

"Push on his chest, Bert," said Doc. "Just keep pushing up and down. Don't stop. Push hard."

Angie was crying and between sobs said, "I love you, Wolf. Please come back to me, please."

The room was silent. No one was doing anything except Bert, who had now crawled up on the bed, and kept up his steady rhythm as Wolf blankly stared into space.

CHAPTER 1

Wolf saw a brilliant light. He thought for a moment. *'Where's that coming from? It's nighttime."*

Then he saw a purple shadowed figure in the center of he light and smiled to himself. "Efrem, is that you? You've come to take me home again. You've got a purple robe on."

"Well, maybe, Wolf. We need to talk about that. That's why I have the purple robe today. We've got some important business to discuss."

"What's there to talk about? I'm ready."

"Well, you reincarnated back again to do good for others. Your last three incarnations that was your job but somehow you seem to try to spoil your efforts. The only difference now from when you were a hellacious buccaneer is that you have a shorter blade now."

"I've tried real hard with my people. Angie is with me again."

"I know she is. It was her choice, not yours. Oh yes. You've treated your friends very well but you continue to think you're a warrior. Look what happened when you went to Rome. You started off well then decided to become a legionnaire. Not really helping anyone but you, was it? You did quite well until the pleasures of the flesh turned you into s slave and a gladiator. You died by the blade again."

"Well, if they would have given me a sword I probably would have survived to do some more good.

Efrim laughed. "That sounds like you. What about when you decided to go to Japan and help the downtrodden? You ended up a samurai mercenary during the time of the great shoguns. You died by the blade again that time. This seems to be your destiny. Oh, you've had several other reincarnations but you've always been an outsider within yourself and somehow get off track."

"Do you really want to help those in need? You have the skills to do so right now but you always succumb to the thrill of the adrenalin."

"Oh yes. I really want to make good. I really do."

"You're never going to get ahead in the soul world group unless you make a concerted effort, Wolf," he said as he looked around the room.

"Your friends weep for you and they're grief-stricken. You've failed them with your continued actions and loss of the direction you came to accomplish."

Wolf followed Efrim's gaze, and looking down saw Angie lying across his still body weeping. Doc had his head in his hands and Bert sat on the bed in shock. They were all his friends and he had let them down.

"How can I make amends to them now? If you're here to take me now I'll have to return again to accomplish that."

"What if I left you here, Wolf? What if you had the chance to change?"

"You did accomplish care, trust, love and helpful consideration for your friends. You've accomplished your weakness of the flesh to a great extent. You've not forced yourself on others as you have in the prior lives. Your indiscretions with the Willis girl Misha can be partially excused as an immature body."

"I was only seven years old. I really didn't know what that was all about until she showed me. I paid dearly for that and carry the scars to show for it."

★ ★ ★

He remembered Misha well.

They were the best of friends even though she was part of a slave family on his father's plantation. He played with all the slave children and helped them learn many things.

His father's slaves were treated very well. Better than most all the other plantations. They ate well. Governed themselves through their own leader, Ronald, and wore good clothes and boots. Consequently they were excellent workers and made the plantation thrive. Most of them stayed on as paid help after the war, and many who left returned telling stories of the difficulties of their so-called freedom.

It was when she told Wolf about what she saw her parents and other doing, and it seemed like great pleasures, so they too tried "poking".

It was a wonderful experience and they "poked," whenever they could.

He was nine years old when he was in the henhouse doing his early morning egg-gathering, a chore that was shared with the slaves as well as the family, when his father burst into the henhouse.

Ronald was showing some of the younger men how to clean and scrape the floor when Wolf's father lashed Wolf across the back with his three-foot horsehair whip, screaming, "I'll teach you to be "poking" that young girl."

On the second lash, Ronald said, "Massa! Massa B!"

The third lick cracked through Wolf's shirt again tearing into his flesh as Wolf slumped over the rack of hen-laying cubicles attached to the wall.

"Massa B, maybe the boy didn't know he wasn't supposed to do that."

His father looked at Ronald and said "What?"

Ronald shrugged his big shoulders and said, "Maybe the boy didn't think it was wrong. Did anyone ever tell him? The Misha girl has seen lots of that "poking" going on you know. Our rooms are very small. Maybe they didn't know they weren't supposed to do that. Don't think anyone told Misha."

Wolf's father stared at Ronald for a long time. The slave workers, with Ronald, were frozen in their tracks, wide-eyed, staring at Massa B.

Henry Beaumont clearing his throat said, "Thank you, Ronald. I never thought of that," as he turned around to find the egg bucket on the floor and Wolf gone.

★ ★ ★

Wolf raced through the orchard and into the woods he loved so well and headed to the stream to cool his throbbing back.

He remembered he didn't go back to the house that day, but holed up in his self-made shack just inside the tree line of the forest where he had slept many a night.

It was about dark when Misha and an old slave woman they called Trish came to the shed.

Misha was crying, and the old woman Trish was all business. She was the one who did the healing in the slave compound.

"Hush up girl! Let's see your back, boy."

Wolf already had taken his torn shirt off as it hurt to wear it and slowly turned so the old woman could see his back.

"Well you got three good licks back there boy. I've got some salve that will take the pain away and start the healing, but first we gotta clean you up some. You been in the water have you?"

"Yes'm. Down at the creek."

The old woman cleaned his back with a clean rag and daubed the cuts and welts on his back with some kind of an ointment.

"Don't go lying on your back boy. Keep your shirt off. In a couple of days you'll be good to go."

"Not planning on wearing any shirt, that's for sure."

"Misha. Take this boy's shirt and clean it up in the stream and get it dried out. He'll be needing something to keep the flies off. That's the worst part and damn important.

Misha set down a bowl with some soup in it and said, "I brought you something to eat. I knew you'd be here."

She took the bloodstained and torn shirt and dashed out the door.

"I'm gonna leave this tin with you boy. Get someone to put more on morning and night. Keep the flies off you back. You got that?"

Yes'm and thank you. I appreciate it.

★ ★ ★

It was after dark when he saw the lanterns coming through the orchard from the main house.

He slipped outside and dashed into the timber just far enough that he couldn't be seen, but could watch the approach.

His mother and one of the household help came to the shack and opened the door, swinging the lantern around.

The Shack was empty, of course.

His mother was talking to Gretchen, her house girl, and left a pot of stew on a small table made from scrap lumber.

"Damn old bastard. Whipping his own boy. Come on, Gretchen. I know he's out there. Let's go home."

Outside the shack, his mother stopped and turned around toward the tree line and said. "Wolf, come to the kitchen for breakfast early and bring the pot. There will be food for you."

The lantern slowly made its way the quarter mile to the big house as Wolf entered his domain.

He draped the shirt over his back and tried to rest on his side. The thin blanket made a small tent over him to keep the flies out.

★ ★ ★

He remembered creeping into the kitchen at first light and it was obvious the kitchen help was waiting for him. They hovered around like mother hens, he thought as he smiled to himself.

"You bring Trish's ointment? She said to daub some on you," said Flo, the chief cook.

"Yes'm," he said as he set the little tin on the table.

"Let's see what you got Massa Wolf."

Wolf had his torn shirt draped across his back and carefully pulled it off.

"Damn, Massa Wolf. Like Trish said, you got some good licks hack here."

"Bring me a clean towel and some warm water. We need to do some cleaning up here."

The other three ladies were staring at his back all wide-eyed.

"Irma, damn it, get with it. We don't have all day and you two get moving on breakfast right now."

The ladies were all busy and mumbling to each other in a dialect they had conjured up to communicate with each other from various tribes the slaves represented.

Wolf understood most of what they said and smiled to himself at their heartfelt concern.

Flo cleaned his back carefully with warm water and soap then rinsed and dried it clean.

"You're not bleeding anymore, Massa Wolf. Trish's goop is doing its job. That shirt of yours isn't fit for a field hand, though, but I fixed you up something that will work," she said as she picked up a piece of blue linen that appeared to be a remnant from some sewing project.

She folded it in half and deftly cut a slit in the center, draped it over his head, stood back and smiled.

"That'll work just fine for now. It's nice and loose and will keep the flies and skeeters off you. In a couple of days you' be fine, Massa Wolf."

She turned to the ladies in the kitchen and said, "Now bring this boy his breakfast."

★ ★ ★

He remembered that day well as he smiled to himself. That was when he made the decision one day he would leave the plantation and go to the city.

Efrim smiled. "Yes you remember it all right. Well, it's decision time Wolf. You think you got what it takes to go back?"

"What do you have in mind, Efrim?"

"There's lots of evil out there now Wolf after the war. You think you're up to really doing something about it?"

"Yes, tell me what I have to do and I'll do it."

"You'll be what you've always been---a warrior--- but if we reincarnate you this time it's fighting evil not for pleasure or for gain," he said as he stared at Wolf.

"Oh, there will be some benefits along the way to keep you going as long as you do a good job."

"How do I find this evil you're talking about?"

Efrim laughed and looked around the room at the grieving people. Shaking his head, he said, "You won't have to look for it Wolf. It'll find you."

"You'll have to prepare yourself, both spiritually and physically to cope with it in many ways. You must keep your eye on your goal. If you're not prepared...we'll meet again when you fail.

"I won't fail. I'm ready."

"You just think you're ready, Wolf. You read the newspapers, so your guide tells me, and you know what's going on in the new frontier."

"If you intend on surviving you'll need to be prepared in many ways. Oh, you have the knowledge from prior lives right now but you won't remember that if you go back. You'll have to understand the forces you are up against. This time you must be proficient to meet the worst. You think you're up to that? The quest will have some benefits as you go along, the better you do."

"I'll make sure I'm ready. I'll prepare and I'll treat my friends with love and respect. I'll not fail you."

Efrim laughed and said, "You're not failing me, Wolf. You're failing yourself. Only your faith and belief is your protection when everything seems wrong. You know that. Your redemption relies on that.

"You'll be leaving your friends within the year, but remember they will always be our friends, wherever you may be."

"I'll have to leave them?" "Yes, your quest will follow what you determine. There's no hanging back. You'll see soon enough. You'll find your way."

"OK, if that's what it takes. I will and I can do it." "Well let's see if you're really up for it," he said as he slowly faded into the ever dimming light.

CHAPTER 2

Wolf's eyes fluttered and he saw Bert sitting on his bed and Angie crying on his chest.

He coughed and said, "Damn it's hot in here."

Angie pulled back with a gasp and flung herself on Wolf.

"Oh, thank you God. Oh thank you."

Everyone in the room was in shock.

Doc said, "I thought we lost you there, man. You were a goner."

"I need some rest right now. Angie, Can you stay with me?"

"Of course. I'm not going anywhere."

She turned to one of the girls and said, "Tell Gee I won't be in tonight." She then turned back to Wolf and rubbed her eyes.

"I guess I'd better finish up what I came here to do, Wolf. You still need some patching up," said Doc, as he slowly shook his head in amazement.

CHAPTER 3

Wolf stayed in his room for several days and read all the newspapers his staff could find. He knew within himself he had to prepare for whatever life would now bring him.

He exercised heavily every day and sought out people he thought he would need to learn from to prepare himself for whatever he would encounter. Somehow he knew that was vitally important.

The businesses were doing very well and his share from the plantation was steady now that he and his younger brother Richard, who ran the plantation, had matured into a great loving and trusting bond.

He only shared his new perception with his brother and Angie, who were both distressed by his thoughts and efforts.

He was still without direction but knew that would come at any moment.

He had always been an excellent shot with a rifle and shotgun but the handgun was something that he knew he would have to perfect to survive what he thought was coming.

He went to an old gunsmith he knew well and spent many hours over several days to find only the best rifle and handguns to use and how to use them well.

He rode his favorite mare, 'Blondie,' out to a place he had set up to use for target practice everyday. He and Blondie were so close that she knew what he was going to do before he acted. They were a great pair and then he added her stall mate, Ruby, to the everyday jaunts. The constant attention and sharing made the three of them very close and the horses became accustomed to the shootin on or off their backs. They seemed to enjoy the exercise and learned to anticipate what he was going to do from the saddle.

Speed on the draw he knew was critical and he practiced constantly on the range and in his room above the tavern and restaurant.

The gunsmith had told him that most encounters with gunfighters he heard about, was within five yards so Wolf concentrated on the short shooting range. He knew he needed to increase his speed on the draw when an idea came to him.

He had the gunsmith cut off the barrel to five inches and modify the cartridge ejector to accommodate the shorter barrel. He had him heat and bend the hammer up to almost ninety degrees.

He went to the saddle shop that made holsters and gun cases as well and showed him the design he wanted for a new holster for the shorter gun. It had an open slot down the front of the holster that would allow the barrel to clear he holster and pop out before the gun was completely out of the holster. The barrel only had to move about two inches and it was clear and cocked.

It took two layers of heavy leather and a small metal plate to hold the holster in form to hold and secure the revolver.

The change was dramatic on the shooting range. The new hammer allowed him to lift the revolver out of the holster by the hammer, cocking it as it elevated to the slot.

He could now get two shots off so fast, and hit his three-inch target, that it almost sounded like one shot. The new practiced motion made the first shot dramatically faster and by "fanning" the new hammer with his left hand the second shot was immediate.

He practiced day and night and the motion became instinctive.

The gunsmith had the new smokeless powder cartridges that were three times more powerful than the black powder cartridge and it made shooting much more accurate.

The gunsmith also got a rifle from Augusta that had a scope mounted on it that increased the magnification by eight times.

The lever action rifle was the same .44-40 caliber as the carbine but was made heavier, and had a longer barrel and could accommodate more powerful loads than the carbine.

The carbine was only affective up to one hundred yards but the longer rifle with higher power custom ammunition could reach three hundred with accuracy.

Price was no object. Wolf only wanted the best because he felt he needed the best to survive.

He bought two revolvers with fourteen-inch barrels that were as accurate as the carbine up to 100 yards and powerful with the smokeless ammunition.

He learned how to load his own ammunition and bought powder and bullets for the scoped rifle. The .44-40 caliber cartridges were available everywhere and easy to obtain, but the special rounds for the rifle would have to be handloaded.

★ ★ ★

At one of the Chinese restaurants he frequented he learned about a man that had an incredible skill with his hands and body and searched him out.

During the many training sessions he had with the man, Wong Tu, he learned the man, much older than himself, and much smaller, could and did throw Wolf to the floor with ease. His moves were simple and fast and his facial expressions never changed. He just nodded and smiled when he helped Wolf off the floor.

His sessions increased and his skill became much better, but never attained Wong's ability.

He told Wong about his past as a knife fighter and told him about his stab wound and how it happened.

Wong just smiled, and shaking his head, and said, "that's a very amateurish action, Wolf, and easy to defend against. Let me show you how to turn it into your favor."

Wong showed him many disarming techniques and deadly skills that could be used when attacked by someone with a knife.

Wolf smiled to himself as he went home after his last training session with the blessing of Wong Tu. He, somehow knew would be leaving soon, and the man instinctively knew what Wolf's journey would encounter. The man was extremely intuitive and sent Wolf off with encouragement and admonitions.

Wolf was better prepared, but he had to continue his practice daily.

CHAPTER 4

I t was seven months after his injury when he heard about some people from up north that had to flee their homes.
They had come downriver from up in the Kansas country, and were headed to a city on the gulf coast.

Wolf met the folks and liked them immediately. They had ranches in the Montana country and were run out of their holdings, and town, by a cattle baron who kicked them off their ranches. It was leave or die.

The two families had land plots that they had staked out and registered with the newly formed state. They had their paperwork with them showing the recording numbers from Montana.

The Jamisons claimed they had one hundred sections of land and almost three hundred head of cattle on it and another parcel lf fifty sections in another more northern area where they raised eighty head of sheep along with a small herd of cattle. The sheep were not liked by the local ranchers but with the demand for wool they produced cash.

The Swensons had a larger plot of one hundred and twenty sections and about three hundred and fifty head of cattle in the lower country that they shared in the winter when the high country was snowbound.

The properties were well watered with rivers and ponds and their boundaries were rivers, waterways and mountains.

The Swensons' property abutted the town of Northland, which was brutally controlled by one Oscar Thorndale, the local cattle baron, the man who literally stole their ranches without a bill of sale or title to the property. The owners were just run off.

Wolf immediately knew where his quests would lead him and made arrangement by buy their properties and had a local lawyer draw up a deed and bill of sale for the properties and livestock.

The sellers were shocked at Wolf's generosity and fairness and couldn't have been happier.

They wrote letters of introduction for Wolf addressed to the local pastor, banker, dry goods store owner and saloon owner/operator. They also wrote letters for the saloon's barman and other small ranchers in the area who were fearful of what was going to happen to them.

Their ranches were just too small for the cattle baron to consider at this time, but their time was coming. The Swensons' and Jamison's' ranches however were large, profitable and prime targets.

Wolf told them he would deliver the letters in person.

The Jamisons and Swensons blessed him furiously and wished him the very best. They told him about the many brutal gunslingers old Thorndale had and the crooked sheriff who was in his pocket.

Wolf was in for a brutal arrival.

★ ★ ★

Practice and preparations continued at an elevated pace as he waited for the early spring to start him to move north.

Angie, Wolf's brother Richard and Wolf arranged to move funds to Wolf as he needed them and got letters of credit and background from the family's banker.

CHAPTER 5

Spring came faster than he had hoped. The day finally arrived when he spent the day and night with Angie. When he would return he didn't know but he couldn't take her on the journey he knew was ahead.

★ ★ ★

When he mounted Blondie, she knew they were going a long way. She looked at the fully packed Ruby and they looked at each other with apparent understanding that all was practice before. This was the real thing.

The three of them had become so close over the last year that it seemed they understood each other.

The carbine was sheathed on his right and the scoped rifle was completely enclosed in a leather scabbard on his left.

Over the saddle horn, a one-piece heavy leather sling hung on each side. On the right was a very short double-barreled shot gun that had been sawed off at the end of the wooden forearm and the stock was cut off to the handgrip. Four pouches, for birdshot and heavy buckshot, straddled the gun.

On the left side was one of the long-barrel handguns secured in its own holster. He had a similar, but soft holster, hung over his left shoulder and down his bac that would accommodate the long gun. He was ready to move.

CHAPTER 6

He had studied and carried all the maps he could locate and found the Swensons' and Jamison's' knowledge of the western territory invaluable.

He would follow the Red River northwest through Texas then north into and through the Indian territory to the Arkansas River and follow it northwest through Colorado. When he saw the great mountain ranges they talked about he would head north to the Platte River then through the Nebraska country into Wyoming. He would then ride north to Fort Smith in the south of the Montana area, then north to Northland.

There should be many trails near the rivers where cattle, people and stagecoaches would use and he would try to find and follow these trails as far as he could.

The Swensons' and Jamison's' knew the Montana area well and gave detailed information on where to cross the area and how to approach their ranches unseen.

The whole trip was through hostile country that teamed with people of all types. It was best to avoid as many as possible and try and remain as inconspicuous as possible.

CHAPTER 7

The weather held well for almost a week when it appeared that a big rainstorm was in the making.

Fortunately, he found a small rock outcropping just inside a tree line that made a small cave into the rocky hillside.

He stopped early to prepare and put his packs in the cave and made a tent, like awning over the entrance by cutting three poles with his machete that would wedge one of his tarps on each side and another pole in the center. The side poles were wedged up with the two saddles and the end tied tight to ground stakes.

He collected wood and staked the horses in the trees where they could browse for food.

The smoke from his small cooking fire easily leaked out of the small cave into the twilight.

He was dinking a cup of hot coffee after dinner looking into the storm when Blondie snorted.

Alert, he drew his small revolver and held it cocked under his rain poncho as he looked at the horses, who were staring into the night.

Three men on horseback slowly rode up to his camp through the tree line.

The two outriders were looking in all directions and obviously focusing on Blondie and Ruby.

The man in the middle was intently watching Wolf, who was

sipping coffee in his left hand. The focus of his revolver under his poncho never left the man.

Something down deep inside Wolf said, "Evil will find you."

They were a bearded, scruffy bunch, wearing well, worn saddle ponchos.

"Evening gents. A bit wet out there isn't it?"

It was then he saw the woman on a tether stumbling behind the outrider on Wolf's right

The young Mexican woman was shivering under a soaked woolen shawl over her head. The fear in her face was obvious.

"Care to sit a spell? Seems like your lady friend could use a hot cup of coffee. How about you boys?"

The two outriders chuckled and looked at their obvious leader in the center.

Their horses were not much and their obvious attention to his two well-muscled, healthy mares made their intentions obvious.

It was then the leader reached under his poncho for his gun and was knocked off his horse with Wolf's first round.

Their horses started to move erratically as each of the shocked outriders tried for their guns.

The woman dropped to the ground and rolled into the trees.

Wolf's second shot took the man on his left who was trying to control his horse.

The third man on the right was tangled up in the woman's tether when she rolled into the trees and couldn't get his horse turned around to face Wolf and he went down easily.

Blondie and Ruby were accustomed to the shooting and hardly moved a muscle.

Wolf got up grumbling about the three holes in his rain poncho as walked over to inspect the three would-be killers.

The second man Wolf shot was still coughing from the chest wound when Wolf kicked his gun away from the dying man.

Fluent in Spanish, he walked over o the fearful woman and said, "Its okay now. Come on over to the fire and warm up. There's hot coffee there for you.

She looked at Wolf for a long time before she spoke.

"Are you going to hurt me too?"

Wolf smile and said, "No, senorita I'm not going to hurt you. I think you've probably been trough enough of that," as he untied her tether.

With that, he walked over to the nearest horse, and with its reins, tied it to a tree.

The second one was easy to catch and he tied it as well.

The third horse, the one the second outrider was riding, had run out of the tree line and was standing, looking back.

Wolf told the lady to come to the fire and she got up, walked over to the man that had her tethered and kicked him, cursing as she did so.

Satisfied, she walked over to the fire where Wolf was adding some wood.

They wrung out her heavily soaked shawl and put it near the fire to dry.

He then stripped the best poncho off the leader and draped it over her shoulders.

The woman was crying but the coffee, and the poncho collecting heat from the fire relaxed her and she no longer shivered.

Wolf cut off a piece of jerky and handed it to her.

She looked wolf in eyes for the first time and said, "Thank you, thank you. These are terrible men. They've been robbing, raping, taking our women and beating us for months."

"Who's us?"

"Our little pueblo."

"What pueblo? Where is it?"

"It really doesn't have a name. It's about two days south of here. They were going to sell me to the Indian up north. They've been doing that to our women.

"Oh my God. How long has this been going on?"

"I don't know. I think forever but it started just after Christmas when they came to our pueblo," she said as she munched on the jerky.

"How many people live in your pueblo?"

"I don't know. I think about fifty."

"Why didn't your people do something about it?"

"They took all the guns we had in the pueblo when they first came. We only had three or four, I think. We're farmers. We grow everything we need. Milk the cows, raise chickens and hogs. We lived well before they came."

"Now they come every Saturday and eat our food, drink our wine and tequila and rape our women. They leave us nothing. They take the young girls to sell to the Indians. We hide them as best we can. That's why they took me. It's to show our people that no one is safe."

"How many of these men are there?"

"Beside the three here there are about fifteen or so.

"Where do they come from?"

"They arrived at the spring in the fall I think. We always got our best water from the spring. Now we don't even go near there. We have to wash our clothes and collect water way downstream.

"You don't have a well in your pueblo?"

"Oh yes. We have two wells, but the water isn't as good as the spring water."

"The men are trying to dig another well but it takes a lot of time."

Wolf stared into the fire a long time and finally said, "Maybe we should go to your pueblo and have a look."

CHAPTER 8

The woman was a good rider. She was on one of the three horses and they led the other two. They had collected all the guns and in searching through the saddlebags and belongings they recovered extra ammunition and cash in gold, silver and paper. Wolf gave it to the lady, he now knew as Susan.

★ ★ ★

Two days later, the horses had settled into their new routine as they broached the hill overlooking her pueblo.

Wolf said, "We'll stop here for awhile. I want to see what you have down there.

They sat side by side on the knoll of the hill looking down at the pueblo.

Susan was fascinated looking through Wolf's brass collapsible telescope that magnified images about four times.

She commented about the children and people she saw through the scope and giggled at what she saw.

The pueblo was a simple place made up of one main street lined with attached adobe living quarter on each side.

On the western end, directly lined up with the main street about fifty yards from the living quarters was a white adobe church with a bell tower and a well.

Her story of how the people had saved to build the bell tower and buy the church bell told the religious commitment of the people.

The local priest also doubled as a doctor of sorts. Everyone in town knew each other like family.

North of the pueblo were poled corrals for their horses and about eight wagons of different sorts.

There was a large enclosed area with chickens and another enclosed area near the corrals where there were several hogs of various sizes.

★ ★ ★

This was a pueblo of hard working subsistence farmers.

A plan was forming in Wolf's mind. Susan had told him on Saturdays several men from their spring camp east of the pueblo would ride into town announcing their arrival by firing their guns into the air and buildings. This was their playpen.

The only cantina was on the south side about half way down the main street.

Wolf lay back on the ground and pushed his scope together and put it in its case and after looking at the sky for a long time and finally said, "Okay. Today is Wednesday. We have three days to get ready to end this problem. I need you to convince your people that we can end this but they are going to have to do exactly, and I mean exactly, what I tell them to do. Do you think you can do that?"

"Yes, ---without a doubt. We're dead if we don't do something. People are talking about abandoning our pueblo."

"Okay, let's go."

CHAPTER 9

They dropped down off the hill and entered the little pueblo from the west. When they rode in from the church a shout went up and people started coming from everywhere.

"Susan, Susan," they cried as they ran up to her.

Susan jumped down from her horse, holding the reins, and hugged the first lady to arrive.

"Oh my God. It's you. Oh thank you, Lord."

The next twenty minutes was chaos.

As Susan was telling her story and pointing at Wolf, who quietly sat on Blondie, the townspeople started to look at Wolf more and more.

Susan finally walked over to Wolf and said, "Come on, they all want to meet you and I have a place for you to stay."

★ ★ ★

The horses were corralled, watered and fed. Wolf's quarters were in a woman's small apartment, nearest to the church.

Wolf insisted on taking all the guns he had collected from the three men to his quarters along with his gear and supplies.

A small fiesta was planned for the evening to celebrate Susan's return and her new friend whom everyone appeared to hold in great respect.

The food was plentiful and Wolf thought he had shaken hands and hugged everyone in town at least three times.

He watched the people in their excitement and thought, *this had better work out.*

★ ★ ★

All the men were crowded into the small cantina by eight o'clock in the morning waiting for the meeting Wolf had asked for.

Wolf had drawn a fairly detailed layout of the town and had paced off the width of the street and the distance to the church from the cantina. He was as ready as he could be.

The cantina had two swinging, saloon type doors that he pushed open and stepped into the cantina as a hush fell over the crowded room.

"Buenos Días, amigos," he said.

All the men smiled and started talking at once.

Wolf walked over to a heavy, handmade wooden table and started dragging it to the far side of the cantina.

Many hands immediately appeared to help him move it.

He was now looking directly to the two front doors. A bar, serving area, was to his left and numerous tables had been stacked against the wall to his right to make room for the men.

Wolf looked at each of the silent, waiting, men in turn and finally said, "You want to save your pueblo?"

The room echoed in "Si, Si, Si."

"You want to save your women and children?"

The chorus got louder.

"You want to end this robbery, brutality and rape for good?"

It was a shout now.

"Okay. I'm going to tell you how we, and I mean you and I, are going to do it."

I'm going to show you a plan that will work. I'm going to show you how we are going to do it without any of you getting hurt, hopefully. Are you up for that?"

Heads looked at each other, nodded and they all said, "Si, Si."

They were all in agreement as Wolf looked around the room of nodding heads.

"Okay here is what were going to do. You must, and I repeat, you must follow the plan exactly as I lay it out. If you don't follow the plan things could go very bad for everyone and I mean everyone in your pueblo. Do you understand that?"

Heads nodded and the men mumbled to each other, but were in agreement.

Wolf laid his drawn out plan of the pueblo on the table.

"Okay here is what we have to do to make this work."

CHAPTER 10

He went over his plan in detail and asked for questions after each segment of the plan.

The men could see the real possibility of eliminating their threat forever and making the pueblo a new, happy, prosperous little village as it once was. They could see that they could now possibly recover the four young women the men had taken to their camp.

Wolf asked who's the best with a rifle? and hands went up everywhere.

Wolf smiled and said," I want you to tell me who's the best. You'll have four carbines. Who're your best shooters?"

The men talked among themselves and finally four men came forward.

"You think you know how to shoot?"

"Si senor, we were good hunters we can shoot."

Wolf lifted the empty carbine from the table and said, "Show me. The rifle is empty. Check it yourself. Take aim at that picture on the wall and get off three shots.

The first man took the carbine, hefted it, and levered the action.

"Could use a little oil," he said.

"You're right; the man that used to own this gun didn't take very good care of it. That will be your first order of business, to clean it up and get it operating smoothly.

The man shouldered the rifle like he knew what he was doing

and dry fired three times. He held the rifle steady between shots and lowered the rifle when he was done.

"You got a job," Wolf said as he handed it to the next man.

★ ★ ★

Each of the men went through the exercise and each demonstrated they knew how to shoot the carbine, and well.

"Okay, here's the deal. I'll give you four carbines to use. You clean them up and get them ready to fire. I'll want them back when this is over. You'll have many rifles and revolvers when this is over to protect your town. I suggest you four show everyone how to shoot when this is over.

"We can get some target practice in before they come." They all nodded like it was a good idea.

"Well, what's you name again," Wolf asked the man who spoke.

"Jesus, senor."

"Well Jesus, they took all your guns away didn't they?"

Jesus nodded.

"They're only what, three, four miles away? If they hear shooting, they'll know you have guns.

"You'll then have a war on your hands that you can't win and you will lose everything including your lives."

They all started talking at once, nodding and shaking their heads.

"As I showed you, you will only be shooting, maybe thirty feet. If you can't hit anything at thirty feet I need someone else," he said as he smiled.

The men all laughed, and Jesus blushed.

He repeated the selection for men who could shoot a revolver accurately.

He had three handguns from Susan's captors and they could shoot his long revolvers. That gave them five.

He then spoke to an elderly man everyone said was a good shot, but he was lame and couldn't climb the ladders that Wolf had planned to get the men on top of the buildings they would be shooting from.

"Senor Vargas. Everyone say you're a good shot but too old."

Everyone laughed and the old man shrugged his shoulders.

"That's great, because I have a special job for you."

A murmur went through the crowd as the men looked at each other.

"They come to the cantina first when the come to town. Is that right?" he said looking at the crowd.

They all agreed.

"Senor Vargas, you my friend will be the man to greet them."

"We will tip this big table on its side. You will be behind this table with a short shotgun loaded with buckshot."

"The table will stop any stray bullets from hitting you. We will put tables by the front doors so they will only open a couple of feet, narrowing your target."

"Somebody is going to try and get in here when the shooting starts. You'll blast him right out the door with a load of buckshot."

"I don't think you'll have a second visitor, but if you do, you have a second barrel for him."

"You reload and wait. Think you can do that?"

Vargas was smiling from ear to ear. Everyone in the room was jubilant and slapping each other on the back.

Every door in the pueblo would be barricaded except for the Cantina's.

Remember everyone, this is only going to take a matter of a few seconds and it's over.

"You have nine guns and your first shot should be true. Don't shoot the horses. You'll want them.

"Remember everyone and I mean everyone on the roofs. No peeking or you're dead. You wait for my shot from the bell tower. I'll shoot the leader, the guy dressed in black on the black horse. When you get up to shoot, they will all be looking at the bell tower and not you.

Remember, I get the black horse and tack, and the man's guns.

You get everything else. Don't shoot my horse," he said with smile pointing at the ceiling.

All the men laughed.

"Keep in mind the procedure after the shooting. It's very important and must go smoothly and rapidly. You men that aren't shooters you'll be on the wagon detail I outlined. The timing and the speed in which you get it done is important, so make sure when you move the wagons into position they operate well and can be moved fast. It's very important that we seal off the street so no horses get out."

"Are you ready?"

A cheer went up from the crowd. They slapped each other on the back and headed to the bar for a drink.

"This afternoon we start to prepare. No one gets drunk until this is over. You must be sharp. There's nothing to celebrate yet."

CHAPTER 11

Saturday finally arrived. The people of the small pueblo had worked diligently to prepare for that afternoon's event. They knew if was a do or die situation. They were at the end of their tolerance.

Susan had been up in the bell tower all afternoon watching through Wolf's telescope where the men would come out of the low country was and head to their pueblo.

It was a warm day and the fevered pitch everyone had been living under made it more uncomfortable.

It was late in the afternoon when Wolf joined her in the bell tower with his scoped rifle and they traded off watching the road while talking about what the people would do when they had their lives back.

Susan was watching when Wolf heard her gasp.

"They're coming," was all she could say.

Wolf yelled down to the men, lingering around near the ladders with their armament, and they all froze with the announcement. Planning and practicing was one thing but this would be the real test.

The men scrambled up the ladders and Wolf yelled, "No sombreros."

Some of the men had forgotten to take off the huge hats that had become a way of their life. The big sombreros would be easily seen from the street and it would be a death warrant to the pueblo.

The men crouched down low as instructed and went to their assigned places on the flat roofs of the living quarters on both sides of the street.

Their targets were only the ones across the street so they wouldn't have to expose themselves above the small parapets. They did well in practice, now it was show time.

Susan crouched below the opening of the bell tower, and Wolf took his wide brimmed, light grey, plantation hat off, as it would be easily seen, and sat at the edge of the opening so only a portion of his head and one eye could watch the men approach. There were ten of them and they were moving quickly to their fun and games.

"There are ten of them, Susan."

"Oh my God. What will we do? I'm afraid."

"Exactly as we planned. This will work out just fine, you'll see. Fear is a lie. Remember that."

★ ★ ★

The terrible ten came into town shooting and yelling.

The ladies were in the streets as planned and rushed into their homes and barricaded the doors.

The men took it all in stride that things were normal.

Wolf watched the men on the roof to make sure no one tried to peek over the one-foot parapet on the edge of the roof.

They were all looking at the bell tower.

As predicted the boss man on the black horse was in front, and had a big grin on his face.

He slowed as he came to the cantina and prepared to dismount.

All the men were near the cantina now.

Wolf eased the tip of his rifle over the sill of the bell tower and watched the man intently through the scope.

Only your faith and courage can save you, when you are in trouble.

It was time.

★ ★ ★

The men on the roofs maintained discipline, and Wolf lined up on the black shirt just as the man lifted his foot out of the stirrup.

The leader hurtled off the back of his horse and his companions all started shooting at the bell tower.

All hell broke loose.

The men on the wagon detail burst into action and shoved the wagons into the street, blocking an exit from both ends. It took three wagons on each end to do the job but they got it done, and fast. It went unnoticed as bullets were raining down from the rooftops and men were falling off their horses.

The first hail of bullets knocked five men off their horses and the rest were firing back as fast as they could.

It was then they realized the street was blocked at both ends. This was a fight to the death, where they stood.

The remaining men were all wounded and on the ground, trying to use their horses as cover.

One man made a dash through the cantina door and was blasted back out into the street. The action was not lost on the others.

It was over in a matter of seconds.

The men started looking over the parapets to see if anyone was moving. One man was trying to get his gun and was shot by a rifleman.

The procedure now was that all the men would catch the horses and tie them to any hitching rail in town.

The wagons were moved back to their original location at the ends of the buildings and the ten men were dragged off the street to the west, out of sight of the main street. Everything appeared normal within minutes.

They had been instructed to try to match a man to his horse if possible and to remove their shirts and hats and stack them by the dead owners. Everyone was wearing jeans of some kind, so the pants weren't necessary to remove, but the rest were needed for the next day's charade.

The women were moaning and the men were acting in various

moods. Some were ecstatic and others were sorrowful, but the job, done according to plan, had succeeded.

★ ★ ★

Susan returned to the telescope detail to make sure no one else came to town.

Wolf climbed down the ladder from the bell tower and passed through the church.

The priest was at the alter praying in his low mumbling voice and he looked at Wolf as he passed. Wolf nodded to the priest and crossed himself.

"Your services are not needed, father," he said. "Everything went as per the plan. This town is free again. Tomorrow we will get the girls."

"Bless you, my son," he said as Wolf hurried out the door.

★ ★ ★

The townspeople were nervous. They were worried that others from the spring camp might come to town to see what all the shooting was about.

By dark the people relaxed and fires started and food was disbursed at the cantina. The emotions were mixed among the gatherers but everyone was happy with the results. They had never seen such carnage in their lives and they were the ones that did it.

The women were making many trips to the church and the priest had his hands full.

Most people ate quietly knowing that the next day was another matter, and more dangerous.

Wolf did his best to encourage the men who were now starting to come around to the understanding that they themselves actually beat the terrible spring camp gang, but they were apprehensive about what was yet to come.

CHAPTER 12

Sunday morning the church was packed with everyone in town including all the children.

There was no liquor served Saturday night as Sunday was going to be a whole new game plan.

★ ★ ★

The spring camp group usually left town, and headed back to the spring late in the morning, after raising hell all night, so that was the time they had to move.

Wolf rode the black horse with the man's black shirt and hat. He had six other good revolver shooters dressed in the clothes of other men from the spring.

They weren't too sure if they had the horses matched up to the man, but chances were that would go unnoticed as they rode into the spring camp.

★ ★ ★

Wolf was in the lead when they neared the camp. The men were tightly strung out behind him and were nervous as this was a confrontation they had never done before.

Wolf had told them what to do, and instructed them the best he could, but the time was short.

"Just think about the shot, nothing else. Remember you're saving the girls from your town. You'll be heroes. What you are about to do is vital and necessary. This will end it forever."

★ ★ ★

With their heads lowered, so as not to be recognized too early they slowly rode into camp.

There were four men here that Wolf could see and they were busy playing cards and talking around the dying morning fire.

They shouted greetings to the returning men and Wolf waved to them and turned his head looking around the camp.

His men were behind him and slowly moving in.

Wolf rode right up to the men playing cards and looked at them.

They realized Wolf was not their pack leader, and they went for their guns.

Wolf dropped both men before they could shoot.

Everyone was shooting now and the other two spring men dropped to the ground.

Wolf looked around and said, "Is everyone alright?"

The men all looked at each other and when they realized they were unscathed they started to cheer and yell.

CHAPTER 13

Wolf sent one of the men back for the wagons that were following them to the spring.

The four girls were tied in a small enclosure made of tree branches and cactus that kept them from escaping the ten-foot corral. They didn't appear to be over twelve years old.

They were crying, and their clothes were dirty and torn. They were emotional wrecks.

How anyone could do this, he wondered.

The men were off their horses now checking on the bodies and releasing the girls from their cage. It was an emotional time for the close-knit community.

Wolf was off his horse now and tied his horse to a nearby tree, stripped off his black shirt and hat and throwing more wood on the fire added the clothing to it. He had played the role of an evil person and tried to distance himself from the hollow feeling it left in him.

Everyone was hugging each other as Wolf led the stallion down the creek from the spring.

He was about a hundred yards away and well out of sight of the camp when he tied the horse to a tree where he could nibble on green grass, and he sat on the riverbank staring into oblivion.

His thoughts were a jumble. He wasn't a very religious man before he left on his quest but he could feel the protection of something that was helping him accomplish what he set out to do. It was nothing physical but was and incite or suggestions that registered in his mind.

He slowly did his now-daily prayer as he took off his clothes and waded into the cool stream. He needed to clean his body from the last few days' efforts. It was more than dirt or grime he was removing---it was a cleansing of his soul, he thought.

★ ★ ★

He was sitting on the bank of the stream with only his undershorts on staring at the water when he heard a soft voice say, "Wolf?"

He turned to find the tear-stained face of Susan.

"Why are you here, Wolf?"

"I just needed to be away. I just needed to try and get back to normal a little bit. This is a celebration of your people, Susan. They need their own time without a stranger and I needed to wash some of the grime off the inside of me."

"You're no stranger, Wolf. You're just as much as a part of our pueblo as anyone. You were the one that brought us back from the brink of hell and dragged us into the sunshine. You're part of our group, no matter where you are, or where you go. They'll be talking about you for generations. You're part of us, Wolf."

"Oh, I'll never forget your pueblo, with no name. I'll never forget you and the people I've met. Yes, you're a part of me now. No question about it."

"How did you get all these horrible scars, Wolf? You have them all over, and the ones on your back, you could only get one way. You've led a hard life I think, but by seeing your horses and gear I think you were pretty well off, somewhere."

"Oh yes, I was pretty well off indeed. I led a tough life that I chose for myself and now I find myself being some kind of a warrior for a Supreme Being or force. I'm really not sure. But it's my destiny. Your story of your pueblo somehow fit into my quest and I had to respond. I was drawn to it. I'm afraid sooner or later this quest will be my demise."

★ ★ ★

After a long conversation, Susan got up and said, "Let's go, Wolf. The people are going home. They have the spring camp completely cleaned out, like you suggested, like it was never occupied.

CHAPTER 14

An interesting thing happened when they returned to the pueblo. There was no celebration. Everyone headed to the church before they unloaded the wagons, which were now lined up in front of the white building.

Wolf made his way into the church declining Susan's efforts to get him to sit up front, eased his way into the back bench with the old men of the town.

He sat next to Vargas. The old man smiled at him and Wolf patted him on the back and said, "You did real good, Senor Vargas."

Vargas smiled and said, "I was a little worried when that animal came through the door but I hit him with the first load that stopped him in his tracks and tipped him over backwards. I thought, 'what the hell' and fired the second barrel and that slammed him back out in the street for everyone to see. I reloaded quickly and waited but no one else tried the cantina."

"He went flying. That's for sure. They got the message that old Vargus was inside."

Vargas smiled, and patted Wolf on the leg. The priest was getting underway.

★ ★ ★

It seemed that food came out of nowhere. Tables from the cantina, and several of the residences, were in the street outside the cantina that showed they had done this many times.

The ladies were in their realm. They chatted and laughed their way through the whole ordeal with a smile on their face, as they assisted and cooperated with each other.

The men kept out of the way and drank beer and tequila and sang songs. These folks were happy in their town, and with what they had. Life could offer them nothing more.

★ ★ ★

Wolf moved out of the limelight and made his way to his quarters. This was the celebration of the townspeople for their newfound freedom, and the recovery of the four young girls.

Some young men were doing their best to be mariachis and the folks were cheering them on.

The closed door of his quarters couldn't keep out the noise from the happy town. Even the young children were up and playing in the street.

★ ★ ★

He was lying on the thin mattress on the iron bed, only in his undershorts in the warm evening, with his eyes closed. He was thinking about moving on, when the door to his room was quietly opened and someone entered.

Instinctively, his hand moved to the revolver on the floor by his bed when he recognized Susan.

"You scared me when you walked in. I wasn't expecting anyone."

"I know. I saw you move out and go to your room. I'm sorry I didn't get to talk to you much during the fiesta. It gets pretty crazy sometimes."

"That's ok. You have a lot going on right now. It's amazing how resilient you people are and how you can pull together when you need to.

"This is a great pueblo."

Susan pulled her cotton dress over her head and lay down alongside of Wolf.

Wolf said, "You know what you're doing?"

"Oh yes. I should have been here a long time ago."

★ ★ ★

Monday, Wolf worked with the men to make a sturdy packsaddle that would hug the black horse's saddle.

He rode the horse a lot that day, getting to know him. He was a strong stallion that looked like he was from a Mustang herd, but obviously had not been cared for too much. He was a easy rider, and the two of them got to know each other well that day, and the stallion liked the attention that Wolf gave him by patting and talking to him the entire time.

He would work out well.

CHAPTER 15

Tuesday morning arrived with a clear sky and gentle breeze from the west.

Wolf was putting the saddles on his three horses, when several men came up to him.

"Senor, won't you stay awhile? You're welcome here with us. We'd like you to stay."

"I'm sorry but I have to move on. I have places I need to go and things I need to get done."

"Si senor. I think we understand you. Please let us help you pack your horses."

The three horses were now tied outside his quarters and he was working on getting his packs together when Susan walked in and looked at all his equipment.

"Wolf, why do you keep all these guns? You can't possibly use them all. Why do you do that?"

Wolf took a minute to contemplate an answer as he looked at the rifles and revolvers he had wrapped so carefully.

"Susan, I really don't know. Somehow I think I have to save these for something in the future. I've learned not to doubt my thoughts, but to act on them with intelligence and understanding."

"Sometime and somewhere I will need them for something. I just don't know what that is yet."

★ ★ ★

The three animals were saddled and loaded. They looked at each other and Wolf could tell they knew they were going a long way.

The farewell to the town brought everyone into the street, waving and throwing kisses.

Many of the older women hugged him and said, "Vaya con Dios, senor.

The priest had come to him earlier in the day and blessed him for what he had accomplished in the town and said an interesting thing to Wolf.

"I think you have a long and dangerous journey ahead of you, my friend. I hope and pray that you make if successfully."

"I have the feeling that you know evil and are in search of it. I hope you maintain your vigilance and faith to get to where you're going, and God willing, you lead a long and happy life, my son."

★ ★ ★

Wolf looked over at the priest, who was standing on the steps to the church, and touched his hat in acknowledgement of the man, and what he knew the priest understood.

The last person he looked at and for a long time was the pretty Susan.

She had tears in her eyes and Wolf had all he could do to hold back his.

She knew by the look he gave her that he would not forget her. She was a part of him now. They had shared everything from the beginning to the end. She knew more about him than anyone else in the pueblo.

She crossed herself, and kissed the cross between her breasts and held it out toward Wolf, in blessing.

He blew her a kiss and touched Blondie to move out.

CHAPTER 16

The three of them settled into a rhythm they all understood and were comfortable with.

The stallion was a little miffed, Wolf thought when he rode Blondie, rather than him, but he got used to it.

Wolf would trade off along the way riding each horse in turn for a few days, so everyone knew they were equal in his mind.

Exercise was an important part of his day and when Wolf would get off to walk and jog each day the horses would trot along behind like they enjoyed what Wolf was doing.

When he was sprinting, Blondie was right along side of him watching him all the way. It was a game to her. Like a little race.

He had to get north, back to the Red River, so his direction was almost due north, but angling slightly to the west.

They were making good time without interruption of any kind. He saw dust off in the distance created by a small wagon train working its way west.

★ ★ ★

He was more intent on watching the horizon for any other activity and his mind was wandering about the events of the past, when he noticed the stallion, he was astride of looking off to his right.

He glanced to the right and saw all the horses were looking to their right as they moved forward at an easy lope.

Wolf looked in that direction and saw a huge wolf-easily running parallel alongside them in the tall grass about fifty feet away.

The strange thing about the wolf is that it was not aggressive and was loping along just watching the horses. He wasn't sneaking or stalking, and sometimes bounded up above the grass in full view. This animal was not on the hunt.

Wolf looked to see if there was a pack following them and searched everywhere without seeing anything.

Wolf, in a low voice, said "whoa," to the horses and they all started slowing down without taking their eyes off the big animal.

The wolf stopped and looked at them with great interest and wagged its tail.

Wagged its tail, thought Wolf. Wild animals just don't stand there looking at you and wag their tails.

The horses were not near as fearful as Wolf thought they should be if there was a threat, and they obviously didn't detect any.

They sat and watched the big guy who slowly made its way toward the horses.

Wolf got off Blackie and tied his reins to the pommel on Blondie's saddle and stood watching the big wolf.

It was then, he determined, this wasn't a wolf. It was some kind of a crossbreed. The head was too thick and the jaw and mouth too wide for a wolf. The hair was grey wolf color but shorter.

Wolf said in a low voice, "hey boy. Where you think you're going?"

The animal wagged its tail in response. He was not dangerous Wolf thought, so he went to the saddle bags on Blondie and cut off a large piece of jerky and slowly walked toward the critter, talking to him all the time.

★ ★ ★

Wolf walked within ten feet of the animal and made the

determination this was a dog. It was a damn big dog that was a cross with a wolf somewhere along the line.

Wolf squatted down on the ground and looked back at the horses that were standing perfectly still, watching the action.

Wolf put the end of the jerky in his mouth, clamped his teeth, and cut off a half inch piece that he chewed on, making pleasant sounds.

The big dog's eyes never left him and his tongue slavered across his lips.

Wolf took the piece of jerky out of his mouth and offered it to the dog.

The dog took a couple of tentative steps toward Wolf then backed away whining a little.

Wolf threw the jerky to the dog and he grabbed it immediately, gave it a couple of chews, and then did something rather strange.

He put his nose straight up in the air and swallowed. He coughed a couple of times and he looked at Wolf expectantly.

Wolf repeated the process and the dog now was within five feet of Wolf, wagging it's tail.

When he swallowed this time with his strange extended neck, Wolf saw it.

★ ★ ★

There was something binding around the big guy's neck that was hidden by the long hair. It was almost the same color as the dog's hair but it was defiantly a collar of some sort, and a too tight of one at that.

Either the dog was in captivity or he had the collar on for so long that he grew too big for it, but it had to come off if he was going to survive.

Wolf extended his hand, palm down, and talked to the dog, signaling for the dog to come and have a sniff.

The big dog reluctantly moved forward and sniffed Wolf's outstretched hand, pulled back looking at Wolf, who had not moved, and came forward for another sniff.

This time the dog nuzzled Wolf's hand.

Wolf gently moved his hand to the side of the big head and scratched behind his ear. The dog loved it and his tail was wagging fast now.

After getting the dog closer, Wolf was petting the dog and touched the collar. It was tight against the skin and the dog was reluctant to have him touch it.

This was going be difficult and had to be done quickly, if it was going to get done at all.

Wolf went back to petting and scratching the head and neck and making more contact with the collar all the time.

He finally sat back on his haunches and took out his folding knife attached to the back of his gun belt.

He opened the skinning blade and held it in his right hand as he caressed the dog's head with his left.

Slowly he worked his fingers under the round hard collar and while caressing the dog with his right he slipped the sharp skinning knife under the collar and jerked it away, cutting through the collar.

The dog yelped and jumped back and started to growl as Wolf put his hand on his gun.

It was when Wolf looked at the collar, he saw it was made from woven horsehair and secured with a knot.

This dog probably came from some Indian tribe. If he was a pet or a captive, he didn't know.

Wolf talked to the dog and showed him the collar and the dog shook his head and moved his neck around. He looked at Wolf and wagged his tail.

Wolf cut another piece of jerky and handed it to the dog that gave it a couple of chews and gulped it down with ease. The dog realized what had happened and wagged his whole body as he walked up to Wolf.

Wolf patted the dog and then started looking over the neck. It was raw. The collar had embedded itself into the skin of the dog.

Wolf looked the dog in the eye and said, "I'm glad I found you, big fella."

The dog just looked at him and then wolf thought, *"I didn't find you, did I?"* you found me.

★ ★ ★

The dog immediately was friendlier and Wolf got up and started walking back to the curious horses, the dog followed watching Wolf's every move.

Wolf walked up to Blondie first as she would be the most likely one to accept the new recruit. She watched them approach with her ears forward in a curious gesture. Wolf walked up and put a hand on the dog and the other on Blondie's and started talking to both of them.

The dog reached up to sniff her and Blondie dropped her head to the dog's nose. They had made contact and the dog gave her a quick lick on her nose which startled the horse but she immediately put her nose back down to the dog.

Wolf got down and patted the dog and said, "I think we'll call you Jake."

Contact had been made and accepted. Wolf thought these animals know a whole lot more than a human will ever understand about such things.

The operation was continued with Ruby then Blackie with various successful results.

Wolf said, "I think it's time for me to walk a bit and strolled off with the dog at his side and the horses following as they normally did, when he was off walking or running.

The dog continually looked up at Wolf as they walked and he talked to the dog, using the name Jake constantly, and stroked its head from time to time. They were becoming a team.

★ ★ ★

When Wolf mounted Blondie again and the moved off at a leisurely lope the dog ran ahead, with his nose down, and scoured the area on each side of the trail they were following, constantly looking back to make sure they were still all together.

★ ★ ★

Late in the afternoon, Wolf saw a covey of grouse working their way through the grass and he took the lead rope for Blackie and looped it over the saddle horn of Ruby. Ruby and Blondie knew what was going to happen as Wolf edged ahead on his mount, pulling the short shotgun, from its holster.

He called to the dog to come, and the dog stopped and looked at Wolf in wonderment.

Blondie knew the drill. They had done this numerous times when the birds were dusting in the late afternoon, and she slowly increased her speed to where the birds were working the ground.

With the touch of his boot, Blondie tore into a dash straight for the birds.

Wolf was standing in the stirrups now, with the shotgun leveled just above where the birds were.

They burst out of the grass and Wolf shot the first one on the rise and leveled at the one moving to his right, taking it easily with the wide pattern of the short barrel.

It hit the ground and started to run, but the dog seeing it flee dashed in and grabbed it and shook it violently.

Wolf was off his horse picking up the first bird and looked for Jake.

"Hey Jake, Where are you?"

Jake stood up in the tall grass and looked at Wolf. It was obvious he was making a meal of the second bird.

Wolf got back on Blondie who was waiting for him and lashed the bird on one of the leather stringers on the saddle. He reloaded the shotgun and eased it into its sheath by the saddle horn.

★ ★ ★

The first night Wolf thought would be interesting to see what

Jake would do but he settled in well near the fire as the horses, which were strung together worked their way through the grass.

Jake responded to his name well. The dog was obviously smart and Wolf guessed his weight to be well over eighty pounds. He would probably gain some weight, now that he could eat better and the daily running would muscle up the already powerful dog.

It was on their third day together that they saw a small settlement in the distance. It was made up of six wooden structures in a row and had a well near one of the buildings at the end of the street.

There were three houses in back of the row of buildings that appeared to be the main street.

They slowly rode into town and stopped first at the well to water the dog and horses and Wolf scanned the town.

Some people came out to see who had arrived and Wolf waived to them and they returned his wave.

The nearest building was more or less a general store and there was a stagecoach notice on the front wall so this town must be on a stagecoach route.

Wolf left the horses near the well and walked into the general store and looked around.

Surprisingly enough, there were ample supplies for obviously more than the town needed.

"Afternoon, sir," said Wolf to the man in the store who was putting supplies in bins behind the counter.

"You've got a nice store and you sure have a lot of supplies for a town this size."

"Well there're lots of folks that live in this area and they need a place to get things they need. Just passing through?"

"Yes sir. We're headed up north and just spotted your town, and thought I'd take a look."

"Name's Roberts, Who might you be?"

"They call me Wolf. Kind of a nickname, I guess. I can use some beans and flour if you have it, and maybe some salt."

"I've got it all. How much do you need?"

Looking around the store surprised Wolf at the variety of things the man sold.

"How often does the stage come through here?"

"It's kind of irregular but they come through just about every week or so. There's lots of traffic going west now days."

"I need to hit the Red River again. I kinda got sidetracked so I'm headed north to catch it again."

"Just go straight up that trail by the well where your horses are," he said as he looked out the window. "Damn fine horses you have there, mister. Don't see many like that in these parts. I bet you paid a pretty penny for them."

"Had the two mares for quite some time but the black stallion is a new acquisition. I figure it's just as cheap to feed a good horse as a poor one."

"Well that's true, but I'd be a bit careful in these parts. Lots of ex-army guys wandering around and of course the damn Indians and outlaws. They'd all like those horses."

"Thanks for the advice. I try to be extra careful and keep pretty much to myself," he said as he picked up his supplies and went out the door.

They headed north for about three miles and found a good place to spend the night, with plenty of daylight to set up camp and get the horses taken care of.

The old man is right, he thought. Better keep an eye open. Jake should be a help with that, for sure.

CHAPTER 17

While looking through his scope on the fifth day he saw and small solitary building if front of a well near a clump of trees by a small river and decided to go see what it was all about. They could always use fresh water.

★ ★ ★

As they approached the building he saw three horses tied to the hitching rail in front.

The well was almost directly in front of the building and they stopped there first.

Wolf got down and looked into the well. The water lever was only about fifteen feet down, probably supplied by the stream behind the building.

He worked the bucket up and down giving the horses, and Jake all they wanted.

The water was surprisingly fresh, so he filled the four water kegs, the packhorses carried and the two canteens he had on his horse.

He walked the animals over to the clump of trees to get them out of the sun where he tied Blondie to a tree with a loose loop that would allow her to walk in any direction. The three of them were now separated on their own trees and browsing on the green growth underneath.

It was time to see what this place was like.

★ ★ ★

He called Jake and stepped inside and stopped to let his eyes adjust to the dim light.

There was a long counter in front of him with racks behind it for storage of many items that were for sale.

There must be a lot of these places around this open country, he thought.

A thin bald man stood behind the counter. He was hunchbacked and wore spectacles would look like.

He stared at Wolf as he entered, and had a fearful look on his face. He wasn't a big man and looked like one might imagine as a storekeeper.

There were two tables over to Wolf's left among all sorts of large articles for sale. The nearest table had two men sitting at it drinking something out of cups and eating from two plates of food.

They wore revolvers that were tied to their legs and wore army boots. These men looked like the gunslingers he had heard about.

They were a scruffy pair with dirty hands and face.

Wolf thought about leaving when he heard a woman yell in Spanish and saw a big man lying astride a screaming woman that he was pinning to a pile of feed sacks.

A low rumble was coming from deep inside Jake so Wolf calmly put his hand on the dog to quiet him. The dog had been leaning against his leg and Wolf guessed it may be the first time Jake had ever been inside a building.

The man was cursing her and muffling her with his big hand. It was an obvious rape in action.

Maybe he wasn't going anywhere.

CHAPTER 18

Wolf quietly commanded to Jake, "Come."

Jake knew instinctively that this was serious when he heard that tone of voice.

Wolf walked quietly over to the two men sitting at the table and said, "You boys just sit nice and quiet while I go have a talk with your friend over there," while he nodded his head in the direction of the commotion on the far end of the room.

They both laughed, and the man on Wolf's left, who had the nearest gun, said, "Yeah?" and reached for the gun high on his hip.

The man had just touched the handle when he was staring with wide eyes down the barrel of Wolf's cocked revolver. The other man had his fork halfway to his mouth and had frozen in action, with his mouth open, and wide eyes staring at the revolver not more than ten inches from his partner's eye.

"Yeah," was all Wolf said.

The man froze and slowly took his hand away from his revolver, never taking his eye off the big hole at the end of the barrel, and said, "Well okay, if that's how you feel about it."

Wolf slowly reached down and removed the man's gun from its holster, then looked at the other man who was still frozen in place, and said, "Friend, put your gun up on the table real slow like with two fingers."

That man was now staring down the barrel of Wolfs gun. He

coughed, and said. "Jesus H. Christ. I never seen nothin like that," as he slowly put the gun on the table.

Wolf had tucked the first man's gun in his belt, and picked up the gun on the table and said, "Like I said, you boys just sit nice and quiet. Maybe you should pay a little more attention to Jesus H. Christ."

He looked at Jake and gave the command, "Guard" and pointed at the two men sitting at the table.

Jake snarled and looked at the two men who were horrified at the huge snarling jaws snapping in front of them.

* * *

Wolf and Jake had worked on every day on that Guard commad. Wolf would take Jake to their supplies that were under a tarp each night and tell him to guard, pointing and patting the supply stash. He first started out by sitting with him and pointing around the area and doing his best growl. Jake would follow suit.

Now their supplies were as safe as being in a vault each night and Jake loved his job. He knew it was his alone and no one was ever going to get to what he was protecting.

Wolf smiled as he took the two guns to the other table and set them down. Those men weren't going anywhere.

Wolf slowly walked toward the wrestling going on at the far end of the room. He glanced at the storekeeper and touched the brim of his hat in greeting and said, "Storekeeper, you just keep your hands on the counter. Okay?"

The storekeeper only nodded.

Wolf walked quietly to the commotion and reached down and pulled the man's gun from its holster.

The man turned his head in shock and said, "What the hell---."

Wolf hit him across the back of his head with the man's own gun and tucked it in his belt.

He turned around as saw the two men frozen to their chairs and staring at Wolf as he reached down and grabbed both of the unconscious man's boots and dragged him off the woman and across the rough wooden flooring to the table where the two men sat. He was a big heavy man to drag.

He's going to have a lot of splinters in his dick to think about for awhile, he thought as he smiled to himself.

He dropped the man's feet when he got to the table and said, "Maybe you should teach this guy some manners."

The big man was coming around and sat up swearing at Wolf and said, "I'm gonna kill you, you son of a bitch."

Wolf didn't say anything. He just kicked the man under his chin and saw teeth fly out of his mouth.

Wolf didn't wear the western cowboy boots that were the common footwear. He continued to wear his work boots, which had a round toe and one inch flat heal. The toe of his boots were double layered with a steel inlay built in for safety in working.

Wolf reached down and undid the hold-down strap on the man's leg. He unbuckled the belt and dragged it out from under the prone body and walked to the other table and sat down.

In Spanish, he called to the woman who was struggling with her disheveled clothes and asked her to come to his table.

He called to Jake and he came over wagging his tail for a pat of appreciation, which he well deserved.

★ ★ ★

She was a young girl of about twenty years old. She was wiping her face and eyes that had been slapped around.

"Do you have some good food here, senorita?" he asked.

She started by thanking Wolf profusely and said she had fresh beans and she would take down some carne asada that she had drying and would shred it up and make him a good meal.

"How about flour tortillas?"

"I'll make them up fresh for you, senor."

"First go get yourself cleaned up and wash well. Then fix my meal, okay?"

She dashed through a door behind the counter and disappeared.

Wolf looked at the big man's gun belt as it was too light and found it only had three cartridges in the bullet loops on the belt.

The man was out of ammunition. Then he looked at the two men sitting at the next table, and noticed they too didn't have bullets in their belts.

He got up and walked over to the table and said, "Boys, it appears you may be in the market to buy some cartridges for your guns. Is that right?"

The man on Wolf's left said, "Well we're thinking about that. What do you care and what do you care about the 'greaser'?"

"What's a greaser?"

"The spicko, Mexican whore."

"Never heard those terms before."

"Maybe you ain't been around much mister."

"You boys got money to buy your lunch and ammunition?"

The two men looked at each other, which answered Wolf's question.

"Get your money out, boys and show the storekeeper that you have money to pay for things."

The two men just looked at each other.

"Well, if you don't have any money how do you expect to pay for your meal and ammunition?"

"We'll take care of that," the man said.

Wolf reached down and picked up the two plates on the table and set them on the floor and said, "Jake."

Jake moved right in and wolfed down everything on the plates and licked them so fast they were sliding along on the floor.

"Mister storekeeper, I think these boys here were about to rob you and probably kill you when they got done with their meal. Probably going to make off with the woman too, would be my guess," he said as he returned to his table.

The storekeeper nodded and said, "I didn't trust these guys. I've seen the likes of them before too many times."

"Well maybe your problems are over. Let's hope so."

Wolf watched the two men at the table, who were waiting for their friend to get up.

Wolf was too.

The big man sat up and looked around the room for Wolf, and reached into his boot.

Wolf knew what that was, and had the man's gun lined up on him sitting on the floor.

A roar from his left alarmed him, and he saw the storekeeper had just unloaded the single barrel of his shotgun into the big man.

"That son of a bitch was going to kill someone. That's for damn sure."

"Yes sir. I think you're right, mister storekeeper. Good job."

The two men were on their feet now looking at the storekeeper, who was popping another shell into his shotgun.

"I think they have the message now sir. You can put your gun back under the counter."

Jake was up looking at everyone, and looking at Wolf for assurance.

"Easy Jake, everything is fine," he said as he held out his hand to the big dog.

You boys sit down there and wait until I've finished my meal, then you can drag that no-good friend of yours and haul him away.

★ ★ ★

He had the woman sit down with him, while he ate. She told her story of how she happened to be there.

It seems she had been sold to the storekeeper by some local Indians who frequented the store for supplies and whiskey that they traded her for.

"You want to leave here?"

"Yes I do. I want to be back with my family."

"Where is your family?"

"South. About one day."

"How've you been treated here?"

"Not too bad. He's always really nice when we go to bed, but I don't want any more of that."

"Maybe this is your day to go home. What do you think?"

"How can I pay the man for what he paid for me?"

"You think you have to?"

"I don't know. It's all very confusing."

"Well think about it. There's a horse out front that'll be available and you could leave if you want to."

★ ★ ★

With his meal finished, and the supplies he requested on the counter, Wolf walked up to the storekeeper with the three guns and holsters slung over his shoulder.

"How much do I owe your sir?"

"It seems I probably owe you stranger. I don't even know your name."

"They just call me Wolf. I want to pay for my meal and supplies and I want to buy some supplies for the woman here as I think she wants to go back to her family. I know she's been here awhile and I think probably the time she's spent with you has paid you in full for what you had to pay the Indians, but I'll give you another twenty dollars for her release."

★ ★ ★

The storekeeper was looking at the woman now, who had her head bowed looking at the floor.

"Is that what you want to do, Millie?"

"Yes sir. I miss my family and my friends. You've been pretty good to me while I was here, but I want to go home now."

Tears came to the storekeeper's eyes and he said, in a husky voice,

"Well, if that's what you want, I guess its okay but I'm going to miss you. If you ever want to come back, I'll treat you real well, Millie."

★ ★ ★

Wolf paid the storekeeper and said, "You're a good man sir. I don't even know your name."

"Names Wilson," he said as he extended his hand.

"Mister Wolf it's been a real pleasure meeting you and thanks for what you've done for both me and Millie."

★ ★ ★

Wolf had the two men pick up their dead friend and cart him out the door. Wolf instructed them to carry him well out into the yard and lay him down, well away from their horses.

He then helped Millie load her supplies, which were more than enough for one day and had her water the dead man's horse well.

He took the carbine out of its scabbard and levered it. It had one cartridge in the magazine.

He put four more of his own in the magazine and made sure she knew how to use it and sent her on her way with a hug and whispered in her ear to watch her backtrack in case the two men tried to follow her.

"Don't stop till you get home or to a safe place. You can't trust these guys and they'll want your gun, supplies, horse and you."

She squeezed him and said, "Gracias."

The two men were swearing and complaining all the time about taking the big man's horse but Wolf just said, "He doesn't need it anymore."

He took the other two rifles and their scabbards and hung them on Blackie's and Ruby's saddle horns.

"You boys load your friend on one of these horses and head east. I don't want to see you turn in any other direction or I'll come after you. This ground is as flat as a pancake, and I can see you for miles, so get going."

★ ★ ★

The storekeeper was standing in the doorway with his shotgun, as the men wrestled the big guy up on one of the nervous horses, and then they argued as to who was going to walk and who was going to ride.

They finally decided they would double up on the remaining horse.

Wolf smiled. He knew that wouldn't last long.

They left without watering their horses and moved at a rapid clip into the east.

Wolf looked at the storekeeper and said, "How long you think it'll take them before they dump their friend?"

"Not long, I'm sure."

Sure enough; they hadn't gone three hundred yards when the horses stopped, and the dual rider got off the horse, and pulled the big guy out of the saddle he was draped across.

They both laughed at the tragedy. The three would-be robbers were real friends in deed.

The two men turned south as Wolf predicted to chase the woman who had at least a three-mile head start.

"I worry about Millie."

"I don't think those guys will catch her. Their horses have been standing in the sun for hours and they didn't water them before they left. They'll run out of energy long before they catch her and I told her to watch her back trail as I figured they would do just what they did."

"Mister Wilson, you're a real gentleman. I wish we could have met under different circumstances, and I wish you the very best of luck out here."

"Thank you, Wolf. Likewise," he said as Wolf was mounting Blondie.

CHAPTER 19

They finally hit the Red River. It seemed like it had been forever since they left it.

They headed northwest near the south bank of the river and on their second day Wolf saw a wagon train going west in the same direction they were heading.

It seemed like a good idea to travel with them if possible as they were bordering the Indian Territory and the more protection the better.

They moved into a nice lope and Jake had no problem keeping up. They covered the three miles or so and headed for the lead wagon and the group of men heading the train.

Wolf pulled alongside the men who had been watching them for long time and said, "Mind if I join you folks for a few days? How far are you going?"

"Don't mind at all. We can always use another gun in these parts."

"Had any trouble so far?"

"Yep. We've been attacked twice so far, but thankfully no serious problems. Seems the Indians around here still have mostly bows and arrows, but with everything going on, who knows when they'll get more rifles. The Indian wars supplied them with a bunch, and these guys that trade with the Indians, are always supplying them with more."

"Just drop back and find yourself a place to settle in. we're going to stop in about two hours for the night. These folks need a lot of sleep as the days are hard and hot. Lot's of folks walk a bit and they need to get cleaned up a little in the river. We'll hit somewhere near the river for the night. Got a man out front looking for a spot."

"Okay. Thanks for your help. I'll be no bother and have my own supplies. It will be kind of nice to talk to some folks that aren't the wild ones I've seen so far."

The men chuckled as Wolf moved off to the side and stopped.

The leader of the wagon train said, "You see the guns that guy's carrying?"

"Sure did. I spose he needs em, traveling alone."

"What kind of a hat is that? Never seen one like it before, and I thought I've seen em all."

"Don't know, but I think it's one of those plantation hats I've heard about that the big plantation owners wear."

"What on God's green earth is a wealthy plantation owner doing traveling all along in this country?"

"Damned if I know. See that dog of his? Hell I think it's a wolf."

"Acts like he's pretty well mannered for a wolf."

★ ★ ★

There was a little gap in the train, and Wolf moved into it. The dogs were barking at Jake and Wolf had to keep him quiet. These dogs were lean from the long march and no contest for the likes of Jake.

"Hey sonny. Where you heading?" said a woman driving a four-horse team behind him.

Wolf turned in the saddle and looked back. She had a long light blue dress on with a bonnet to shield the sun and grey hair stuck out over her forehead and down the sides of her head.

"I'm headed up Montana way, ma'am. I'm going to cut north when this river runs out, and head north to the Arkansas River.

"Sounds like you got a ways to go yet."

"Yes'm, but I'll get there."

★ ★ ★

They circled the wagons at night in a field of grass that their stock could feed on.

The old woman came to Wolf and said, "You can eat with me tonight if you want. I'm a pretty good cook. What do you have for supplies?"

A little of everything I guess. Enough for me to get by on and I usually shoot a bird or two during the day and maybe a rabbit. Jake my dog is a big eater and a hell of a hunter. As a matter of fact he's out looking for dinner right now. I see a couple of the dogs followed him. I hope they're all right."

"They'll survive I imagine. Come on over to my wagon and we'll fix us something to eat."

She had a hundred questions for Wolf. He tried his best to answer them, without going into any of the sordid details. He made his trip sound like everything was going smoothly in every respect.

"Well, Wolf, you have a long way to go yet for a single rider. Why don't you tag along with us? We have a lot of great people in this group and I think you'd get along just fine."

"Well ma-am, I've got a little property up Montana way and intend on raising some cattle up there."

"Well that's a good reason as any I guess."

His horses mingled with the others in the grass, and they had collected enough water from the river, for everybody.

Wolf and Jake slept under the woman's wagon that night with their supplies and listened to the men talk around the various fires within the circle of wagons.

The going was slow with the wagon train. It never moved faster than a walk.

Jake got nervous with the slow progress and was constantly heading off the trail to hunt on his own.

Wolf could tell that he had eaten well all day and wouldn't be hungry again at suppertime.

★ ★ ★

It was on the fourth day when they were passing some hills on their left, and the river was on their right.

Jake came back to the train in a wild sprint, that Wolf knew meant trouble, and he yelled at the wagon master to keep an eye open towards the hills.

Pretty soon they could hear yelps from a war party and the master called for an immediate circle of the wagons, which was done in an amazing fast fashion.

The horses were driven into the circle and the men armed themselves for the attack that came almost immediately.

The Indians circled the wagons attempting to frighten the people into submission, but that was not even dreamed of, as the rifles started to bark.

Ma'am, you know how to load a carbine?"

"Damn right sonny. You need loading?"

Wolf had two of his carbines out now and dumped a box of shells in his hat and handed it to the woman.

"You sit right there and load when I hand you a rifle. When you give it to me, you tell me how many rounds you put in it. Got that?"

"Hell yes, sonny. Go for it."

Wolf edged up close to the back oh her wagon and peered around the corner as he brought the rifle to his shoulder. The only thing an Indian would see is a small part of Wolf's head and the rifle.

It was easy shooting. They came past in a straight line from right to left and he hammered away dropping them as fast as he could track and squeeze the trigger.

He counted his rounds and gave it to the woman to load and picked up the second rifle.

"How many did you get, sonny?"

"Seven ma'am," was all he said as he continued to fire.

The old woman chuckled and jammed cartridges into the carbine as fast as she could.

Wolf continued to sight, track and shoot.

My God, there must be at least fifty Indians in this war party the way they're streaming by, he thought.

Wolf handed her the second rifle and she gave him the one she was loading, and said, "six. How ya doing?"

"Missed one, I think, but he's not going to go too far."

The old lady chuckled and continued loading.

Wolf turned around and was back in business, but after knocking down a few more the Indians veered away towards the hills.

They stopped at about two hundred yards, out of range of the carbine, and one large, heavily painted man was gesturing with his arms and pointing at the wagons. He was not giving up.

The men started talking about the next attack when Wolf had an idea.

He slid the scoped rifle out of its scabbard on Blondie and leaned against the wagon, resting the barrel on the edge.

He looked through the scope and judged the distance at about two hundred and twenty yards. A couple of yards in either direction would not change his aim point.

He put the crosshairs where he thought they should be at that distance and slowly squeezed the trigger.

The roar of the big gun brought everyone's attention to Wolf and then, in dead silence, they looked at the Indians, the SLAP was heard by all, and the well painted man was knocked off his horse.

The remaining Indians in the party looked back at the wagon circle and galloped into the hills leaving their leader on the ground.

Everyone looked at Wolf as he put his rifle back in its scabbard, and a cheer went up.

The men went out to collect all the rifles the dead Indians carried and brought them back to their group.

Several men were counting the bodies where Wolf had been shooting and kept looking back towards the old woman and Wolf.

"I knew you were a little different sonny. You got the best horses

I've seen and you sure have a lot of guns with you. I saw you shoot. You're a serious man, and yes I believe you'll get to Montana on your own after all.

"Thank you, ma'am."

Wolf stayed with the train until the Red River started to peter out. He had reached the headwaters and it was time to find a crossing and head north to the Arkansas River.

He gave the old woman a hug and thanked her for her hospitality. She had tears in her eyes when she said goodbye and wished him Godspeed and safety.

★ ★ ★

It was all Indian country now. He would have to keep his eyes open to survive the next several days. It was time to move fast, if possible.

CHAPTER 20

The wagon master told him that the Arkansas River was over two hundred miles north and suggested stopping at a small town north of where they were now and rest a day or two so he could make a fast dash to the Arkansas.

He learned he would be going through Kiowa country, then Arapaho, before he hit the river. There were a few forts up that way and hopefully the Indians weren't too plentiful or warlike. It was best to keep moving.

They had made about fifty miles when Wolf spotted the small town, the wagon master had told him about, and how to find.

It was still early afternoon when they rode into town.

The town sported its usual saloon and gambling hall, a church, schoolhouse nearby and several stores all made from unpainted rough lumber.

Wolf stopped at the general store to get supplies he knew he would need over the next couple of days as they dashed north to the Arkansas.

The store owner/operator was a congenial fellow and happy to sell Wolf anything he needed.

The store had almost anything anyone would want in that part of the country, so Wolf asked the man, "You must have a lot of neighbors around here to keep this much merchandise on hand."

"We sure do. The problem is getting paid from those folks," he said as he patted a tall, compartmentalized box that held dozens of small tablets of some kind.

"What are those?"

"There IOUs from all the folks around here. They only collect money when they sell cattle, stock or produce and that's when they can pay me. I on the other hand carry them until they can pay, and believe me, sometimes that's very difficult."

"I bet it is. You have a good heart, I'm sure."

★ ★ ★

Wolf collected the items he needed and went out to his horses and tossed Jake a small piece of jerky the storekeeper gave him for his dog.

It was far too early to stop so he mounted and headed north.

★ ★ ★

When they had ridden about five miles north of the town he slowly rode over a rise, always cautiously, and spotted a small ranch in the distance and headed for it.

There was a sturdy main house, a small barn in a clump of trees, a corral with two horses and some cows in it and a large fenced in area that must have been a chicken coop as there were chickens running around everywhere.

Between the chicken yard and the house was another fenced area that could only be a garden, as it was full of greenery of various types.

What caught his attention was the well, directly between him and the house. It was a place he could water his horses and fill the canteens and water containers.

He slowly rode up to the well and called, "Hello the house."

A blond-headed boy of about ten years old came outside and said, "What do you want, mister?"

"I'd like some water for my horses, if it's okay with you folks. I won't be bothering you any, just water my horses and I'm on my way. Sure would appreciate it."

"Well that's a little difficult, mister. The damn bucket fell into the well and I have to get water with this bucket here," he said as he pointed at an old steel bucket with a rope attached to it.

"That's fine. I can use that bucket. What happened to the other one?"

"Rope broke and it fell in the well."

"Was that a steel bucket too?"

"What difference does that make?"

"Well if was a regular wooden bucket most people use in their wells, maybe we could fish it out with the bucket you got there. The wooden bucket will be floating around in the water I imagine."

The boy was quiet for awhile and finally said, "Well, maybe so."

"Your pa try to fish it out?"

"My pa is in the army. Expect him home anytime."

Wolf knew just about everyone who was in the army had left long ago and if this boy's dad was alive he should be home by now.

"Well let's have a look at what you have, and see if we can do something about it, as long as I'm here. Bring the bucket you have," he said as he got off Blondie.

The boy hadn't missed looking the horses over and as he brought the bucket he said, "Boy, you sure have some great looking horses mister. Where'd you get them?"

"I had the two mares for a long time, and only recently did I get the stallion."

"Boy, they sure are nice ones," he said as he handed the bucket to Wolf.

"What's your name, son? They call me Wolf."

"Is that because you got that big damn Wolf with you?"

Wolf laughed and said, "No. He's not really a wolf. He just looks like one. The wolf must have gotten mated up with a big dog of some kind."

"My name is Jason."

Wolf checked the knot on the bucket and went to the well and looked down. The water was only about twenty feet down.

"Boy, that's a great water table. You have some streams around here?"

"Got one on each side only a few hundred yards away, why?"

"Your water table is real high. You must have good water around these parts," he said as he let the bucket rope slide through his hands.

The steel bucket hit something in the water before it got into the water.

"Your bucket is still floating around down there. Let's do a little fishing."

"There's no fish in there, mister."

Wolf smiled, looked at the boy, and said, "We're going fishing for a bucket."

★ ★ ★

It was on the third try that he knew he had the wooden bucket firmly against the plank wall of the well with his full steel bucket underneath.

He slowly, hand over hand dragging both buckets out of the well and reached in with his free hand and grabbed the wooden bucket, pulling it out and setting it on the rock well housing that rose about three feet above ground.

"It looks like we caught a big one, Jason."

The boy was all smiles and said, "Wow, that's great."

Wolf dumped both buckets of water into the small dry water trough alongside the well and all three horses and Jake were on it immediately.

Wolf looked the rope over and said, "No wonder you lost your bucket Jason. The rope is completely rotten."

It was then he looked at the crank device that was made of wood to spool up the rope and bucket out of the well and said, "You know Jason, you have to keep all that wood up there wet."

"What for?"

"Well if you don't it's going to dry up and fall apart then you're going to have this whole apparatus down in your well. Then you'll have a real problem. See how these boards are separating here," he said as he pointed them out and looked at Jason.

"I guess so. That's important?"

"If you don't keep this wood wet, you won't have a well at all one day."

Wolf dropped the metal bucket back in the well and pulled it up.

He threw it on the wooden drum that spooled up the rope and poured some on the end sections. The water cascaded back into the well.

"You got some more rope around here, Jason?"

"Just this one, and a few short pieces we use for the horses and cows.

"Let's use this one to get your well back in operation and next time you go to town get some more rope."

"You been to the town?"

"Sure have. Nice town. You go to school there?"

"Sure do."

"What grade are you in?"

"Well, I guess maybe four, but part of my work is in five."

"That's great. What subjects you like the best?"

"I guess arithmetic. The teacher is real good in arithmetic. She's real smart."

"That's what teachers do, Jason. They teach you and tell you things you don't know so you can use those things every day."

"Ya, that's what ma says. But some of it is a waste of time, I think."

Wolf was cutting away the old rope and keeper knot on the rope drum as he talked.

"Well let's see, Jason. I've only been here a few minutes and you've learned how you can fish your bucket from the well, right?"

Jason just looked at Wolf.

"You also learned that you have to keep this rope drum wet or it's going to dry out and fall apart. Isn't that right?"

"Well, that's different."

"No it's not. Everything she tells you, or teaches you, is something you don't know yet. That's how you learn."

"You sound like my ma."

"Where is your ma?"

"She's inside."

"Well pal, your ma is right. You need to learn everything you can from that teacher because those things you learn from her are going to be things you will use your whole life. The more you learn, the better you will do in life."

"You sound like my teacher now."

"Well you don't know me Jason, but I know what I'm talking about. You'll just have to take my word for it," he said with a smile.

"Okay. I've got the new rope on the wooden bucket and drum. Let's see how it works."

They talked while Wolf wound the drum up and down and Jason hauled water to the almost empty stock tank in the corral.

The horses went for it immediately, which told Wolf they weren't getting much water

★ ★ ★

Jason hauled water to the chicken coop and poured water on the garden near the house. It appeared everything was in need of water.

When he started pouring water on the ground by the four thin shade trees on the west side of the house, Wolf stopped him.

"Jason, what you're trying to do to water those trees is all wrong. It's just a waste of water. I'll show you how to water those trees so that they really get water. What you're doing now is of very little help to the tree."

"They need water too."

"Yes they sure do but, believe me, what you're doing now isn't going to help them much. I've raised many trees and I'll show you how it's done, okay?"

"You really raised a lot of trees?"

Wolf thought of the plantation and the orchards and all the trees on the property.

"Oh yeah lots of trees. Let me show you something. You know what the roots look like under the ground?"

"You are kidding? How would I know that?"

"That's some of the stuff you'll learn in school, Jason. Let me show you what the roots look like under the ground where you can't see them," and he started to scratch on the ground with a stick.

"You see what the tree looks like above the ground?"

"Well sure, I can see that."

"Well it looks just about the same underground."

"How you know that?"

"That's some of the stuff you'll learn from school, and from other people, that know things."

Wolf was explaining about the drip line and where the tree roots really needed water and how to get it to the roots, when Jason yelled, "Here they come!" he said as he looked off in the distance.

CHAPTER 21

Jason started to run for the house and Wolf stopped him. "Who are those guys Jason?"

"They come around here every so often and they do bad things to ma."

"Why don't you just run them off?"

"They took our gun away. I gotta go to ma."

"Hold it pal. You take my horses and lead them behind the house and don't come out until I call you. Trust me, Jason," he said as he held the boys shoulders, and looked him in the eye.

Jason didn't know what to do so Wolf gave him Blondie's reins, pulled the carbine from the scabbard and said, "Blondie go," and pushed Jason toward the house.

Wolf called Jake to his side and had him lie down beside him, behind the well housing. He took off his plantation hat and knelt behind the stone well housing with Jake.

He peeked over the edge, behind one of the thick wooden, upright rope drum structure, all the time talking to and calming Jake, and waited to see what was going to happen.

Three men were riding at a fair lope towards the house. The lead man had a revolver in his hand and was waving it around to his two outriders. Everyone seemed to be in a jubilant mood.

When they were about fifty yards from the house they started shooting at it. Wolf could hear the slugs hit the heavy walls of the house, and one ricocheted off the stone well housing. They were yelling and laughing like damn fools.

At thirty yards Wolf eased the carbine to the top of the stone housing and lined up on the lead man.

They were coming almost straight on and had picked up speed in their enthusiasm.

The first shot knocked the lead man off his horse.

The two outriders were in a quandary. *This had never happened before,* and they kept on coming. Now they were shooting at the well structure.

The second shot knocked the man to Wolf's right down and he swung to the remaining man who was trying to turn his horse toward the barn, lying low in the saddle.

The man never made it to the barn and now the three horses were looking at their riders, breathing heavy, and wandering around.

★ ★ ★

Wolf dropped his head on the stone well casing and said, "Lord, where do all these people come from. I'm not even to my goal and you try me almost every day in every way."

He knew instinctively it was a test of his will and faith.

★ ★ ★

Wolf called, "Jason, its okay to come out now. Bring the horses back."

Jason looked around the corner of the house and saw Wolf looking at him.

"Come on, pal. Those guys won't be bothering your ma anymore, okay?"

Jason ran to the wellhead stared at the three men lying in the dirt just a few yards away.

"These guys always shoot your house up when they come?"

"They sure do. I'm always patching up the holes to keep the flies and mosquitoes out."

"Well, I guess you won't have to do that anymore."

"I never seen anybody shot before. Sure felt like shooting them myself, from all the pain and misery they give to ma. I know my pa would go out and hunt them down."

"Well, you and I saved your pa from having to do that I guess."

"We gonna bury em?"

"What do you think? Think they're worth burying?"

"Hell no. Just like to see the coyotes and the birds get em."

"You got a shovel and a spade?"

"We gonna bury em now?"

"No. Right now I'm going to show you how to water those trees we were talking about."

"I gotta go see ma," he said as he turned and ran for the house, yelling, "ma, ma, did you see that ma?"

★ ★ ★

Wolf looked at the men in the field. No one seemed to be moving, so he led his horses over to the shade from the barn, where they could eat the grass and told Jake to stay with them.

Jake wasn't happy about that as he kept wanting to go and check the men he saw lying on the ground.

Jason came out of the house rubbing his eyes. He obviously had been crying, but didn't want to show it.

Wolf walked over to him and patted him on the shoulder and said, "Why don't you get that shovel and spade now?"

★ ★ ★

Wolf showed Jason where to dig the holes around the trees. Each hole would be big enough for one bucket of water and the four holes were placed evenly around the tree just inside the drip line.

"What are we gonna do with those guys out there, Wolf?"

"We aren't going to do anything, Jason. I'll take care of them in a minute. I'm just waiting for their horses to settle down and as you can see they're coming up to your corral where your horses are. They smell the water. I'll tie them to the corral and it looks like you'll have three more horses to feed."

"What about those guys lying in the sun?"

"You think we should be worried about that?"

"I don't know. We can't leave them lying around out there, we'll have a bunch of coyotes here and they'll kill the chickens and probably Oscar."

"Who's Oscar?"

"The dog you saw earlier. He's in the house now. I think he thought your wolf Jake was going to eat him."

Wolf laughed and said. "No, Jake isn't going to hurt anyone unless I tell him too, and I sure don't want him hurting Oscar. I'll take care of those guys. How far are those rivers you talked about on each side of your place and which one is the biggest."

Jason pointed east. "That one over there is a pretty big one. The water really moves fast. Ma won't let me swim in that one so we go over there," he said pointing to the west. "I got a great swimming hole over there. You should see it."

"Maybe I will, pal. Right now I gotta go catch you some horses. You get to digging and then we'll talk about how to water."

★ ★ ★

Wolf walked slowly up to the first horse that was now almost to the corral. He was talking quietly to the horse, which didn't seem to be the slightest bit nervous.

He took the reins that were dragging on the ground, and tied him to the corral, where the horse could get his head in the now-almost full, water tank.

He looked the horse over and checked his saddle and pack.

There was a lariat tied to the saddle, which was unusual for a traveling man. This horse must be used for working cattle, Illegal or otherwise.

The other horses didn't miss the fact that their companion was drinking water and started for the corral.

They were caught easily, and another horse also had a lariat. All the horses had saddle scabbards and rifles.

Wolf removed the scabbards and rifles and carried them over to the barn where his horses were.

He then slowly went to each man and confirmed that in fact they were dead.

They were all unshaven and ill-kempt. They obviously were living on the move in the area, as they had their bedrolls and supplies packed on each horse.

★ ★ ★

Wolf went back to the corral and got two of the horses and led them to the first man.

He unbuckled the man's gun belt, found the revolver and re-buckled the belt, hanging it over the saddle horn of one of the horses.

With the lariat he looped it over the man's feet and boots and tied the other end to the saddle horn of the horse.

He led both horses to the second man. The horses were looking back at what was being dragged.

He repeated the process and moved to the third man.

This man got one leg in the same loop of one of his companion's, and his other leg in the other loop of the second horse. Now the two horses were dragging all three men between them.

Wolf walked between the horses, talking to them, and headed for the large river, which Jason had told him was less than a mile away.

CHAPTER 22

W hen Wolf got to the river he untied the three men and tied the horses to a tree, down low, so they could eat the lush river grass.

He then searched each man.

I found one boot gun and a derringer. He also found lots of smoking and chewing tobacco and some cash, which he someone would get to Jason's mother.

He threw the three men in the river and watched as they rapidly moved downstream until they were out of sight.

Wolf mumbled a blessing to the outlaws and wished them well wherever they were headed.

He rolled up the lariats, mounted one of the horses, led the other and headed back to the house.

★ ★ ★

Jason was hard at work when he got back and just completing the third hole under the first tree. He had followed the instructions to a tee and had the small mound of dirt almost all the way around the tree from the digging.

"Hey Jason, You're doing great. In just a couple of weeks you won't even be able to see the sunlight through these trees. Look how sparse the leaves are now. I want you to get a good look at that, so when you see how well they're growing, you'll know you accomplished that."

Jason smiled with pride and asked, "What you do with those guys?" "Took em swimming."

"I'm going to get something to put in those great holes you're digging. I'll be right back."

He went to the enclosure where all the chickens were and got a square-end shovel that had been used to clean up after the chickens, and scratched together a shovel-full of chicken droppings.

He went back to the tree and dropped some droppings in each hole, picked up the steel bucket and went to the corral.

He started dipping water and filling the holes, when Jason said, "You really think this is going to make a difference, huh?"

"Guaranteed, Jason; you'll start to see s difference in just a few days. You watch. You're going to be surprised."

"You grew a lot of trees, huh?"

"Oh yes. We have a big orchard and lots of shade trees. Of course we have a lot more rain than you do here so that's why I'm showing you how to get the best out of what you have."

"What you leave for?"

"Got some work to do Jason."

★ ★ ★

The three holes he had poured water into were only half full now indicating good soil. *"This is going to work,"* he thought.

Jason had finished with the fourth hole now, and they both worked on getting the dirt circle around the tree sound so it would hold water when it rained.

"See how that water is soaking into the ground, Jason? That water is going to the roots you are trying to water. When you dump it on the ground you only get a couple of inches of soil wet. That really doesn't do much good and wastes water. Our little dam here, around the tree, will catch all the rainwater and keep it from running off, and fill up the four holes you dug. From time to time you'll have to clean out these holes and just add the dirt to the dam."

"Every once in awhile you drop some chicken droppings, or a little horse or cow dung in there. Not too much, because it's going to go right down to the roots and you don't want to burn them up with too much animal shit. Okay?"

"You fill these holes up again, pal. I've got to take care of your new horses."

★ ★ ★

Wolf unsaddled each horse and took the saddles to the porch and stood them on end, saddlebags and all.

He then worked up a simple halter for each horse from the left over rope from the well bucket job, and put them in the corral with the other two horses. No one seemed disturbed by the newcomers, so Wolf went to the barn to sort out what he had taken off the horses.

★ ★ ★

Jason had gone into the house and came running over to Wolf and said, "Ma wants to know if you will stay for supper?"

"Well that's real nice of your ma, Jason. You tell her, sure. It's a pleasure."

Jake had accepted Jason as a friend now, and went right to him for a pat.

"Jason, you take the saddle bags off and go through them and keep what you want. You'll probably find some ammunition in there as well."

"Don't have a gun."

"I'm working on that right now Jason. You'll have one when I get done."

If you folks don't want the horses, you can always sell them. The saddles too. Someone is always looking for a horse, and those three aren't too bad. You should get some decent money for them. The saddles are pretty good too, so you should get a good price for them as well."

"What if they ask where we got em?"

"You tell them you got them from me. It's as simple as that. I'll even work up a bill of sale for your ma so she won't have any problems."

I imagine we're gonna have chicken tonight for dinner. You like chicken?"

"Sure do, but why don't you eat one of those antelope out there grazing in all that nice grass?"

"I've tried sneaking up on them but I never got close enough, then those guys took our gun away from us. Ma's even been afraid to go to town."

"Do you know how to clean out an antelope, and skin it, and cut it up?"

"Sure do and ma is really a good butcher. She knows how to cut em up, hang em, dry em and everything. She does some butchering, and about everything else I guess. She's a hard worker."

"You want antelope for dinner rather than chicken?"

Jason laughed and said, "their too far to shoot and impossible to sneak up on."

"You want antelope for dinner?"

Jason looked at Wolf with a strange impression and said, "Sure do, but how we gonna get one?"

★ ★ ★

Wolf got up off the ground and went over to the far side of Blondie and pulled out the scoped rifle.

As he walked to the corner of the barn Jason said, "Wow, I've never seen anything like that before."

"Not a whole lot of these rifles around, Jason. I think maybe we should shoot that female over there on the left. She looks real healthy and probably got some fat on her, and should be tenderer than those bucks standing around. What do you think?"

Jason laughed and said, "Ya, I guess so."

Wolf leaned against the small barn and steadied the rifle in the taught sling. The barn gave great stability for shooting.

He judged the antelope to be about three feet high at the head so adjusted accordingly, pulled to the center of the chest cavity so as not to destroy any meat and slowly squeezed the trigger.

In the quiet they could here the bullet hit its target with a slap, and the doe dropped.

"Guess you better get your knives, Jason. You got some work to do."

Jason was jumping up and down saying, "Wow! Wow! Wow!"

And he ran for the house.

★ ★ ★

"He dashed inside and said, "Ma, did you see that? We're going to have an antelope to eat. Oh wow."

His mother smiled and opened the drawer that had the knives in it and said, "oh yes, I saw it alright. It looks like we're going to have some meat on the table for awhile, so you be sure and thank that man."

★ ★ ★

Jason dashed out of the house and ran over to Wolf and said, "Boy that was great, Wolf. Ma wanted me to tell you thanks. We can sure use the meat. Ma's great at smoking and jerking it so we can keep it, thanks."

"That's ok, Jason. Is it ok if I take a bath before dinner? It's been a few days away from a river and I sure could use a bath."

"Well the tub is in the house, Wolf."

Wolf laughed and said, "I don't need the tub Jason. I can use that little water trough by the well. That's perfect."

Jason looked over at the well and back at Wolf and said, "Well, okay I guess."

★ ★ ★

Wolf got his necessaries and headed to the well while Jason was cleaning out the doe.

He was standing in the small wooden water trough when Jason came back dragging the antelope. Jason looked at Wolf and said, "Jesus, Wolf, your buck naked."

"Well aren't you usually buck naked when you take a bath, Jason?" he asked smilingly as he lathered his face.

"Well ya, but someone might see you out here like that."

"Wolf looked all around as said, "Well I don't see anybody, and if they don't want to see me buck naked then they don't have to look I guess."

"Golly, Wolf. You got a whole bunch on scars all over your body," Jason said real quiet like.

"Yes I do, Jason. Each and every one of them represents something and they aren't very good memories."

"I better get this doe into ma, I'm thinking."

"Good idea."

Wolf completed shaving with the razor-sharp flat blade on his folding skinning knife that he kept honed to perfection.

He rinsed off and dried the best he could with his small towel and walked moccasin-footed back the barn.

★ ★ ★

Jason's mother hadn't missed the view of Wolf standing naked at the well.

She didn't remember ever seeing anyone built as fat free, and muscular, as that man Jason called Wolf.

It looked like he had a lot of scars on his body that she couldn't really make out from the house, but the ones on his back were obvious.

That man has led a hard life, she thought.

There was something about him that churned inside her that she just couldn't make out. It felt like he was supposed to be there.

★ ★ ★

Wolf knew he was going to spend the night there because it was clouding up and it looked like a heavy storm on the way.

After getting permission from Jason he put his gear and horses in the barn. They had plenty to eat and had enough water till morning.

He stacked his rollup bedroll on top of his pack and covered everything with one of his canvas tarps.

He went through the rifles and revolvers from the three men to select something for Jason's family.

CHAPTER 23

Wolf walked up to the house and knocked on the door, which was immediately opened by Jason with a big grin on his face.

"Come on in, Wolf. Welcome to our house. That's my ma over at the stove. Man, we're going to eat tonight," he said licking his lips.

Wolf was surprised by the beauty of the lady. She was probably in her early thirties, just a couple years older than Wolf. She wore a long housedress that still showed off her buxom, shapely figure that was very appealing, covered by a well-worn and stained apron.

She was about three inches shorter than Wolf's five foot nine and had thick shiny black hair that was pulled tightly back into a big bun on the back of her head.

She seemed familiar, like he already knew her, *but that's impossible*, he thought.

Wolf was unconsciously appraising her, when smiling, she said, "Is it okay?"

Wolf mumbled a little and said, "Sorry ma'am. Yes, its okay indeed."

Jason looked back and forth between the two of them. He'd missed something, but he didn't know what it was.

"I'm sorry, Mister Wolf. I'm just in the middle of getting some of this cut-up antelope in the skillet. You and Jason sit down and I'll be with you in a minute."

"Jason, you get that bottle of red wine we have in the cupboard so Mister Wolf can at least have a cup of wine while he's waiting for dinner."

"I'm not mister Wolf, ma'am. That's just a nick name. My name is Wolfgang Beaumont. Everyone just started calling me Wolf when I was a kid, and that's what I go by most all the time. It saves trying to explain things."

I'm Sarah Hudgens. Where are you from, Wolf?"

"New Orleans, ma'am."

Please, just call me Sarah, okay?"

"Yes ma'am, I mean Sarah," and they all laughed.

"I was just raised to always call a woman ma'am."

Jason arrived with a big grin on his face, and a half bottle of some kind of red wine Wolf had never heard of.

"Get the man a cup, Jason. He can't drink it out of the bottle."

"Yes ma," he said as he scooted over to the little cabinet in the kitchen.

★ ★ ★

Sarah came and sat with them from time to time while she was cooking dinner, and she was a delight to talk with.

She came from Kansas and was on her way to meet her uncle in Texas, when she met up with her husband, who went to war several years ago and never returned.

Jason said, "I wish he'd hurry up and get here. It sure would be nice if you could meet him, Wolf."

Wolf looked at Sarah, and it was obvious that she knew he wasn't going to return. Jason just held it in his mind as wishful thinking. If he believed he was really going to return or not, no one knew.

"Wolf said, "Well, Jason, you're the man of the house now you know. You have to take care of your mom, and do everything you think your dad would have done if he was here. I can tell there are things he didn't get to teach you so maybe we could talk about some of those things tomorrow."

"Waiting for your dad is great, Jason, but you have to be the man in the house now. I bet you were just a pup when he went off to war, huh?"

"You think he's coming back don't you, Wolf?"

"I don't know, pal. I hope so. But the war's been over for some time now and lots of the soldiers went home already, you know."

"Ya, a couple has stopped by here on their way to their places. I hope he comes home."

"We all do, Jason."

"You going to show us those guns you hauled in the house?"

"We'll do that after dinner when we have time to talk about it. Right now I can't think of anything other than that great smell of your mom's cooking."

CHAPTER 24

The dinner was far better than he expected. There were fresh greens and tomatoes and cucumbers.

The steak was browned then cooked with onions and fresh-cut chives and tomatoes.

The bread was fresh and obviously baked that day. There was even a small amount of butter they had churned themselves from the milk from the four cows they had in the corral adjacent to the horses, where they could all share the same watering trough.

There was even a small amount of honey. It was like a family dinner, and all three of them realized how easily and happily they fit together.

After dinner, Sarah said, "Jason, go and gather some eggs for breakfast before it rains, please," and Jason dashed out the door with a small wicker basket.

"Sarah, please let me help you to clean up here. This has been the best meal I've had since I left New Orleans and I'm sure appreciative. It's the least I can do."

★ ★ ★

The water was already hot and she poured it into a tin tub she had in the sink and swished around a small remnant bar of soap.

Conversation was exploratory, the telling of their lifestyles. Sarah did not think her husband Richard would return. He loved this country and if he was alive he would have been home long ago. She just hadn't convinced Jason that that was a possibility. Tonight was the first time he acknowledged that perhaps things were different than what he thought. Maybe he was maturing into understanding.

By the time they had finished with the dishes and cleaned up the kitchen, Sarah said, "I have to cut up some of this meat and smoke it and jerk some of it. It's too warm to keep too long."

"You could get me another pail of water so I can start soaking the meat in salt and pepper to get it ready to dry. I'll soak it for a day then hang it in the sun and then it'll last a long time. You can take some with you on your trip, if you're still going," she said as she was looking down at the hindquarter on the counter by the sink.

Wolf was surprised by the comment, and for a while wished he could stay as he looked around the house. This is a great family. They just needed a strong leader.

He did not respond immediately and said in a low voice that only Sarah could hear over the crash of thunder and lightning. "I'll have to tell you what I'm doing. I don't want this to end either, but it came on all of us awful fast and hard.

★ ★ ★

Wolf laid the two rifles and two holsters with revolvers on the table and waited until Sarah was through with what she was doing with the fresh meat.

Wolf and Jason talked about some of the things Jason could do around the ranch, and Wolf said, "Come on, Jason, I want to show you something," and headed for the door.

The door stuck something and Wolf noticed the top hinge was loose from the jam as he opened the door and went out onto the porch.

"Where're we going, Wolf?"

"Just out here Jason, I want to show you something you did today."

"What did I do?" he said in a defensive manner.

"Nothing you did wrong, pal. Something you did really well."

Wolf walked him to the edge of the porch staying far enough inside to stay out of the heavy downpour.

"Watch when the lightning strikes again and lights things up. I want you to look at the tree that you dug the holes in and put the little dam around."

They only had to wait a few seconds and the lighting lit up the sky and the thunder crashed.

"Wow, the tree well is full of water."

"Sure is. You see the other trees aren't getting near the water that your tree is. That tree is going to grow to be a big strong shade tree this year. When you finish with the others they will too. That's what I was talking about when we dug the holes and made the dam around the tree," he said as he patted him on the back.

"Those trees will keep your house a whole lot cooler in the late afternoon sun. You'll see."

Jason ran in the house and said, "Ma, you should see the water that tree is collecting since we dug the holes and put the dam around it. Wow, it's really getting water now and fertilizer too. Boy those trees are going to be big in no time."

Sarah smiled, looked at Jason and said, "Well, I guess you learned something didn't you? You're always saying there isn't anything to learn in school and now all of a sudden you're learning all sorts of stuff. Maybe you should pay more attention in school. You'll be surprised what you'll learn."

"That's the same thing Wolf said," Jason said, shaking his head like all of a sudden it was coming to him.

Sarah smiled and looked at Wolf, who winked at her.

★ ★ ★

They sat around the table and Wolf was showing the guns he had selected for them.

"The rifles are the common 44-50 calibers and the pistols are Colt .45s."

"This is the holster that I selected for you, Sarah."

Before he could continue both Jason and Sarah laughed, and Sarah said, "I didn't think I was that fat. The belt is huge."

"Yes it is and there's a reason for that. Let me show you," he said as he stood up and motioned for her to stand as well.

"Jason, what's the first thing you do when you pick up a gun?"

"Make sure it's not loaded."

"No, that's the second thing you do. The first thing is, you point it in a safe direction. Then you see if it's loaded.

"I've unloaded all of these guns but I want each of you to point it in a safe direction then check to see if it's loaded.

Sarah and Jason each took turns going through the exercise of checking each gun to Wolf's satisfaction.

Wolf walked over to Sarah and looked her in the eye and felt that she was looking intimately deep inside him, like she knew him.

He draped the belt over her left shoulder and let the holster hang down in front of her dress. The gun was now just below her wasteline facing right, and he pushed everything in place. *Damn, she's got a nice body,* he thought.

"I know you're right handed so this is how you wear it."

"How'd you know I am right handed?"

"I see how you move and what you do. You cut and eat with your right hand. Not too hard to figure out."

Sarah just looked down at the table and smiled.

"Here's what you do, Sarah. When someone comes to the house you go right out on the porch to meet them. You can drop this over your shoulder in seconds. When you walk outside you put your hand on the butt of the gun and lift it just a little bit with your thumb on the hammer. You know how to shoot, don't you?"

Sarah smiled and looked at Wolf and said, "Of course I do."

"Show me how you would pull the gun out and shoot it at someone."

Sarah surprised him with her quick reaction and had the gun in her hand leveled straight ahead.

"Now shoot it three times. It's not loaded of course. You checked that."

She pulled hammer back and pulled the trigger. She repeated it three times.

"Sarah, you notice when you pull the hammer back the gun doesn't stay on target? It wanders around as you reach for the hammer with your thumb. Let me show you how to handle the gun in the event you have to use it."

★ ★ ★

Wolf went through the training to show her how to use both hands to hold the gun to reduce the movement from recoil and to use her left hand that was gripped over her shooting hand to thumb back the hammer.

"See how you stay on target now? Practice that a few times and you'll have it. Those guys had plenty of ammunition so practice everyday, first with the gun empty, and then shoot a few live rounds. Jason you do the same thing, but here's the secret for you, Jason."

"If your mom goes outside with her gun you know it's serious. You take one of the rifles there and go over to the window on the left side of the door," he said pointing to the shuttered window.

"You cock the rifle and stick the barrel outside the window. Not too far, just a couple of inches. When your mom is talking to whoever it is. You say in a loud voice, "I've got the one on the left.""

"Now they'll know you guys a dead serious. If that happens the word will get around and you'll have no problems from that point on."

"Pay attention to your dog at night he hears and smells things that you can't. He'll tip you off to any intruders. Do not go outside after dark if there is someone there. You talk to them through a window and each of you have a gun pointed at whoever is there. You'll have to trust me on that folks."

★ ★ ★

Wolf loaded and hung Sarah's revolver in a handy location that she could get to in an instant. The rifles he put in the corners of the front of the house.

They were ready.

CHAPTER 25

"Okay, Jason. Its bed time, so clean up and jump in bed son. I think tomorrow's going to be a busy day."

"You can't go out in the barn tonight, Wolf. It's going to be cold and wet out there. You might as well stay here in the house tonight where it's warm," Jason said as he went to the sink and poured water, to brush his teeth and wash up before going to bed.

"I'll be ok, pal. You just get good night's sleep."

"Well my bed is too small for both of us, but mom's got a big bed," Jason said, while scrubbing his teeth.

Wolf looked at Jason in surprise and then at Sarah, who was in mild shock as well.

"Yes we have plenty of room, Wolf. You're welcome to stay here tonight. No sense in going out to the barn when you have a comfortable place to sleep," she said looking Wolf directly in the eyes.

Wolf had nothing to say and just sat down at the table in bewilderment.

Jason finished up and went to his corner in the front of the house. Oscar raced in and jumped on his bed and Jason pulled his privacy curtain around his bed and yelled, "Good night, ma. You too, Wolf."

Sarah who was already adding some wood to the fire to keep the house dry and warm for the blustery night. She turned the damper down and walked to the small bedroom in the rear near the kitchen area and looked back at Wolf who was still sitting at the table in the light of the small lantern.

Sarah took a lantern off the wall in her bedroom and lit it. She looked at Wolf nodded her head to him to come into the bedroom, and slowly disappeared into the small room.

★ ★ ★

The room wasn't what he expected. It was clean and the bed was smooth with a blue blanket on it. It was carefully and privately preserved for her own domain.

"Boy you've got a nice room here, Sarah."

Sarah looked at him. Put her finger to her mouth for silence and closed the door into the room and slowly walked over to a little chest of drawers in the corner and set the lantern on its top. She slowly started to undress facing the small mirror over the dresser, watching Wolf at all times.

Wolf watched as she pulled the long dress over her head slowly revealing a firm body that could only be supported by her energetic daily life.

She pulled three long pins out of the bun on the back of her head and her black hair fell to below her shoulders.

She picked up a hairbrush and started brushing the curves from the bun out of the hair, and pulled it over her shoulder and brushed it down over her full bosom.

Her eyes never left Wolf's reflection in the mirror the whole time she was doing it. She wanted this man to know he was wanted.

Wolf slowly walked over to her while watching her in the mirror and whispered, "You trying to drive me crazy, Sarah?"

"No, Wolf. I'm just trying to let you know that you're wanted here and that I want you here. I thought that when you first walked through the door. I think you had some feelings too if you will recall. I felt like I already knew you."

"No one and I mean no one has ever done that to me. You are

closer to Jason than even his father. To us you're a dream come true. I want you---no, we want you to stay."

Wolf put his arms around her and had his hands on her stomach. He kissed her on the side of her neck and just held her.

"That's the nicest thing anyone has ever said to me, Sarah. I don't even know how to reply."

"Don't reply, Wolf. Just get undressed and we'll get to bed."

"I can't believe Jason suggested this," he said shaking his head and moving to the single wooden chair at the foot of the bed.

"Maybe he knows more than both of us. I was shocked myself when he said it, especially since he was witnessed so much from those men you eliminated. I really can't believe it."

Wolf hung his gun belt over the back of the chair and took all his clothes off except for his knee-length, tight fitting shorts that were an advantage in sitting in the saddle all day, and dropped them in the corner of the room.

Sarah went over and picked up his clothes and hung them on a hook in the wall and stared at him for a long time.

"Better get rid of those pants Wolf. Looks like you might break out of them at any moment," she whispered with a smile.

CHAPTER 26

I t was nothing like he expected, or experienced in the past. Sarah just moved close to him and caressed him in total silence, all the while staring at him in the dim candlelight.

Wolf actually made love to Sarah. It was one of the few times in his life. It was slow, tender and very meaningful. Everything they did to each other was a caress, not a mechanical function.

The two of them fit like a hand in a glove, and nothing was overlooked.

Sarah had an outstanding body and she kept it close to Wolf all night.

He could smell her and their lovemaking and feel her warmth. Even in his weary state he had a hard time falling asleep with his mind whirling.

★ ★ ★

Wolf was surprised when he opened his eyes and found the bed empty and the smell of coffee in the air.

It was first light and he looked at his gold pocket watch, the only real symbol of his true past, wound it and read the time. It was 5:30 and by the sound of things, both Jason and Sarah were in the kitchen.

He found the water basin on the chest of drawers was full of warm water and a small remnant of a bar of soap on a towel next to it. The ceramic water pitcher nearby was full of cold, clear water, all accomplished by Sarah while he slept.

Wolf dressed, and casually opened the door, and walked into the kitchen. Both Sarah and Jason smiled and Jason said, "Good morning, Wolf. How'd you sleep?"

He noticed Sarah was waiting for the reply as well with a smile on her face, and he said, "Never better, Jason. Thanks for asking."

There were six eggs on the counter and Sarah poured Wolf a cup of coffee "Have a seat, Wolf. Breakfast will be ready shortly," she said as she slid a large heavy ceramic pot out from under a kitchen counter.

She reached in and pulled out a whole bacon side and laid it on the kitchen counter with a thud.

"Wow, you sure aren't short on bacon I guess," he said as he looked at the huge slab.

"I do some butchering for a neighbor and he pretty well keeps us in bacon as well as a little cash. We butcher his hogs and he sells it to townspeople and neighbors alike."

Sarah took a knife out of a drawer and went to work trying to cut the bacon into strips. She was having a hard time so Wolf walked over to her and said, "Let me see that, Sarah."

The knife was too dull to cut the bacon easily and he said, "I think we need to sharpen your knife," as he laid it down and pulled out his razor-sharp Bowie knife.

Sarah was amazed at how easily the big knife cut through the side.

"How many slices to you want, Sarah?"

"One each for Jason and I. You cut as many as you want for yourself. Now that's a sharp knife."

"Well I'll get yours sharp for you today. You can't work with a dull knife. You should know that as a butcher."

"Well, I just haven't gotten around to it I guess with all the other stuff going on around here."

"We'll get it taken care of," he said as he wiped his knife and sat down at the table with his coffee.

★ ★ ★

After breakfast while Sarah was cleaning up the kitchen, Jason and Wolf sat at the single table in the house drinking coffee.

Wolf said, "Hey, Jason how's that buckboard you got out there? I need to get some stuff from town and I thought you and I could get your horse hooked up and take a ride into town. How does that sound?"

Jason was grinning from ear to ear and looked at his mom and said, "Okay with me. Is it okay with you, ma?"

"Sure. You boys go to town and have a big time. I'll stay here and slave away," she said with a big smile on her face, and a look of admiration and love at Wolf.

"Well let's get saddled up then, pal. The day is moving on."

As they walked out the door Wolf had his hand on Jason's shoulder talking to him.

Sarah has tears in her eyes as the two of them headed to the barn to get the buckboard carriage.

★ ★ ★

Wolf called Jake over to the house, fed him and told him to sit on the porch and gave him the guard command.

Sarah said, "What's that all about?"

"It's something that Jake and I've worked out on this trip. I've given him the command to guard this area, and believe me he will guard this area. No one, and I mean no one is coming on this porch."

Sarah looked at the snarling do, going through the exercise he and Wolf did with the Guard command.

Jake then looked at Wolf and got his praise which he answered with a lick on Wolf's hand and then looked at Sarah while wagging his tail.

Oscar was behind Sarah looking around her at Jake, obviously in fear for his life.

"That's the darndest thing I've ever seen. I mean he's one mean-looking SOB and that snarl of his brought goose bumps on my neck."

"He'll look after you, Sarah. We'll be home before you know it."

CHAPTER 27

Wolf was surprised at how meticulously Jason hooked up and checked all the harness for the horse and rig. He was equally a good driver as well.

Wolf took one of the carbines with him and a small leather pouch of rifle cartridges.

When Jason asked about it, Wolf said, "I'm riding shotgun pardner," in an old growly voice that made Jason laugh.

They talked about a lot of things. Wolf talked about some of the things that needed fixing at the ranch and told Jason they would get a few things to fix those matters up.

Jason looked at Wolf and said, "Ah, Wolf. I don't think we have much credit at the store in town. Ma hasn't brought them any money lately. I'm not sure we can get what we need."

"Don't worry, pal. We'll take care of it. They got a saddle shop in town too?"

Sure, and a real good one. The old guy that runs it makes saddles, boots and all kinds of stuff."

"Let's go there first. I have to get a proper halter for Blackie. The rope one I made needs replacing. The rope is too hard on his head."

★ ★ ★

It was a short trip to town and Jason was busy pointing out all the buildings and telling Wolf what they were.

The schoolhouse was down near the end of town close to the church and he was excited to point it out and tell Wolf where he sat in the schoolroom.

They pulled up to the saddle shop and got down from the buckboard. Wolf put the carbine under the seat out of sight.

Jason was right. The man running the store was busy cutting leather in the rear of the store and without looking up said, "Howdy folks. Be with you in a minute."

Wolf slowly walked around the store looking at all the supplies and finery.

He found the steel clips he was looking for to tie to the ends of a rope and easily clip the end on a halter or bridle. He picked up ten of them and put them on the counter. He then went over to the side where there were three types and sizes of rope on big spools on a pipe.

There were markings on the floor for footage, so all you had to do was pull out as much as you wanted and cut it off.

He said, "Jason, give me a hand over here, will you?"

Jason was busy feeling one of the saddles the man had made and said, "Okay," and walked over to Wolf.

"You and I are both a little short of rope, Jason, and I thought we should get some. I think this one is good. You can use it on the stock and it sure will work if you have to replace the water bucket rope. We're going to cut one fifty foot piece and four twenty foot pieces, okay?"

"Sure. How're we going to know how long they are?"

"See those marks on the floor and the numbers along side them? Those are measurements for the rope. I want you to take this rope out to ten feet, then come back and get the rope where I'm holding it and go out to ten feet again, okay. Then I'll cut the rope."

"Ya sure. Then we'll have a twenty-footer, right?"

"Right; we're going to do that four times, okay?"

"Okay."

Wolf noticed the man cutting leather didn't miss any of the

conversation and finally finished what he had cut and walked over to Wolf, looking him up and down.

It was obvious the man was assessing Wolf. He'd seen a lot of people pass through his shop and was a pretty good judge of people.

"Haven't seen you around here before, mister; I see you're with Jason here. You know the Hudgens do you?"

"Yes sir and we need a few items so Jason and I came to town to get them."

"I need a halter as well, sir. Jason and I'll finish cutting up the rope we need, unless you want to do it?"

"No, you boys go ahead. I trust you. I know Jason. He's a good boy, so I'm not concerned."

They finished cutting and coiling the rope they needed and asked if they had any nails and hammers and things like that.

"No, you can get that at old Jamison's place. He's got about everything there.

"You don't have any steel files or anything of that nature, do you?"

"Nope. Jamison is the guy."

★ ★ ★

They made their way to the general store that presumably was run by a Mister Jamison and walked in.

"Hi Jason. How are you and you mother doing son?"

"Ah---just fine, Mister Jamison." Jason responded.

"What can I do for you folks today? Say, you're the guy that came in here a few days ago. You said you were heading up north somewhere."

"Yes sir. That was me. We need to pick up some things for the Hudgins today."

"Mrs. Hudgins has an outstanding balance of, lets see." he mumbled as he turned back to the IOU tablets.

Jamison looked at the cabinet behind the counter that he'd shown to Wolf when he was in the store earlier.

"Ah, yes. Here it is. She has a balance of $18.35," he said, as he looked up at Wolf with his eyebrows raised.

"Thank you Mister Jamison. We'll be taking care of that today and we want to make a cash purchase of a few items, and because you don't have to carry the Hudgens on this purchase, I believe you give your cash customers a nice discount. Is that correct?" he said looking Jamison in the eye.

"Well yes indeed. Just what do you need?"

★ ★ ★

The counter was full of items that Wolf requested. James was busy writing down the items on the list for pricing.

"We need one of those tin containers over there. We want to fill it up with beans. Can you do that and weigh it so we know what we have?"

Jamison was excited. This was the biggest sale he had in months. "Oh course, sir," he said as he got the tin and headed to the bag of beans.

Could we borrow a few boxes from you sir? I think the flour, sugar and coffee and the like need to be in a box. Jason can bring the boxes back to you when he comes into town next time."

"Of course. I'll take care of it."

Jason was over looking at the soft goods of blankets and pillows and clothing.

"Boy, look at this pillow, Wolf. This is sure a lot better than the one ma has."

Wolf smiled at Jason and said, "Yes it is, Jason. Think your mother would like this?"

"Oh boy would she ever, Wolf."

"Then I think we should get it for her don't you?"

"Your mother needs some other things tooI think Jason," he said as he picked up a white apron. "This for instance," he said as he smiled.

"Boy, ma really needs a new apron alright."

"How we gonna pay for all of this, Wolf?"

"Don't worry. Somehow it will get handled, pal," he said as he walked over to a stack of blankets and quilts.

"Do some of the ladies around here make these quilts, Mister James?"

"Yes. The church has a group of ladies that do quilting. They're beautiful aren't they?"

"They sure are. How much are they asking for this big multi-colored one here?"

"There should be a tag on it somewhere."

Wolf opened the heavy winter quilt up and searched for a tag.

The tag said $9.00 and the name Bessie Morgan.

"It says here Bessie Morgan and the price is nine dollars."

"Well I've had it for her for quite some time. I think you can buy it for seven."

Wolf looked at Jason, who was taking it all in and winked at him.

Jason got close to Wolf and said, "What's going on, Wolf?"

"I think we should get this quilt for your mom. I'm thinking about getting two good blankets too for winter and I see that wooden trunk over there, I think that would be great to keep them in. what do you think?"

Wolf went over and opened the wooden chest. It was four feet long and two feet deep and almost three feet high. It was a big chest.

It was solid and appeared airtight and had been lined with a sweet-smelling wood, he was not familiar with.

"What's this wooden trunk over here, Mister Jamison?" he said pointing to the trunk.

"A lady brought that in some time ago. It's a cedar chest. She brought it from back east but she didn't like living around here with all the damn Indian problems so took the stage out of town and went back east again.

"How much you have to have for it? You've probably had it for quite a while and it isn't earning you any money sitting here."

Jamison walked over to Wolf, and talking in a low conspirator voice said, "Sir, with all the things you've purchased and the tools and hardware and now the quilt and blankets the charges are over eighty dollars. You sure you are going to pay cash for these things?"

Wolf took the man by the arm and walked him over to the counter. He unbuttoned the lower button on his shirt and pulled out a thick leather pouch that as attached to his pants belt with a rawhide cord.

He opened the pouch and pulled out a wad of bills and took a hundred dollar bill out and handed it to Jamison.

Wolf kept around four hundred dollars in the pouch and another three thousand in a money belt below his belt line of his pants. He knew he would need serious money to get started before he could get funds from New Orleans.

His brother lamented that Wolf may get killed for it, and Wolf said, "Well I won't need the money then will I?" He and his brother laughed about that.

Jamison didn't miss the roll of bills Wolf had. He was dumbfounded.

Mister Jamison, take this on account. When we're finished here we'll settle up. We're paying cash and we expect a good price on these goods. They only work for you when you sell them, and today is a good day I think so I want you to remember that when the Hudgins come in. Okay?"

"Oh absolutely mister---I'm afraid I don't know your name."

"The name is Wolf," he said as he smiled and patted the proprietor on the arm.

Looking the man in the eye, he said, "Now how much is that chest?"

CHAPTER 28

The buckboard was loaded as they headed home. Jason was quiet and couldn't get over all the things they had purchased in town. He kept looking over his shoulder to make sure it was still all there.

"Think your mom's going to be surprised, pal?"

"Wolf, she's not going to believe this. I don't believe this and I saw it happen. Old Jamison never had a day like today before, I bet. He couldn't give me enough candy. I took a bunch to give to ma. I can't eat all that stuff."

★ ★ ★

When they came over the ridge they could see Sarah in the garden with hoe in hand, working the rows. When they got closer they saw she had her new holster set hanging on a post by the garden gate.

"Boy, ma's gonna be surprised. I can hardly wait to see the expression on her face."

"Look, you and I will just start unloading the wagon, and don't say a word to her. She'll know something's up, when we start making trips to the house. Remember don't say anything, okay?"

Jason just shook his head and said, "Oh wow. You really like my ma, don't you?"

"Sure do Jason. I like her a lot. You're a lucky boy to have her as your mother."

"Is that why you're doing all this for us? I mean, I've never seen so much stuff all at one time, in my whole life. Why don't you stay with us? I think that would be great and I thing ma would really like it, too."

"It's a long story pal. We'll see how it works out.

I really want to help you guys out as much as I can. You're part of a quest you'll never understand."

★ ★ ★

They pulled the buckboard right up to the porch, by the front door, and without saying a word to Sarah they started hauling the boxes into the house.

Sarah looked up from her gardening, when they made the second trip, with Wolf and Jason hauling the large wooden chest up the single step of the porch to the house.

"Hey, what's going on?" she shouted.

Neither Wolf nor Jason responded and just walked in through the now open door.

Jason giggled when they got inside and they carried the chest and set it down at the foot of Sarah's bed.

"Oh boy, is she gonna be surprised," Jason said.

Sarah came through the door just as Wolf and Jason were headed out for another load. "What's going on with you two?"

Neither responded and just picked up two more boxes and hauled them into the kitchen.

Sarah was standing in the middle of the living area with her mouth open staring at the boxes and bags stacked up in the kitchen area.

"Hey you two. Stop right now. What's going on? Where did all this stuff come from?"

Wolf just looked at her as he leaned the new shovel up against the house and said, "Old Jamison said you were good for it, so we thought we'd get you some supplies you were short on."

She looked at Jason real hard and said, "Jason, what's going on here? You know damn well we can't be buying this much stuff from Jamison. You guys have to take it back right now, so get with it."

Wolf looked at Jason who was now back to the empty buckboard and said, "Hey Jason take the wagon back to the barn will you? Don't forget to brush down the horse real good."

Jason looked at Wolf with a big smile and said, "Okay, I'll take care of it."

Wolf then grabbed Sarah by the arm and steered her to the back bedroom and closed the door. He put his arms around her loosely so he could look into her eyes and still hold her firm.

"Nothing's going back, love. You really needed some things around here, and I wanted to give those things to you. You and Jason are very special people to me. It's as simple as that."

"Wolf this stuff had to cost a fortune. How could you do that? Oh my God what's that chest at the foot of the bed?" she said when she spotted it.

"I don't know. You'd better take a look."

She walked around the bed and stood looking at it and stroking the shiny top.

"It's beautiful. What is it?"

"Give you something to sit on in here besides that old wooden chair."

Sarah reached down and opened the chest, and gasping, just stood mesmerized. It was full of sheets, blankets, the big bright quilt and on top was the new apron.

"I can't believe this."

"We both thought you could use a new apron."

She threw her arms around Wolf with tears in her eyes and said in a trembling voice, "I've never had anything like this before. I just can't believe it."

"Well believe it. You've got a lot of putting away to do and I want to show Jason how to fix that front door of yours before it falls off."

"How can I ever repay you?"

"Lord, there's no repayment needed. It was my pleasure. The gift is in the giver, you know. I don't know how to say this but you've played a very important part in my life in just the short time I've known you. I can't possibly repay you for that."

"Wolf, stay. Please stay. I want you to stay more than anything and I know Jason would love it."

"Believe me, I'd love to stay. We need to talk about that so you'll know what's going on in my life now. You're an important part of that I think."

Sarah was busy in the kitchen, putting things away and making happy sounds as she did so.

"Beans! Wolf, you got beans. We haven't had beans in a long time. We love beans, but they weren't in our budget. Oh my God, you got a lot of beans. We're going to have steak and beans for dinner tonight. I'm going to start them right now," she said as she scooped out double hands full and dropped them into a pot. "Oh my God we're so lucky," she mumbled to no one.

★ ★ ★

Wolf showed Jason how to jack up the edge of the big heavy door to the house to make it level and take out the screws, one at a time starting with the top hinge.

He cut a small sliver of wood that would fit into the screw hole, dobbed it with a tiny bit of glue they had bought and drove it in the screw hole.

He explained to Jason how the weight of the door had slowly loosened the hinges and how to correct the problem. Jason got a lot of hands-on experience that was observed by Sarah in the kitchen.

When all the hinges were tight Wolf closed the door and it again fit into the lock space.

He then showed Jason how to knock out the steel hinge pins, sand them shiny, and put on a small dab of the gun grease they bought.

When they were done Wolf swung the door back and forth and it moved smoothly and quietly.

"Hey Sarah, look what Jason did. See how this old stubborn door works now?" he said as he swung it back and forth and let it slam shut on the third swing.

"Good job boys. That's really great," she said smiling at both of them with a dish rag in her hand.

Wolf sent Jason out to the barn to repeat that process on the two big barn doors that needed some help as well.

Jason was excited that he was asked to do the job on his own. *He was learning, boy was he learning*, he thought as he went to the barn.

★ ★ ★

Wolf went over to the kitchen counter, where Sarah was organizing the metal containers that were now full of flour, sugar, beans and coffee, and pressed up against her from behind.

He put his arms around her and putting his hands on her full bosom he said, "I think you're the deepest-down most beautiful woman I've ever met."

"I bet you say that to all the girls," she said while covering his hands and leaning into him.

"I don't know how to say this so it sounds like I think it, but yes, I've known women before. But just this short time with you I've come to understand that there is so much more to lovemaking, than I ever knew existed before. This is a first for me. You have to believe that."

"There's a deep understanding emotion that I never knew, and I hardly know you. You just, all of a sudden when we were lying together became a part of me."

"I know that probably sounds stupid, but I don't know how else to explain it."

Sarah turned around and put her arms around Wolf and kissed

him on the lips with her tongue just licking the inside if his lips and said, "Funny thing you said that, Wolf. I couldn't have done it better myself. There's obviously something here that we should hold on to. I feel I've known you for a long time, somehow, somewhere."

CHAPTER 29

They next week flew by. It moved much faster than all of them had hoped for.

Wolf had tried to explain his quest as best he could when he couldn't really understand it himself.

He told her about the ranches in Montana, and what he had to do and the dangers involved. He tried to explain that he wasn't really sure what was going to happen but he knew he was going to be challenged time and time again by something evil and he had to right it somehow. He also had to do good along the way to compensate for the evil he was destined to fight.

Obviously, Sarah and Jason were a part of that plot plan and he was very happy they fit into his present lifestyle. He would miss them terribly. The intimate sharing of the three of them, holding hands before meals, giving thanks to the Lord, had become an important daily ritual. It was then he realized, that Sarah was a true sole mate. He was beginning to understand more of his quest since his death, or near-death experience. He was finally getting more insight on what he had to do and what he should expect. He just couldn't remember what happened or what he had forgotten. He was happy that he hadn't cut back on his unseen exercise and practice in the barn.

Evil will find you, but there will be rewards along the way, is what he remembered.

He felt he was about to be tested.

★ ★ ★

The sad morning arrived when Wolf had the three horses saddled and packed to move. He still had well over a hundred miles to the Arkansas River and it was all through Indian country.

He knew that with his three well-blooded and formed horses he would be a target so they had to move fast.

Wolf and Sarah's lovemaking had become a rich part of both of their lives as they discovered new things about each other every day.

The explanations of the multiple scars on Wolf's body took up a full evening as she caressed each one and she never spoke of them again as if they didn't exist.

They had worked out that Wolf could write to her when he was settled and mail it in care of Jamison's store to hold for her. The Stage Line stopped there on a semi-regular basis and this was common practice.

★ ★ ★

The horses were well rested and seemed eager to move. They were ridden daily. As Sarah and Wolf explored the area swam naked in the calm stream, made love on the soft grass, and raced each other over the countryside.

Jason had become quite proficient with the rifle during their practice and Sarah proved she really did know how to shoot.

They were much more secure now than ever.

Most evenings, all three of them rode Wolf's horses so they would get exercise and not pull up lame when they headed north and the going got tough. He could not afford any delays or any thing slowing them down.

They must move fast now.

CHAPTER 30

They covered a lot of ground the first day and Wolf thought after looking at his maps that they would hit trails the next day that skirted the southern part of the Arkansas River. It would be safer there for sure he felt.

He moved his horses into a wooded area and spent the evening without a fire. The horses had plenty of grass and browse in the trees, and Jake had caught a rabbit and was enjoying his dinner. Wolf snacked on some of the smoked antelope Sarah had given him for the trip and enjoyed the beans he had stored in his tin cooking pot sealed with twine.

★ ★ ★

They were on the move early and rode steadily north. He could see hills ahead, and by looking through his scope, he could see what appeared to be a well-worn trail skirting the south end of the hills and veering east. That's what he was looking for, and that's where they would go.

The caught the trail at the south end of the hills. It was a well-worn path that had seen a lot of use. It came south on the west side of the hilly country, through a boulder-strewn area. There were horse and heavy wagon wheel tracks going in both directions.

Wolf eased up on the horses and with an easy lope they headed north on the track. It would lead them to the Arkansas River.

★ ★ ★

When they had covered about a mile Wolf alerted to Jake. The dog was out in front doing his scouting job, watching the hills to the east of their path.

Wolf looked where Jake was fixated and saw a lot of Indians, some on horseback and many walking along its ridge.

They had just come to an open area where there a fifty-foot wide wash that ran down from the hills.

Wolf stopped and looked through his collapsible scope and could make out one individual who had lots of feathers on his head and was riding a large pinto horse. He must be the chief Wolf thought.

Wolf put up his right hand in the peace sign and watched as the chief did the same.

Wolf took that as a positive sign and started to move until he heard yips from some of the Indians and a stream of horses started down a winding game trail from the crest of the hill. All the time the chief sat on his horse and watched.

This wasn't going to be good.

★ ★ ★

Wolf knew he could probably outrun the war party that was descending the hill, but he saw several rifles among them and even a stray shot could cripple a horse and they would be in big trouble on the open road.

He looked around to see what he could find as a defense to keep them in the wash.

To the west, on his left there were numerous boulders. One was huge. It was about fifteen feet long and eight feet high and appeared to be fairly flat on top. He would head for that one.

He urged the horses behind the big boulder and nudged Blondie against the rear side, telling her to stay, which he knew she would.

He instructed Jake to lay down and stay, Ruby and Blackie followed suit with Blondie.

They all looked at Wolf in confusion and he just talked to them in a quiet voice enforcing the stay command.

He pulled out the carbine and put it over his shoulder with its strap. He dug in the back pack where he kept his ammunition and pulled out the small leather bag with the high-powered cartridges for the scoped rifle.

He undid the buckle holding the cover on the scoped rifle and pulled it out.

He then stood in the saddle and laid the ammo bag and the scoped rifle on top of the boulder, which was now waist high and crawled up on top.

The Indians were nearing the bottom of the hill and Wolf could make out thirteen on horseback, and several with rifles. The bottom of the hill looked to be about five hundred to six hundred yards from the boulder where he now sat.

He didn't know the order of things, but felt they would charge in the order they came down the hill.

This was going to be a coon shoot.

★ ★ ★

When he was a boy and they would go raccoon hunting he learned how to shoot coons.

The dogs would run the raccoons up a tree and if he shot the coon at the top of the tree the others would see it fall through the tree and they would all scatter. If he started shooting the coon at the bottom of the tree and worked his way up he might get the whole pack.

This was going to be the same.

If he shot the lead horseman the others would scatter and he would lose the advantage of keeping them all in one arena. He would have to start with the farthest Indian, and he would have to wait until he knew he could make all his shots count. To be safe that meant about three hundred yards. He was deadly at that range.

He had jacked a round into the chamber and replaced it from the organized pile he had made in his hat on his right side.

He was watching them through the rifle scope as he sat cross-legged on the boulder with his elbows braced on his knees and the sling held tight.

They would be coming straight on, which was a great advantage and he would just have to be patient.

★ ★ ★

The first man was at the bottom of the hill looking back at the others and urging them on with his rifle by swinging it in the air.

The man in front was the obvious leader and the others charged after him.

Wolf could judge the distance by knowing he height of a horse through his scope, and waited until the first man hit his mark of three hundred yards.

The leader was there faster than Wolf would have imagined.

Wolf tracked each man as he crossed his imaginary line until the last man appeared.

Wolf made what he hoped was a good elevation adjustment and squeezed the trigger.

The man was knocked off his horse.

Wolf then went from left to right on all the trailing men.

All of the shots counted as a man down except one, who he didn't shoot. That man saw his friend go down and went back for him. He was off his horse and kneeling by the other man's side.

He only got off three more rounds, when the field of view through the long scope made it too difficult to hold on his target.

He put the rifle in his lap and picked up the carbine, jacked in a shell and aimed at the last three men coming on.

He hit the man on the left, then the one on the right, and now the leader who was riding a beautiful red horse. The man was the only one charging and he was only thirty to forty yards away still swinging his rifle.

Wolf put the carbine to his right shoulder and with his left hand pointed over the charging man's head twice.

Curiosity caused him to quickly glance back, and when he didn't see any of his riders he swiveled his head from side to side and saw them all were lying in the wash.

The man was serious now.

He dropped the reins and put the rifle to his shoulder to make a kill shot but was too late.

With the rifle flying he was knocked off his horse.

The big red horse, which Wolf could see was a stallion, came to a stop and looked back at his rider.

★ ★ ★

There were only one or two men who that showed any signs of moving and weren't worth trying to shoot again, so Wolf gathered his supplies and worked his way off the rock onto the waiting saddle on Blondie.

Talking to his animals, he dropped the leather pouch into the saddle bag and slid to the ground.

The scoped rifle was hot, so he hung it in a nearby tree to let the barrel cool and walked into the killing field.

His first target was the red horse. This was a magnificent animal.

He talked softly and walked slowly up to the heavily breathing stallion who didn't seem too excited, but its ears still flicked back and forth.

He finally made contact and scooped up the pair of reins and caressed its shoulder and neck talking to it all the time.

The big stallion was about the size of Blackie and probably a mustang. He had an army saddle and bridle and an army rifle scabbard.

Where the man got this horse would be something Wolf would never know.

He led the horse over to a tree and it moved easily, strangely without fear. Wolf had a way with animals.

Firmly tied to the tree, Wolf started back into the killing field again.

The lead man's rifle was a carbine, but in poor condition. Indians were just not into caring for their guns in any way.

The second man also had a carbine, so Wolf took both of them and put them together in the center of the wash.

The third man had a flintlock. Wolf bent its barrel and dropped it in the sand.

The fourth man was lying in the middle of the wash with a quiver over his shoulder and a bow that had a reverse curve to it.

It was a beautiful piece of workmanship and obviously not of Indian origin.

The quiver had ten heavy arrows with steel broad-heads. This was not Indian craft.

Wolf pulled the bow and it was heavy. It had to pull in excess of a hundred pounds. It was a beautiful piece.

He added those items to his pile and moved on.

He found only one more rifle worth keeping, and bent three more flintlocks.

The rest of the bows were of light weight and Indian made. Many of the arrows were not even straight so could only be used at a short distance.

The man was still sitting by his friend when Wolf neared him and the man jumped to his feet staring at Wolf.

Wolf made him the peace sign and signaled for him to sit with his friend.

The man smiled and complied, holding his friend's head in his lap.

Wolf became aware of wailing in the distance and looked up at the hills where the war party came from. Squaws were stumbling down the winding game trail and the chief was slowly following on horseback.

Wolf made his way rapidly back to his stash and picked up the items and carried them to his horses.

He cleared the rifle chambers and tied them on top of Ruby's pack.

He unstrung the bow and tied it to the top of her load.

He got the scoped rifle, which had cooled considerably, into its case and searched the ground rapidly for brass casings for the rifle to reload.

He had to move.

The chief was walking his horse through the men in the wash without glancing at them.

He was headed for Wolf.

Wolf walked out into the clearing in front of his shooting boulder and stood with his arms folded watching the man.

The chief was flanked by two walking men, both wearing knives.

From his experience he knew these men were not coming for a friendly visit.

Wolf turned to look back at his boulder and slipped his Bowie knife up about an inch, taking it out of the secure hold-down position and turned back to the men.

The chief sat his horse and started talking and waving his arms around.

A distraction.

How many times had he seen this attempt?

Wolf looked at the chief and nodded his head as if he were paying attention but all the while concentrating his peripheral vision.

On his right was a maybe thirty-year old overweight man who appeared to have a dull look about his face.

The man on Wolf's left was about the same age, and had a mean look about him. He was huskier by far.

Both men wore buckskin leggings to the knee and were bare-chested except for a rawhide strings with trinkets around their necks.

These two were there to kill Wolf with their knives. No question about it. They just needed to get close enough that they thought they could move faster than Wolf could draw his revolver.

Wolf looked down toward the ground in front of him with his arms still folded and watched the two men while he slowly lowered his right hand to his knife on his left side.

The man to his left was about ten feet away. The man to his right had worked his way to within six feet of Wolf.

The fat boy reached for his knife while Wolf was staring at the ground.

With his left hand, Wolf took his hat and tossed into the face of the man who now had his knife out, and lunging with a powerful backhand swing, slashed through the man's gut from side to side.

The other man was on his way.

With Wolf's return swing, to his left, he threw his knife into the gut of the charging man, whose eyes popped open in surprise.

The man was making a classic thrust of his dagger to Wolf's midsection.

How many times had he seen this?

This was a classic move that he and Wong had worked on at least a hundred times when Wong was showing Wolf defensive moves. This was the real test of what he had learned from the skilful Chinaman.

It was all in slow motion now. It was just like in training where he learned his concentration controlled the movements and timing.

Wolf vaulted back and with his left hand he grabbed the man's wrist with the knife, pulling it past Wolf to Wolf's right.

The forward momentum of the man put him right where Wolf wanted him to be.

With his left foot Wolf kicked the man's left leg out from under him.

The leg went with Wolf's follow through, and the man was now airborne.

Wolf moved into the man and with his right hand he grabbed the heel of the man's knife, and with both of his hands, turned it directly to the man in the air.

Wolf rode the knife down with all his weight and it sank into the left chest, cracking ribs as it went through. The man's hand was still firmly gripping the handle.

Wolf looked back at the other knife fighter and saw he had both hands trying to keep his guts from falling out.

The chief wasn't talking anymore. He was just staring at Wolf, and Wolf returned the stare as he pulled his knife out of the man's gut and carefully wiped it on the dead man's buckskin pants.

He got up, leaning on the knife in the man's chest and casually slipped his blade back into its sheath. He walked over to pick up his hat, his eyes never leaving the chief.

He bent down and retrieved his hat, brushed it off, and while looking at the chief he kicked the left leg out from under the big man holding his gut.

The man went down howling with a splash and his innards spilled out on the sand.

Wolf slowly walked to the chief and quickly reached up and grabbed his buckskin jacket and jerked him off his horse.

The chief was an older man. It would be hard to guess his age but he was starting to turn grey and had deep lines in his face from the sun and weather.

He straightened the man up and looked him in the eye from about eighteen inches away, knowing this man's comfort zone was probably ten to twelve feet.

The man didn't show fear, just resignation.

The squaws were moaning and running around in the wash from one warrior to another when….

"Hey, mister."

CHAPTER 31

Both the chief and Wolf turned around in shock to see a young squaw walking up to them.

She appeared to be in her mid-twenties. She was about six inches shorter than Wolf and had on a knee length buckskin dress with beading around the open collar.

She had black hair that fell over her shoulders and green eyes.

Wolf thought *the green eyes were different for an Indian.*

"For Christ's sake, don't shoot me mister."

It was then Wolf realized his gun instinctively was in his hand and pointing at the threat.

"Who are you?" Wolf asked.

The chief was silent and just stared at the woman.

Another squaw was yelling at the lady in a language Wolf didn't understand, and the lady turned and yelled back at her in the same language then turned her attention back to Wolf.

"I'm Elizabeth Cobb. They call me Betz."

"You're a part of this tribe?"

"Hell no. they attacked our wagons and killed everybody but me. I've been a captive for over three years and I want out. Will you take me? These people are a bunch of degenerate bastards. If you don't take me they'll kill me for talking to you anyway."

The chief said something to her that sounded authoritive and she responded in an angry fashion.

"What did the chief say?"

"He called me a name that's the same as whore, and told me to get back."

"You speak the language well?"

"Hell yes. I'm educated. I speak the Kiowa, Arapaho and I'm pretty good with Cheyenne as well as Polish, French and some German."

"The tribes are all supposed to be friendly now but there are lots of radical factions like this one led by that asshole Little Bear you're talking to. Nobody wants to have anything to do with him or his tribe."

"He's not a chief?"

"Hell no. He may be a sub chief of some kind, but I don't think he's recognized by anyone. Will you take me?"

★ ★ ★

Wolf thought this lady would be a great treasure in crossing the Indian country. She knew the language and customs and looked like an Indian.

She says she's been educated, and it sounds like that may be true. By the way she talks she's no dummy.

"You know how to ride?"

"Of course. I rode long before I came here."

"I want you to do something for me. I want to tell this chief, or whatever he is, exactly what I think. I want you to make the same gestures I do and make it sound as close to my inflection as possible. You think you can do that?"

"Damn right I can. Let's do it and get the hell out of here."

★ ★ ★

Wolf got real close to the chief, well inside the chief's comfort zone, so he could hit his chest with his finger when he was making a point.

He explained how he saw the chief, and gave him the peace sign from his heart.

The chief gave the piece sign but he lied.

It was the chief's fault all these warriors were dead, Wolf said, as he swept his hand across the wash.

It was his fault that the women had lost their men and were in mourning.

It was his fault he brought his two knife fighters to their death. He was a failure, and a liar. He had cheated his people.

"I am the Wolf and I spit on you," he said as he spit on the ground in front of the chief.

Betz did an amazing job. She followed all his gestures and ended by spitting on the chief's buckskin jacket.

"Let's go," she said.

CHAPTER 32

She was to ride the new red stallion because she knew the horse and the horse knew her and her smell.

When she got ready to ride, she said, "This isn't the best thing to ride in," as she pulled her buckskin dress up to her waist.

She had nothing on under the dress.

Wolf said, "Let me show you."

He reached down between her legs and grabbed the bottom on the dress in the back, and pulled it up through her crotch and said, "Hold this in your right hand. Put your left on the pommel and put your left foot here on my knee," he said while patting his knee.

She smiled and did as he told her.

Wolf had his hand on his knee as well, and with the knee boost and his arm she shot into the air and easily dropped in the saddle.

She looked for the stirrups, which were a little long, and said, "I can do without stirrups for today. We can fix them tonight."

Wolf looked at the saddle, and being an army saddle it had buckle adjustments for the stirrups so that different men could use the saddle in a hurry.

Wolf made the quick adjustment on her left side, and she called it good.

Wolf had been talking and touching the horse all the time he was working on the stirrup, and he repeated the process on the right side.

"We're ready to move," he said as he went to his horses.

★ ★ ★

As they were moving out, many of the squaws, who had heard the dressing down Wolf and Betz, had given their chief where now yelling at him, and shaking their fists in his face.

The chief was going to have a bad day.

When they were underway Wolf said, "Where're you from? That opened a floodgate of almost non stop talking from Betz. She obviously had a lot to say and no one to say it to until that day, so Wolf just listened in patience.

He noticed that all the time she talked she was looking the terrain over. She didn't miss a thing. She was a real Indian guide and very valuable to Wolf to get where he was going.

★ ★ ★

She was from Philadelphia. Her dad was a butcher and a prominent sausage maker and they did very well.

Somehow her father got into some kind of a jam that made him leave town, so he liquidated what he could and took the family off to Wyoming where he had a cousin who had a ranch. They met a family from somewhere in Virginia that was headed west, so they traveled together.

When they were attacked the Indians killed everyone but her. The only thing that saved her was her looks and appeal.

The first thing they did to her was throw her down on the ground and then all the men raped her and left her for dead.

The man who rode the red horse she was on came back for her and threw her over the saddle on his horse.

"I guess he decided I was too good of a fuck to let me die out there in the flatland." The comment shocked Wolf. He'd never heard a woman talk like that. She was obviously smart and she spoke well and intelligently, but he couldn't believe what she was saying.

"When he got me to the camp, the men started on me all over

again. It was brutal. They liked to smack me around while they were fucking me. I guess that made them feel more like a man. Shit, I don't know."

Wolf was staring at her in shock and she caught the look.

"I'm just telling you what it was like. Look, I like to fuck. I mean I really like it, but when you got eight or ten guys banging you and slapping the shit out of you at the same time, that's not really a lot of fun."

She was waiting for a reply but Wolf was at a loss for words. This was the hardest woman he had ever met in his life. She was at the opposite end of the spectrum from Sarah. He needed this woman to get him to Montana, but what price was he going to have to pay?

She obviously had led a very hard life in the last three years and that probably made a dramatic change in her, he rationalized. That's the only excuse he could think of.

"Well you sure had it hard, that's for sure. When did things settle down for you? "I latched on to Bezos."

"Who's Bezos?"

"You know that bow you have strapped on Ruby?"

"Yes, what about it?"

"That belonged to Bezos. It was my dad's bow. He bought it in Philadelphia and paid a lot of money for it and the arrows. He loved shooting it and was pretty good with it.

"Bezos is the guy that ended up with it. Bezos is, or was, a big guy, and no one really gave him any trouble. That's why I went to Bezos.

"How did you go to Bezos?"

"Well it's like this. I was getting fucked four and five times a day by different guys. That wasn't so bad, but they slapped me around and the other women were getting mad at me because they weren't getting fucked at home. Their men were on me all the time."

"I finally got a friend, and she understood that I didn't like getting beat up. I didn't like taking the men away from their squaws, so I needed help."

"Some of the women started helping me a little. My clothes were all torn up by these damn animals."

"They'd tear em off me to get a quick fuck. It was terrible. I couldn't keep them together, so my friend gave me my first buckskin dress. I guess that meant that I was destined to be a part of the tribe."

"See, I was the fresh meat in camp. One of the women told me to quit fighting and it would be a lot easier. I was under the impression that some other captives didn't make it because they fought all the time, so I just started letting them have their way and I wasn't getting beat up anymore and things slowed down. She reminded me of a saying we had back in 'Philly', Go with the flow."

"That made sense, so I did exactly that. I'm not proud or happy of what I did, or what I was involved in, but I survived. That's the only thing that was important---to survive," she said in a low thoughtful tone. Hoping to change the subject some, Wolf said, "What's the story on your tribe?"

"Well as far as I can tell, they aren't a tribe. I guess they could be a sub tribe, but I don't know."

"The Arapahoe chief Little Raven worked out a piece treaty with the Kiowas, and the Cheyennes."

"There were a lot of small factions that didn't agree with the treaty and they broke off from their original tribes, and became a small tribe all of their own."

"Little Bear, the guy you met broke off with a degenerative group of dissidents and started his own tribe where anything went. They're made up of mental degenerates and the women they selected were the same. The women understood they were along just to get fucked and cook, nothing else."

Their whole society was based on sex. It wasn't brutal sex, you understand. It was agreeable. They said it was a showing of love and respect and family.

"Sex was open and accepted by all, even with the children, and done anytime and anyplace. Everyone saw it all the time. It was done in the open."

"Hell, their mothers started the kids out very young and trained them. They were taught it was the thing to do to bring love and pleasure to the other party."

"There isn't a three-year-old virgin in the group. The mothers encouraged it and showed them different ways of having sex." "The mothers used sex to get small kids to sleep. They trained them so they would be good at it and get into the group.

"The kids all fuck each other as it is a showing of love and respect, they think."

A shocked Wolf said, "My God, don't the women get pregnant?"

"Oh sure, but the miscarriage rate is very high. I don't know if that's from the man upstairs or the way of their life, or what they ate. All I know it's very high. You hear about it all the time."

"What about you?"

Betz was quiet for some time, and then said, "Well I don't think I can get pregnant."

"We had a few babies that lived and the mothers stayed wet."

"What do you mean, wet."

"Well they don't let their breasts dry up. They keep nursing. There are eight or nine wet women in the tribe. It's the only source of milk."

"I learned in school that the same practice is carried on in several countries of low income people."

"The women share their milk with all the children."

★ ★ ★

"There are about eight or ten of them that are just meat. They go along with anything the men do, and some of it's pretty bad. They're dramatically mentally off balance."

"That fat bastard you gutted back there? He was one of the worst of the bunch. He would always knock me around. You eliminated a whole bunch of really bad men mister."

"I think things might be somewhat different now without that gang of whoremonger degenerates."

"Food was not always shared so the best hunters had the best food and the best women. Simple as that.

"That's why I went to Bezos. He was a good hunter and did very well with my dad's bow. It's a heavy bow. I couldn't pull it myself but Bezos had no problem and got a lot of game with it.

The good thing was people would trade him stuff for meat. Like I said there was little sharing except for times when everything was scarce.

"You were safe with Bezos?"

"Oh sure, but there was a down side too, of course."

"Like what?"

"Well he didn't like getting it on as much as I did and I couldn't get it from anyone else or I'd be dead.

"I had to create ways to get him up to the task."

"How far are we going anyway? Hey, I see horses coming our way and they're pulling a wagon, probably a stage."

★ ★ ★

Wolf looked where she was looking and sure enough he could make out the small dust cloud the teams were creating.

This woman had the eyes of an eagle, he thought.

This was a regular stage run, so it made sense that it was a stagecoach and it was moving fairly fast.

Wolf had Betz get the horses off the trail and moved Blondie to the center of the trail and held up his hand to have the stage come to a stop.

The horses slowed and were blowing and the driver was talking to them, but the man riding shotgun had his shotgun pointed directly at Wolf in the center of the trail.

When the stage stopped about fifty feet from Wolf, he slowly walked Blondie up to the driver's side and said, "Howdy my name's Wolf and I need to tell you what you're up against and what you're going to have to do up ahead."

"What do you mean, Wolf?" said the driver.

The shotgun man never moved his shotgun.

"I'd appreciate it if you wouldn't point that shotgun at me, mister. I'm only trying to help you."

"What you got to tell us, Wolf?"

The passengers were all looking out of the stage now, at Wolf and his entourage standing on the side of the trail.

"Well, the situation is this. I was attacked by thirteen Indians in a war party just below that bluff up there," he said turning in his saddle and pointing at the bluff about eight miles away.

There are a lot of Indians there and fifteen bodies. They don't have any rifles now. I took care of that but there are two guys lying in the middle of the road that's going to present a problem."

"What're they doing in the road?"

"Well Chief Little Bear came to me as I was leaving, with a couple of knife fighters that weren't very good, and they're the ones lying in the middle of the road. There's no way to go around that mess, because of huge boulders. You have to drive through there and I'm sure the two guys in the road will be a hazard for your horses."

"Let's see if I've got this straight," said the shotgun man, with a grin on his face. "You took on a thirteen-Indian war party all alone and then you took on two knife fighters and you killed them all. Is that correct?"

"Yes sir. There is also a hell of a bunch of squaws and children moaning and crying, and it's going to be a hell of a mess by the time you get there."

"I suggest that you stop short and give Chief Little Bear the peace sign and signal for him to drag the bodies off the road, if they're still there."

"The chief and I had a little talk about the peace sign thing and I think that'll work for you."

"You're shitting us, right, Wolf?"

"No sir, I'm just telling you how it is up there."

"You took a squaw for yourself too, huh?"

"I'm no damn squaw, mister. I was a captive and Wolf took me out of there. You'd better listen to what he has to say," shouted Betz."

The passengers were gasping and talking to each other, and the driver and the man riding shotgun just looked at one other as the man lowered the shotgun.

The driver cleared his throat and said, "Well, we're much obliged there, Wolf. Where you heading?"

"Up Montana way. I got a ways to go I guess, but I'll make it, God willing."

"Well this is our regular route. We just go back and forth and I've heard about that Little Bear guy. I hear he's not all there in the head."

"You sure as hell got that right mister," Betz piped up.

"What's your names boys?" asked Wolf.

The driver said, "I'm Carl and the shotgun is Lucas. Thanks for the tip, Wolf. We'll keep our eyes open," he said as he snapped the reins and the horses started to move.

Wolf touched the brim of his hat to the men and to the passengers who were now staring at him out the open windows of the coach.

★ ★ ★

CHAPTER 33

The stage coach was getting close to the bluff Wolf had told them about. They'd been talking about it and were still in doubts about what the scene would look like when they started to see Indian ponies walking around without riders.

"Shit, Lucas, maybe that Wolf guy was telling the truth."

"Keep your eyes open, Carl. It could be a trap you know."

When they turned the next bend it was chaos. There were Indians everywhere, screaming, crying and moaning.'

"Shit, Carl, look at all the Indians."

Carl was pulling the teams to a stop a hundred feet from the commotion and the Indians were now looking at the stage.

"I think that old guy with all the feathers must be that crazy bastard Little Bear," said Carl.

Lucas stood up and raised his right hand and held it there until he got a response from the man they thought was Little Bear.

Lucas then waived his hand at all the people in the trail, motioning for them to move out of the way.

The women were sobbing but they moved, leaving the two men still in the road.

Carl said, "Shit. Look at that. The guy with his guts all over the ground is still alive and the other guy looks like he stabbed himself. He's still got his hand on that knife buried in his chest."

Lucas yelled and pointed to the two men in the road and motioned for the people to move them out of the road.

The chief said something and a bunch of women went and started dragging the two men clear of the road, and Carl snapped the reins to get the horses moving. The animals were now very nervous, with nostrils flaring.

They drove through the herd of Indians and looked up the wash to see that was littered with bodies and moaning women.

The passengers gasped and the lady in the coach fainted.

As the stage picked up speed Carl said, "Lucas, if we ever get into a fight I want that Wolf guy on our side."

CHAPTER 34

They rode on for another hour and Wolf said, "See that bunch of trees up ahead to the left? I think there'll be water there from the looks of the trees. I think we should stop there for the night."

"There's water there, all right," said Betz.

Wolf and Betz worked well together getting the horses unpacked and out in the grass to graze. She obviously knew what she was doing, and told Wolf that all the women worked on caring for the horses. The men just rode them.

Betz had a fire going and was looking through the supplies to see what they could eat for dinner. She was surprised at the amount of provisions Wolf had. It seemed he had everything but the main course.

"Wolf, what are you planning on eating tonight? You've got all sorts of stuff here. We having jerky? You have smoked meat. What is that anyway?" asked Betz.

"Its antelope and it's very good."

"Antelope? I haven't had that in a long time. That sounds good. Where did you get it? Smoke it yourself?"

Wolf thought about where he got the antelope, and thought about Sarah and Jason. It seemed he was now completely lost from that intimate relationship.

"No, some friends I met along the way gave it to me."

"I saw some fish in this little stream here. I thought we may catch a few. They're pretty small but will fry up real good."

"How you plan on catching them?"

"I've got a line and hook and we can dig up a few worms and see how we do."

"Okay, I'll get the bait," she said as she got up, and started looking for rocks on the ground.

Wolf watched her and wondered what she was doing, until she tipped over a large flat rock and started scratching around on the ground it was on.

She started putting something in her hand and walked over to Wolf and showed him.

"These bugs and worms are great for fishing. Give em a try and see how you do."

Wolf was surprised how easily she found bait. She obviously had learned many things from the Indians, she lived with.

★ ★ ★

They had three small fish for dinner along with some smoked antelope and the rest of Wolf's beans Sarah had supplied.

Betz was amazed at how well Wolf ate on the move. When her tribe traveled, they were lucky to have a fraction of what she ate tonight, she thought.

Wolf got up from the fire and went to the stream with soap and towel and took off his clothes to bathe.

He called Jake and sat him by the fire and gave the guard command.

Betz was scared to death at the nasty growl, and said, "What the hell is that about? You gonna put your dog on me?"

Wolf smiled and said, "No Betz, he's here to guard you and our supplies. He knows that if anything goes wrong or if a stranger shows up he'll take care of it. I just gave him his territory to protect.

I suggest you move in normal slow movements as he doesn't really know you yet. Give him a few days."

"I'm glad you're not putting that dog on me. He's big, and I don't think I could take him."

"That's the last thing I'm going to do. I can't believe all the things you told me. Your story is incredible," he said shaking his head.

"Well there's a lot more to tell, Wolf."

"I'm not sure I really want to hear it."

"I know. Everything I saw as an everyday event was completely contrary to my Catholic upbringing. Everything I saw was supposed to be a sin, but those people saw it as a gesture of love and friendship. It's really hard to equate the two."

Wolf shook his head and said, "You going to take a bath? I've got soap."

"Soap? I haven't seen or used soap since I was taken. Hell yes. I'd like to take a bath with soap."

Wolf was in the shallow water washing his hair and body when bets stepped into the stream.

She was a trim, shapely good-looking woman, and he could see why the men liked lying with her. He'd try and keep her sensuous looks and history out of his mind, but it wasn't going to be easy.

"Can I use some of that soap, Wolf?"

Wolf handed her the bar and said, "Of course. Be careful and don't drop it. We don't want it carried away downstream."

"Wow, real soap," she said as she smelled it and lathered her hair.

Wolf had a hard time keeping his eyes off the woman next to him as she cleaned herself. Her dull, dusty hair had come out a bright shiny black.

"Wolf, do my back. Would you? It hasn't seen soap in years."

Wolf did exactly that with his wash rag and when she raised her arms he scrubbed under each arm. He then got close to where their bodies were touching and reached around and started washing her stomach and breasts in a slow easy motion.

Bets smiled to herself, and guided his hand over her body. She could feel his manhood pressed against her back.

"You're doing a great job, Wolf. Want me to scrub your back?"

"Ah, yes, that would be great, as he brought his mind back to the bathing and turned around to give her the wash rag.

Betz scrubbed his back, talking all the time about anything that popped into her mind, especially the road ahead. She completely ignored the scars on his back.

She was now tight against his back and doing his chest and finally reached down and stroked him with a soapy hand.

"I think we're going to get along just fine, Wolf. You're not going to attack me or hurt me, are you?"

"No, Betz, you can count on that."

"What if I attack you?" she said with a subtle laugh and a squeeze.

"That's up to you, Betz."

★ ★ ★

They rounded up the horses, which were strung together on their twenty-foot tethers, and led them well out of sight into the trees.

Wolf checked the dying fire and got out one of his tarps and lay in on the ground and dropped his bedroll on top of it.

Betz had finished cleaning the cooking equipment and was watching Wolf.

He went back to the fire and poured another cup of coffee and asked Betz if she wanted one.

"Sure, I'd love one. I always drank my coffee with sugar and cream. We need one of the wet ladies here to give us a little cream for our coffee," she said laughing.

"You know breast milk is real sweet. Did you know that?"

"How in hell would I know that?"

"How do you know that?"

"Well those ladies need to be nursed on a regular basis, you know. Just like a cow. If they didn't, they started leaking and had a lot of pressure. They'd normally get one of the kids to nurse for awhile, and that took the pressure off. The little kids did it every morning and night and even during the day, but if the ladies were off somewhere

where there weren't any kids around, we would all take turns nursing until the pressure was off. It was just a normal occurrence that went with the wet ladies, that's all."

"One lady, who's not real smart, had a couple of older boys that nursed every morning and night. While they were nursing, they were fucking her at the same time. She loved it and the boys did, too. She has huge tits, and needed a lot of nursing, so she went along with everything. The problem with those young boys is that they can fuck forever. That's just the way it is with the wet ladies.

Wolf shook his head and said, "Well, you'll have to drink it black, I'm afraid."

★ ★ ★

He'd given Jake his guard command and patted the supply mound buried under a tarp, and was getting ready for the night ahead.

Betz was busy putting the fire down for the night as they didn't want it to be seen in the dark.

★ ★ ★

Wolf was under the blanket when Betz said, "I don't have a bedroll you know."

"You'll just have to get in here, I guess," Wolf responded as he rolled over on his side to see what she was going to do.

She pulled her buckskin dress over her head and draped it over the supply stash, and crawled under the blanket and moved up against Wolf. "It's going to be a cold night, I think," she whispered.

★ ★ ★

Wolf was alerted when Jake moved and sat up. He was well tuned to the dog's habits and movements.

He looked at the dog. Jake had his nose in the air and was making a low rumble in his chest.

Wolf immediately crawled out from under the blanket, and by

habit whipped his gun belt around his bare waist and said in a low voice, "What do you have fella?"

He saw Jake looking at the trees where the horses were and grabbed the carbine and put the sling over his shoulder. It was a quiet night with a three-quarter moon. The air was still and all was quiet.

Betz rolled over and said, "What?"

Wolf shushed her and said, "Stay here with Jake. I'm going to have a look.

He decided to pick up the bow and quiver and on moccasin feet dashed low into the woods.

He could hear Blondie and Ruby making noises as they detected him coming near them.

He quieted the horses and got behind a tree where he could see the grass field that extended over a hundred feet to the scrub brush beyond, and waited.

He strung the bow and loosed an arrow from its mossy bed in the quiver and waited.

There it was.

★ ★ ★

A head popped up for an instant in the grass that was about two and a half feet to three feet high, enough to hide a man. He could then see the trail in the moonlight where the man had crawled from the brush beyond.

He waited and watched. There it was again. The man was looking at the horses and didn't want to disturb them. He ducked down and the trail got closer to the horses in the trees.

It was then he saw a second trail about twenty feet behind the man's right.

Wolf looked the rest of the meadow over carefully and couldn't see any more trails. There appeared to be only two of them.

The first man was close now and at about thirty feet away he got up on his knees and looked in every direction.

Wolf thought, *I haven't shot this bow before, but I can hardly miss him at this distance.*

He raised the bow and TWANG! The arrow hit the man in the center of his chest and he went over backwards. The arrow bobbed around above the grass for a few seconds, then stood straight up in the air with the grass.

Apparently the second man heard the bow string and popped his head up to look around. All was still and quiet.

The man made his way to his left to cut the first man's trail and when he got there the grass moved rapidly as he gained on the leading man.

When the second man reached the first man, the arrow that was sticking straight up in the air tipped off to the side.

It was then that the second man raised up, attempting to move the first man, when he was hit in the right side of his chest with Wolf's second arrow and went down.

The grass thrashed around for several seconds, then became still. Neither man had made a sound.

★ ★ ★

Wolf waited for at least a half hour before he moved. There were no more tracks in the grass, nor more men appearing.

When he moved he dropped to the ground and crawled through the grass just like the men did when they approached the horses.

He reached both men and they were both dead. One of the heavy arrows was a pass through.

He raised his head up and looked the field over carefully. There was no movement.

He pulled his knife out to retrieve the valuable arrows, stood up and walked back to the horses, stroking and talking to each of them.

★ ★ ★

Betz first saw Wolf when he was at the stream splashing around cleaning the arrows, but she didn't move.

Wolf came back to the campsite and Betz said, "What's going on?"

"Two guys were sneaking up on us."

"Where are they now?"

"Lying out there, in the grass."

"I didn't hear a shot. What happened?"

"Nice bow we have here," was all he said, and climbed back under the blanket.

"You're cold as ice," she said as she moved her body up to him, putting a leg and arm over him to warm him up.

"They must have been after me."

"No, they were after the horses. Your outfit has an overabundance of women right now, but they sure don't have any horses like ours."

Betz giggled and crawled up on top of Wolf. "Damn you're cold, Wolf," she said.

In a few seconds, she giggled again and said, "I see you're warming up now."

★ ★ ★

At first light, Wolf could smell the smoke and opened his eyes.

Betz had the fire going and the coffee pot was sitting hear the fire. He rolled out into the cool dawn and Betz said, "You up now?"

"I guess you wore me out yesterday. I needed my sleep."

"Want me back in there?"

"No, I've got my morning routine to do before I eat. We've got a busy day today. We're going to find a crossing on the river and head north."

★ ★ ★

Wolf went through his daily exercise program that produced a heavy sweat and then practiced his draw like he did everyday.

Betz came over to him while he was drawing his revolver and watched.

"The first time I saw you do that, I didn't even see your hand move. Damn. You're fast, Wolf."

"I've got to clean up a bit, and then we'll get something to eat. We've got a little work to do before we leave."

"Like what?"

"You'll see."

CHAPTER 35

The horses were saddled and packed. The fire was dead and they were ready to move.

Wolf said, "We have a couple of stops to make first," and headed to the men in the grass.

He got off Blondie and walked the few feet to the men on the ground and said, "You know these guys? These two from your tribe?"

Bets looked at the two young men lying on the ground and said, "Oh yes. I know them. That guy," she said pointing to one of the men, "was a real ass. The other guy was a pretty good guy. Oh yes, I know them."

"What do you want to do with them Wolf?"

"Not a damn thing. The birds will find them shortly and we'll turn there horses loose. They'll find their way home and maybe someone will come looking for them. The birds will guide them," he said as he looked at her.

"I know what you're thinking, Wolf, and yes both of those guys have been on me. There's nothing I could do about that, you know."

★ ★ ★

They found the two ponies not too far into the brush and turned them loose in the direction of where Wolf and Betz last saw the tribe.

"You worried about those two guys being on me, Wolf?"

"Not really but I just can't seem to put it all together. I just don't want to talk about it, okay?"

"Okay, let's get a move on then."

"There's no loss there, Wolf. There's just going to be a shortage of men in that group."

CHAPTER 36

They made good time and hit the Arkansas River again and headed west.

Wolf said, "We have to find a crossing because we need to head north from here, so keep your eye open for something that looks good."

"I've crossed a lot of rivers, Wolf. I'll ride ahead, and try and scout out a good crossing. I know what we're looking for."

"Okay, don't get lost," he grinned.

"Well let's see now. We're on a stage line trail so I think I can find my way back," she said with a smile, and headed off at a gallop.

The trail was as crooked as the river and Wolf moved the three horses he with ease. They covered most of the way at an easy lope that the horses liked. They could cover a lot of ground at this pace.

★ ★ ★

Jake barked and looked down the road in the direction Betz had gone.

Good. Perhaps she's found us a place to cross, he thought.

She came into view at a full gallop. The red horse was really covering the ground. Wolf's first thought was how easily and fast the horse was moving. Then he realized that there was no reason for her to be traveling at that speed. She was waiving her hand and pointing behind her.

Wolf moved the horses into a gallop and headed for Betz.

"What---"was all he got to say.

Betz was screaming that there were three men after her and roared past Wolf and his horses.

She slowed as he caught up and said, "What the hell's going on?"

"I found a crossing but three guys were crossing it coming south and they started after me. Let's go. We can outrun them."

"To where?" Wolf said.

That stopped her.

"We need to find a place," Wolf said. "Follow me."

★ ★ ★

They raced back down the trail they just traveled. Wolf remembered an outcropping from some hills they had passed that looked like it was a place they could defend if they had too.

He spotted what he was looking for. It was about a quarter of a mile south of the trail, and they headed across the flat surface that had lots of small bushes but very little grass on it.

"Where're we going?" Betz yelled.

"Follow me," was all he said.

★ ★ ★

They raced for the outcropping at a full clip, and he could see the three men several hundred yards behind them, trying to take a short cut to the outcropping.

They raced around the end of the rocks down from the hills and Wolf yelled, "Blondie, Ruby, ready."

This got the attention of the two horses. They knew something was going to happen. He then yelled at Betz and Blackie.

When they rounded the outcropping, Wolf looked at the rocks they passed. When they were out of sight of the three men he yelled, "Whoa, whoa," and pulled back on the reins.

The horses were still moving when Wolf pulled the carbine and slid from the saddle.

Jake was just making it around the outcropping when Wolf hit the ground running.

He told Jake to stay and threw his hat on the ground by the dog.

Betz was coming back and Wolf said, "Stay with the horses."

He ran to the outcropping and found a good-sized rock he could get behind and peeked around the edge.

The three men were coming on strong, and Wolf knew the men felt that Wolf and Bets were trapped against the hills.

The man on the left had his rifle out and the other two had their pistols in their hands. They hadn't come to just visit.

★ ★ ★

He waited until the lead man was about forty yards from where he sat and eased the rifle's tip around the rock and sighted on the man.

He was knocked out of the saddle and the man on Wolf's right was now shooting at the rocks, unsure of where the shot had come from.

The men were riding almost straight towards him and Wolf killed him easily.

The third man was cagey. He dropped to the far side of his horse, Indian fashion, and headed to the other side of the outcropping.

There wasn't a good shot at the man, so Wolf did what he had to do and shot the horse in the shoulder.

The horse went end over end with a sad whinny and landed on its back.

The rider, apparently caught under the horse, was yelling and screaming.

Wolf got down out of the rocks and ran around the end of the outcropping.

The two men he had shot out of the saddle were not moving, so he ran, cautiously to the man under the horse.

He could see the man's rifle where the horse took the tumble, so at least the man didn't have that.

Wolf eased around behind the man. He was three-quarters under the horse. Only his head, chest and left arm were visible.

Wolf walked up to the whinnying, wounded horse that was trying to get up without any luck because of its broken shoulder.

Wolf walked up to where the man could see him and the man said, "Help me, please."

"You were trying to kill me. Why should I help you?" he asked as he shot the horse in the head to put it out of its misery. Now the whole weight of the horse was on the man who was groaning.

"No, I think I'll just leave you here for the birds and the coyotes. They need something to eat too, you know. The birds, they go for the eyes first."

★ ★ ★

"You're a hard man Wolf," said Betz, who had come running up behind him.

Wolf turned and said, "I asked you to stay with the horses, Betz."

"I know, but when I saw you running around the point of rocks, I thought maybe I could help."

As they walked away from the man under the horse, Betz said, "I've only known you for a couple of days, Wolf, and it seems you are always in the middle of some kind of a shootout. What the hell is going on? Is it always like this?"

It's a long story, Betz. I just need to survive. That's all I'm doing."

Bets looked at him for a long time as they walked away before she finally said, "You know, Wolf. You and I are a lot alike."

Wolf looked at her with confusion.

"You said you have to do this to survive."

"I've seen you shoot. You're deadly. I've seen you practice. You're not practicing for the fun of it. You're practicing to survive. What that's all about I have no idea, but   if you think about it, we're both in the same boat, so to speak. I had to fuck everybody to survive and you kill people to survive," she said as she gave him a quick hug around the waist as they kept on walking.

Wolf was dumbstruck. She had hit it right on the head. They both were survivors and did what they had to do to survive. He looked at her for a long time as it sunk in.

She was right.

He stopped her, putting his arms around her, and said, "I'm sorry, Betz, I misjudged you. You're right. It's a long story"

"Well, it looks like we have a lot of time on our hands to hear about it."

"I know how to shoot a rifle, Wolf. I want you to teach me how to really shoot a rifle and I want to learn how to shoot a pistol. You've got enough of them."

"We'll talk, but right now how about you rounding up those two horses that are wandering around?"

She looked at the horses and said, "Well, they're pretty good stock but what do we want with two more horses?"

"I don't know. I just think we'll need them, that's all," he said as he walked to the nearest spread-eagled man on the ground.

Wolf had collected all the guns and the two new mares were tethered to Ruby. They were ready to move.

CHAPTER 37

"**W**ell, we know where the crossing is, Wolf. We should be well on our way north by nightfall. We'll be in Arapaho country now. They're pretty nice people generally. I'm sure they have some breakaway groups as well, but I think it'll be easy going to the Platte River, I think you called it, up in the Wyoming country."

They found the crossing that Betz had located when the men chased her. The water was moving gently and the area looked safe.

"I'll go first with one of the new horses. Red here has crossed a lot of rivers. He knows what he's doing and I'm sure you can lead the others across once they see what Red is doing."

"Sounds like a good idea. Go for it."

They crossed the Arkansas with ease and headed due north to the Platte River. They were now on a cattle drive trail where cattle had crossed at the same place Wolf and Betz did.

There were lots of birds near the river, so Wolf had Betz move all the horses slowly as he and the eager Blondie worked the north bank of the river for birds.

About an hour later, Wolf caught up with Betz and the small herd they were now pushing and showed off his six partridges.

"Where's Jake?"

"He'll be along. He's having lunch right now.

The traveling was easy. The first day they saw three different small groups of Indians and Betz called to them in Arapaho and they each waved.

She's going to a valuable person to have, Wolf thought.

★ ★ ★

They had covered a fair distance when on the second day Jake stopped with his nose in the air and looked at a thicket of bushes ahead of them to their right.

Wolf said whoa and eased back on the reins and got off Blondie.

He raised his hand for Betz to stop when she started to dismount.

He eased up behind Jake and said, "What do you have, boy?"

"Jake didn't really growl like this was going to be a fight. He just rumbled a little and started walking over to the bushes, which now started to move and a Negro's head popped out.

Wolf said, "Easy boy," and looked at the man whose hair was starting to turn grey.

"Hey, mister. What're you hiding in the bushes for?"

The man stood up and walked out toward Wolf as the bushes moved behind him and a small lady, also with slightly grey hair, followed the man.

"What in hell are you two doing in the bushes way out here in the middle of nowhere?"

"We didn't know who you were, so we just ducked out of sight. There seems to be a lot of bad folks out here."

"Where're you going?" Wolf asked.

"Well, we were headed up north. We wanted to get away from Mississippi and everything down south."

"Why didn't you go east? Most of the black folks did."

"We heard too many stories about how things were up there so decided to head out this way."

"Where're you from?"

"Mississippi. We were slaves on a plantation there. I worked the horses and the missus here," he said looking at the woman, "she worked in the kitchen. She's a cook."

"It's been some time now since you were set free. How come you haven't settled down yet?"

The man's eyes kept drifting over to the horses and he said, "We tried a few places. I worked race horses in Kentucky for three years. We liked it there, but the farm got sold to some people from back east and everything changed. I was a slave again."

"Well this is Betz up there on that red horse." What're your names?"

The man nodded to Betz, and said, "Glad to meet you Betz. Are you an Indian lady?"

Betz laughed, nodded at Wolf and said, "No, I'm his woman. I was a captive for several years and Wolf set me free."

Wolf was surprised by the comment, but didn't acknowledge it.

The man said, "My name is William Sharpton, but they call me Willie. This is my wife Irma," he said with a slight bow.

I'm Wolf, Willie. We're headed up north. I'm gong to need a horse man and I'm sure I'm going to need a cook as well. If you want, you can travel with us. When we get to where I'm going, you can decide if you want to stay or move on. Your choice. What do you think?"

Irma was already smiling when Willie looked at her and he turned to Wolf and said, "Yessir, I think that would be mighty fine indeed if it's alright with you folks."

When Wolf looked back at Betz, she was looking down at her saddle, shaking her head and laughing.

"What's so funny?" Wolf asked.

"Well, somehow we just happen to have a couple of extra horses that these folks can ride. Can you imagine that," she said looking at Wolf, still shaking her head.

"Well we can walk, if that's okay," said Willie.

"Wolf started to grin now with the realization of the situation. He looked at Betz, shrugged his shoulders and said, "No Willie. You and Irma are riding. Some things are just meant to be. I presume you know how to ride, right?"

Willie smiled and said, "I been working with horses for over twenty years, Massa Wolf, and the wife has gone riding with me sometimes too. Yes, we know how to ride."

"Okay Willie. Those two horses with empty saddles are just waiting for you, and Willie, no more Massa Wolf, okay? It's just Wolf and that's Betz."

A big smile came over both Willie and Irma's face and both said, "Yessir."

Willie headed back into the bushes and came out with two packs.

"These horses have names?" Willie asked.

"Well, yes they do," Betz said. "The one I'm on is Red. That's Ruby there. That's Blondie and the black stallion is Blackie."

Willie looked at each of the horses then at Wolf and Betz and said, "Well, I guess that makes sense," and headed for the two saddled horses Betz was leading.

"We've got a long way to go to get to the Platte so we better move on. Willie, why don't you ride up here with me, and tell me about yourself," Wolf said as he got on Blondie.

★ ★ ★

Willie had been with horses as long as he could remember. He helped herd them when he first started, but his aptitude for getting along with horses moved him into the stables wherever he worked. He trained, shod, cleaned, and worked horses in any number of ways.

"That red horse is pretty long on the front hooves, Wolf. They need trimming real bad. They're pushing him back on his hoofs and he could come up lame or he could stumble," Willie said as he looked at Betz's horse.

"I've got my tools with me, but I don't have any shoes. They come in different sizes and uses, you know, but I can check your stock out tonight when we settle in and see what needs to be done."

"That would be great, Willie. I thought the same thing about Red but we haven't been anywhere to stop and have him looked after."

★ ★ ★

They settled in under a small stand of trees where there was ample grass for the horses. Willie was a great help in staking and tethering the horses for the evening.

They still had sufficient water for another couple of days but would have to find water soon. The Platte River was still possibly two days out.

Willie trimmed Red's hoofs with the help of Betz, who had become attached to the horse, and Willie tightened the shoes on Blackie and Ruby. He proved himself to be trained horseman.

"I talk to them, Wolf. I see you and Betz do too. That's important with a horse. He needs to know you're his friend. These guys that just walk up to them and push them around just don't do well with horses. The horse knows who's good to it and then it's good to him."

"I see you and Blondie and Ruby are real close. They know exactly what you're going to do. When I saw you drop the tether for Ruby and head out with Blondie after those birds, it was obvious she knew exactly what you had in mind and she was going to help. That's what I'm talking about. You're a horseman, Wolf."

★ ★ ★

Wolf and Betz both watched Irma cooking over the fire. She knew just what to do.

She dabbed a little of the bacon grease that Sarah had given him in the skillets and cooked up the birds like a real chef.

"You're lucky, Mister Wolf, that we got the extra cooking gear from those two horses you had. I can make meals a whole lot faster. Your stuff is fine for the two of you but with what we had and what was on those horses we have a real kitchen going here."

Everyone laughed at her statement, but she was right. The meal was grand compared to what Wolf and Betz had been eating.

★ ★ ★

They covered a lot of ground the next day until midafternoon when Jake stopped in his tracks with his ears up, listening.

"What do you have, boy?" Wolf said.

"I heard it, too," said Betz. "Sounded like a scream. It's somewhere up ahead."

"Let's move up slowly until we know just what we're dealing with. I'll keep Jake calmed down," Wolf said as he pulled out the long pistol, got off Blondie and started to walk.

They had moved about a quarter of a mile when it was obvious there was a woman yelling and men yelling in Spanish.

Wolf signaled for everyone to stay put, and to Willie, to get off and keep the horses quiet.

He walked slowly with Jake until they knew where the noise was coming from and Wolf told Jake to lie down and be quiet.

He crouched ahead until he had the lay of the land he was dealing with.

The ruckus was coming from, a wash directly ahead of him to their right.

He slowly worked his way, close to the bushes along the wash until he could see what was going on. He was about thirty feet from the action behind a thick bush.

There were four men, talking in Spanish. They were obviously local Mexicans. Wolf could only make out the legs of two women who were doing the shouting. Their legs were spread open and tied to bushes.

One man, the smallest of the four, had his penis out and was shaking it at the women and laughing about what he was going to do with it. He had an impressive horn, and was waving at the women while the other men were laughing at his antics.

Wolf was trying to decide the best way to handle the situation when an idea came to mind.

He held the long gun in a firm two-handed grip for accuracy and squeezed off a round.

There was dead silence except for penis man who was gripping his gushing penis in both hands.

The other men were reaching for their guns when Wolf, now with two cocked revolvers aimed at them, shouted in Spanish not to move and put their hands on their heads.

The men were frozen in their tracks, taking in the odds of pulling out their guns. They looked at the two Wolf held on them and knew that two of them would die immediately and wondered how fast he could shoot the third man.

They slowly decided to put their hands on their heads, while the bleeding man was screaming at Wolf. He was the man that could be the first to break.

Wolf yelled, "Jake, come."

Jake tore around the bush into the wash and skidded to a halt in front of the three men with a snarl.

The men were all eyes on the snarling wolf-dog, and weren't paying any attention to Wolf who now walked into the wash with one gun on the penis man and the other on the three who were staring at Jake.

"That animal can tear you to shreds in seconds. All I have to do is tell him to kill and you're history, so you do exactly as I say. You understand that?"

The men all nodded except for the man who was gripping the remains of his penis and screaming at Wolf. The original gush of blood from his full member had stopped and he was holding back any more bleeding.

The women were completely silent.

Wolf signaled and told each to take their guns out with two fingers and drop them in the sand. He then had the man closest to the injured one to get the man's gun out of his holster as well, and all dropped their holsters on the ground.

Wolf whistled for Blondie while the men sat in the wash.

★ ★ ★

Blondie moved with the whistle and Willie ran alongside the horses to the wash where everyone was.

The four men were sitting with their hands on their heads and were surprised when the group arrived.

Wolf had only made a cursory glance at the two ladies who were tied between bushes and spread eagle in the sand.

When the horses arrived, Betz dropped out of the saddle, carbine in hand, jacked in a round and after a glance at the men sitting in the wash went to the women and spoke to them in Arapahoe.

The women were yelling about the four men who had attacked them when they were returning to their camp with nuts and apples they had picked.

Wolf ignored their conversation. He didn't understand it anyway, and Betz had it well in hand.

Willie and Irma were in shock at what was going on and stood with the horses talking between themselves.

They had seen the guard command at night when Jake was in charge of guarding the camp, but this was scary. The four men were horrified. One man had his manhood in hand with the end of it hanging off by a shred of skin and he was yelling at everyone in that Mexican language neither of them really understood.

Wolf had collected all the handguns and holster belts and was hanging them on Ruby's pack. Everyone was acting as if it were business as usual, and Willie and Irma just stared at the bizarre goings on.

"Willie, go check on those men's horses would you?" Wolf said to get Willie's mind off what he was seeing.

Betz had the girls released. They appeared to be in their early twenties. One was a heavy blocky woman and the other was a slender lady. Both were a couple of inches shorter than Betz's five foot six inches or so. They both wore the basic buckskin sack dress with beading on the chest area. These ladies were picking apples and nuts when the four men came on them. They got knocked around a bit, and the rest is pretty obvious.

"They live over that hill over there," Betz said pointing. "It's at least a six-hour walk in this direction they told me and longer going back. We'll never make it tonight, so we might as well plan on camping here I think."

Wolf looked over where Betz was pointing and it was a climb all right. He looked at the sun and checked his watch on its rawhide string, and said, "I'm afraid you're right Betz. Tell the ladies that we will take them home tomorrow. We'll camp here for the night so have everyone get ready."

★ ★ ★

It was going to be a warm night with no sign of rain, so tents and shelters were not needed. Two of the captive men's bedrolls were put out for the ladies. The Mexicans would remain tied in the wash under the guard of Jake.

Irma had her hands full keeping all the women out of the cooking, but the assistance made things go much faster as she fried some smoked antelope and some of the birds Wolf had shot that day.

The tied men would get some jerky and water from their own canteens and nothing more.

Wolf had Willie pull the men's boots off and had them in a pile where they couldn't reach them just in case someone got loose. They wouldn't travel very far.

While everyone was eating supper there was a scream from the injured man, and the other Mexicans were laughing hilariously, so Willie went over to see what was going on.

He couldn't figure out what was so funny until he saw the man that was gripping his manhood. The dangling end was gone. Apparently Jake had snatched and the others thought it was hilarious.

Irma had heated up a knife for cauterizing the man's wound and leave what was left of the tube open for urine.

Two of the heaviest Mexicans sat on the man's legs and the rest held him down during the ordeal, which only lasted five seconds.

★ ★ ★

Morning came with the first light, and the ladies had the fire and coffee going with much conversation.

It was decided they would take the four men to the Arapahoe tribe and give them to the chief. He could use them for labor around the camp. The ladies said the men at their camp did nothing. The women did all the work and the men only hunted when things were desperate.

The two ladies, now known as "Yellow Bird" and "Black Crow", would ride two of the horses ahead and announce their arrival. They would return and guide them into the camp. The injured man, who was amazingly still alive, had his manhood wrapped in his bandana and tucked into his jeans. He would ride a horse and the others would walk.

★ ★ ★

The arrival at the camp was amazing. There were about a hundred Indians waiting for them when they slowly made their way into camp with three limping walkers and a moaning man in the saddle.

"Yellow Bud" told them they were welcome and led them to her tepee where she lived with her mother and aunt.

The four Mexicans were yelling at Wolf as they were hauled to an enclosure made of cactus and thorn bushes.

They weren't going anywhere.

★ ★ ★

Wolf pitched their campsite near the stream that bordered the Indian campgrounds.

Their dinner did not include any birds that night because they had their hands full with the captives, so they made do with jerked antelope.

When Betz got back to camp after visiting the village, she reported that the food was very poor. The men had become lazy and were not good hunters, and they rarely had any luck hunting. They were living primarily on wild berries, root grass, apples and anything else the women could harvest. A rabbit or two didn't go far in that compound.

After much discussion, Wolf told them he was going to go for a ride in the evening. There were large hills heavy with trees and meadows near the camp and he was going to check them out.

He figured he had at least three hours of daylight to ride by the time he left his camp, so he moved rapidly into the hills, looking for sign and feeding areas.

He found a large meadow in a small valley between two rolling hills that appeared to be a natural feeding area, and as he crept through the grass and bushes to look it over he was amazed at the game feeding in this little valley. It was a perfect place to hunt.

There were both elk and deer in the lush grass and all he needed was a plan.

★ ★ ★

Betz got Yellow Bird to the campsite and Wolf told her his plan, and what role she and the other women would play in the recovery of game. They needed to be prepared for a busy day.

Blondie was loosely saddled in the evening and Ruby had her saddle and pack saddle on her as well.

They would be leaving early in the dark so the preparation would save a lot of time and possible mistakes.

The pack had everything he hoped he would need and he got to bed before the others.

They were all to wait and see if they heard any shooting. If so,

Betz would lead the others into the hills following the directions Wolf had given her. She also would take Jake to assure that they would find Wolf.

They would use two horses with travois to carry out the game Wolf shot.

★ ★ ★

It was three o'clock in the morning when Wolf woke up. The time was perfect.

He grabbed a little jerky and checked the two canteens on the horses, cinched both horses up with the help of Willie, who got up when he heard Wolf working the horses.

Willie and Irma would be the only ones to stay in their camp to keep an eye on their belongings in this strange environment.

★ ★ ★

Wolf made his way around the base of the hills and followed his recollection to get to the meadow he was looking for.

It was still dark at four thirty, but Wolf could see the sky lighten in the east and knew sunup wasn't far off.

He made his way into the meadow, on hands and knees, and worked his way into a small clump of bushes.

He could now make out several elk and deer through his tubular brass telescope and chose the most likely ones he would shoot.

The air was dead quiet. He moved another fifty yards into the meadow to put him within range of several grazing elk and maneuvered into shooting position so he would be ready at first light when he could confirm what he was shooting.

Two large elk were chosen and their flight path after the first shot was calculated.

The farthest one would be shot first and then the nearest one as he moved away. They were only fifty yards away now and an easy shot for the scoped rifle. The second one would be more difficult as the field of vision in the narrow scope was small and it would make it more difficult to use on a running elk.

★ ★ ★

Betz was lighting the fire at first light when she heard the two shots from the hills behind the camp. She smiled. It was time to move.

Willie already had Red saddled and Jake was jumping around in anticipation after hearing the shooting.

Betz went to Yellow Bird, who had assembled some of the ladies with two travois and they were on the move in the direction Wolf had given Betz.

★ ★ ★

Wolf had the loins from both animals packed. The hearts were in a separate canvas pack for the chief and the medicine man, and the antlers were sawed off the skull to put in front of Yellow Bird's teepee.

The first to arrive was Jake, who was excited about all the meat.

Wolf threw him a large piece of liver that he knew Jake loved, and the dog snatched it and ran into the tall grass to eat.

Betz and the ladies were excited when they arrived. Wolf explained that the antlers and hides would go to Yellow Bird. Meanwhile, Betz carved out the sirloins to make into travel meat.

★ ★ ★

Wolf and Betz were first to arrive in the camp. The women were all talking excitedly when they saw them arrive, but the men appeared indifferent.

Wolf had the whole rear part of the largest elk, legs and hips to the knee joints, loaded onto ruby's packsaddle.

Wolf and Betz had the loins and sirloins wrapped on their saddles.

The women were in a happy mood as they unloaded the heavy double hind quarters of the elk and hauled it off for butchering.

The first order of business was to go to the chief and the medicine man and give them the hearts and livers from the elk. This was symbolic and an important gesture.

Betz did a lot of nodding and talking as she told the chief and the medicine man that Wolf was a great hunter and warrior.

Irma proved herself to be the cook she claimed. The sirloin she trimmed into long strips about an inch thick and when Betz went to put salt and pepper on them to soak in a bucket of water, Irma showed her how to rub the salt and pepper into the meat and let it dissolve into the meat and not dissolve in the water. She then rolled each strip in the fire coals, sealing the meat and then hung the strips to dry.

"We called this Biltong where we came from. It will last a long time and is great eating," said Irma.

★ ★ ★

The entire camp was happy with their new found wealth of meat. The women had carried everything and there was enough to go around to everyone, and they all thanked Wolf for his hunting skills.

The braves took notice and watched Wolf and his companions a lot, and the attention made Willie and Irma nervous.

Everyone had their fill and a large fire was made and everyone sat around the fire in happy socialization of the tribe.

The women stayed together while the braves huddled together on the opposite side of the large fire.

It was a warm night and the fire was just for socializing, not warmth.

A large man got up and strutted around the fire, chest out, heavy in the gut, and surveying all. He was at least six inches taller than the average brave and a good four inches taller than Wolf. It was obvious that he considered himself an important personage and the leader of the braves.

Wolf thought him to be a bully. He had seen him pushing other braves around earlier.

Everyone was quiet in respect for what appeared to be a regular ritual, while the man strutted around the fire.

He walked up to Wolf, who was sitting with Betz, Willie and Irma while Jake guarded their camp, and beat on his chest and talked in a loud voice as he looked around the crowd. The show obviously was for the new arrivals

The big man pointed to a small scar on his arm and another on his chest and talked loudly to all with much vibrato.

"What the hell is going on?" Wolf whispered to Betz.

"He's impressing us with his scars that he is a great warrior and hunter and leader of all the braves."

The big man strutted around the fire to the cheers of everyone, flexing his muscles and pounding his chest.

The chief, who was sitting quietly, said something for all to hear and everyone looked at Wolf in question.

"The chief said I told him you were a great warrior and a very successful hunter. The fact that the tribe has meat for several days is proof of your skills," Betz said.

This got the attention of the big man who strutted up to Wolf, pointed to his scars of battle and laughed as he looked at the crowd and flexed the muscles of his pudgy body.

Everyone was silent.

"He says if you are such a great warrior, where are your scars of battle?"

Wolf groaned and said, "Just tell him he is a great warrior and let it go at that."

Betz explained that Wolf was a private person and acknowledged the big man as a great warrior.

Everyone was talking now as the big man strutted around the fire. Everyone was looking at the chief.

Wolf looked at the chief and the medicine man who were openly staring at him.

"Do I really have to do this?"

"I'm afraid so. You have to prove yourself to the chief. He's the man."

★ ★ ★

Wolf slowly took off his hat and everyone started to murmur as they stared at him in anticipation.

The big man was flexing his muscles again and strutting around the fire in an attempt to draw the attention away from Wolf.

Wolf shed his gun belt and stood up, pulled his shirt out of his jeans and took off his undershirt for all to see.

The crowd gasped at the numerous scars on his arms, chests and torso. As he rotated in front of the fire, the lash marks on his back stood out on the warm glistening body.

He mimicked the big man and flexed his powerful muscles, for all to see. The comparison with the pudgy big man was dramatic. His exercise program was paying off.

He caught the eye of the chief, who was now grinning and nodding, and the people were all murmuring to each other.

Wolf walked up to the big man, who just stood there in amazement.

He asked Betz to interpret and said, "I am a warrior for the great one," as he pointed into the night sky. "I acknowledge one warrior to another. You are a great warrior for your people. I stand before you, and acknowledge your accomplishments. We warriors always love and respect the people we protect. They are important to all great warriors, and we treat them with great respect. And kindness."

After Betz had finished, Wolf put his fist to his heart and lifted it to the big man who was still standing in amazement.

The Indian put his fist to his heart and joined it with Wolf's for all to see.

A great cheer went up from all the people and Wolf looked to the chief and medicine man who were both nodding their heads in appreciation of the gesture.

Wolf put his arms out and slowly rotated around and faced the people and said, "They call me The Wolf," and he tipped his head straight up, cupped his hands around his mouth, and blasted out one of his well-practiced, blood-curdling wolf howls, that were immediately picked up by Jake.

The dogs were all barking and howling now, all over the camp, and horses were whinnying, and stomping, in the paddock.

The people were looking in every direction now, and some who had been sitting stood up. They knew something had just happened but weren't quite sure what it was.

Wolf turned to the chief and said, for all to hear, "The wolves, the dogs and the horses, they know who I am."

He turned and went back to where he had been sitting on the ground with Betz, Willie and Irma and put his clothes back on.

The big man returned to the braves.

Conversations broke out everywhere as people looked at Wolf in amazement. The dogs were still barking and the horses were restless. They had never seen anyone so marked by battle.

Betz leaned in close and said, "Well you impressed the shit out of these folks, Wolf."

Willie and Irma were also staring and shaking their heads.

CHAPTER 38

They had finally crossed the Platte near the headwaters, and where headed north through the western edge of the Sioux country. They were led to believe this was the best way to go as the Cheyenne had made peace with the western Sioux nation and there hadn't been any major Indian battles in a few years.

The Indians had banded together on several occasions, including when the Lakota, Dakota, Northern Cheyenne and Arapahoe tribes banded together and outgunned and outmaneuvered General George Armstrong Custer, killing more than two hundred of his troops a few year earlier in the battle of the Little Bighorn.

The army was dragging Civil War veterans to the Indian wars, but the Indians were not fighting each other much anymore. They had a common enemy.

★ ★ ★

They had been on a well-traveled wagon trail and were making good headway toward Fort Smith. Information from the Jamisons and Swensons, would take them to Northland from Fort Smith.

It was early in the afternoon when they could hear a stage coming from behind them and pulled the horses off the road to let it pass.

Wolf stayed in the middle of the trail and put his hand up to signal them to stop.

The stage slowed and its four horses came to a puffing halt. The shotgun was on Wolf.

"Howdy gents. I'd appreciate it if you wouldn't point that shotgun at me, sir. We're travelers and would like to ask you where this trail leads. We're headed up Montana way."

"Ya, well who are you folks? You're sure a mix. That's for damn sure."

"Yes sir. They call me Wolf and this is Betz," he said nodding at Betz. "And these folks are Willie and Irma. They're going to work for me up in Montana."

The shotgun came down and the two men were staring at each other.

"You that Wolf guy that told the stage about the Indian shootout down in the Arapahoe country?"

"Yes sir. Lucas was the shotgun and Carl was the driver, if I recall."

"Well glad to make your acquaintance, Wolf. Where you headed?"

"Up Montana way. Got a little ranch up there."

"Well, you got a ways to go but this trail will get you all the way to Fort Smith in the south of the Montana country."

"We turn around there and come back this way again. There's a stage stop about fifty miles up yonder," he said pointing with the shotgun, "We stay there for the night, you'll be welcome to join us if you want."

"That's mighty kind of you, boys. What's your names?"

"I'm Josh and the shotgun is Clem," said the driver.

"You'd better be careful. I saw a wolf in the bushes back there," he said as he pointed back down the road. "He looks like he might be stalking you folks."

"Oh, that's Jake. He's with us. He's a wolf-dog, good hunter and lots of help," he said as he called "Jake!" and Jake appeared as if out of nowhere wagging his tail and looking over the stage coach and horses.

"He's not a problem. Your horses are a little skittish, but ours are used to him now. He's just part of our clan."

"We'll see you folks tonight," he said as he whipped the reins.

The passengers were all looking Wolf's group over as the stage passed and Wolf touched his hat to the lady in the door window.

CHAPTER 39

They were back on the trail and making good time again after the dust settled.

Jake was busy scouting ahead as usual. He wandered all around them, keeping them well in sight or smell and hunted at his leisure.

They had covered about thirty miles when Jake came running back to them.

Betz said, "Looks like trouble ahead the way he's looking up the trail."

"Let's get off the trail and I'll check it out, Wolf said.

They rode the horses into the trees and Wolf got down off Blondie, pulling out the long pistol as he dismounted.

"I'll sneak ahead with Jake and see if I can figure out what he's worried about. I'll give a whistle if I need you or when it's time to come in."

"Be careful," Betz said as she watched him move off down the trail with Jake in the lead.

★ ★ ★

They had gone about a quarter of a mile when Jake's chest started to rumble and Wolf whispered to Jake to come back to his side.

Wolf could hear some yelling up ahead so he took Jake into the brush and told him to lay down, which he did. Jake seemed to know what Wolf was going to do in all events, and that puzzled Wolf.

"*That dog amazes me,*" Wolf thought as he slowly worked his way down the trail and closed in on the noise ahead.

He slowly worked his way into the bushes and trees on the side of the trail and made his way to where he could see what was going on.

He was on his knees when he looked around a tree and was amazed to find the stage that had passed them earlier was being robbed by four men.

Apparently someone had gotten the drop on the shotgun and they had all the passengers and Josh and Clem standing alongside the stage with their hands in the air.

The brakes were set and the reins were tied to the bar by the driver's seat.

One man held a pistol on the stage folks and another had a bag into which were depositing their personal items.

The third man was on top of the stage unstrapping luggage and crates and throwing them on the ground. The fourth man was doing the same thing in the freight area on the back of the stage.

★ ★ ★

Wolf worked his way further back into the brush and moved his way around to where he was on the blind side of the stage. He carefully worked his way forward watching the two men who were hard at work taking everything off the coach. They were engrossed in accomplishing the task as fast as possible.

He worked his way to the blind side of the stage, out of sight of everyone and slowly moved around to the rear watching the man who was bent over digging into the freight carrier.

Wolf quietly put the barrel of the long gun alongside the man's eye and whispered to him, "Don't move and don't make a sound," as he took the man's Colt out of its holster.

The man was frozen in his tracks and they were completely out of sight of everyone.

The man was a good six inches taller so Wolf got directly behind him and slowly moved the man around the back of the stage where they could see everything.

No one paid any attention to the big man's arrival until Wolf shot the man in the wrist that was aiming his colt at the passengers and shouted, "Everyone, put your hands on top of your heads, NOW!"

As expected, and planned for, the man on top of the stage stood up and reached for his gun.

He was shot with the long gun and dropped off the top of the stage.

"He wasn't paying attention," Wolf said.

"Now you two, keep your hands on your heads," he added as he pushed the man he'd been standing behind.

"You get over there and sit down. Keep your hands on your head."

"Josh, get that man's gun," he said indicating the man who had been holding the bag.

"Pick up the bag, ma'am, and retrieve your things." You two get over there with your friend and sit down."

The injured man was yelling and holding his wrist over his head to curtail the bleeding and saying he was going to die and needed help.

Wolf looked over his shoulder and quietly called, "Jake."

Jake came tearing into the fray and looked all around and at Wolf who said, "Jake, guard," and pointed to the men on the ground.

Jake leapt toward the men with his best snarl and snapping his teeth.

Clem said, "Holy shit," as he watched the act.

Wolf smiled at Clem and said, "They won't be going anywhere, Clem."

Josh had a gun and Jake had the men well-covered, so Wolf went over to check on the man that tumbled off the stage. He had seen him hit and knew he wasn't going to get up. He was in an impossible position. His head and shoulders were completely doubled over under his body with his butt sticking straight up in the air. No one could survive a fall like that, regardless of being shot.

Wolf whistled for Betz and walked back to the passengers and stage hands.

"I know these guys, Wolf. Sure glad you showed up. I guess ol' Carl and Lucas were right about you."

"You've got some reward money coming for these guys and that's for sure."

"Where you say you're going?" said the lady passenger.

"Up Montana way, ma'am. A place called Northland."

"Northland," she exclaimed. "That's where I'm from. Mister Wolf, you really going up there?"

"Yes ma'am. That's the plan," he said as Betz arrived with the troop.

"I sure would like to talk to you about it tonight, at that stage stop Josh told me about, if it's alright with you ma'am?"

"I'm really looking forward to it," she said with a smile. By the way, my name is Joanna Clark. They just call me Jo."

"You're not the lady that runs that Saloon in town, are you?"

"That's me. How'd you know that?"

"It's a long story Jo. I'll tell you about it tonight. I have some mail for you."

"Mail?"

"Yes, Ma'am, from the Jamisons and Swensons. I'll bring it tonight."

She was a handsome woman with a kind face and bright red hair. She was full-figured and Wolf guessed her to be about forty years old and a little shorter than him.

Betz was over with Irma, tying the man's wrist up tight to cut the bleeding.

At one point, Betz belted the man across the face and told him to shut up, or she'd let him bleed out on the spot.

"You gonna need any help with these guys, Wolf?"

"There's a town about ten miles west of the stage stop on a well-traveled trail. You can take these guys in there for the reward."

"I know the guy you shot the hand off is Tompkins and he's got a good reward. The guy you shot off the stage I think is a guy they call 'Slink'. His name is Bloom."

"The guy with the bag, I've seen his picture as well as the other guy but I don't remember their names. We'll get that at the stage stop." "Okay everybody, lets get this stuff back on the stage," said Josh, as he picked up a crate and tossed it up to Clem.

Willie was already loading the fright compartment.

★ ★ ★

Tompkins was moaning in pain but the bleeding had stopped. A doctor could probably get him put together enough to survive but he'd never handle a gun with that hand again.

All the guns had been collected and the two other men loaded the dead man on the man's horse.

It was going to be a slow walk to the stage stop.

CHAPTER 40

They arrived just at twilight.

The three men were tied to separate trees with their boots removed. Jake was on watch.

Their camp was getting set up, and a fire was going in the stone cooking pit that apparently had been used earlier in the evening by the folks staying at the Stage stop.

Wolf went into the stage stop and found it a small comfortable building with the aroma of a meal still hanging in the air.

Everyone was in a grand mood and the talk was easy.

The room fell silent when Wolf walked in. Everyone was staring at him.

"Evening folks, I don't want to disturb you but I'd like to talk to Miss Jo for a while if I may."

Lucas said, "Hell no Wolf. You're not bothering anyone. We're damn glad to see you. You get those guys here all in one piece?" he said with a grin.

"Oh ya, no problem. I've got em trussed up for the night and Jake is keeping an eye on them. They won't be going anywhere.

You said you had some information on who these men might be?" Wolf asked.

"Got it right here," Lucas said as he picked up some wanted posters and walked over to Wolf.

"Looks like you've hit the jackpot, Wolf. The total for those four is thirty-five hundred. It may be more now as these flyers are a few weeks old, but you're gonna collect for sure."

"Wow, they must be really bad guys with a price on their heads like that," Wolf said looking over the flyers. "They are all are wanted "Dead or Alive"."

"Miss Jo I'd like to talk to you a little about Northland and tell you what I'm going to do up there," he said as he tucked the posters in his belt.

"Sit down Wolf. I'm dying to hear why you're going to Northland. It sure as hell isn't paradise."

"Well I met some real nice folks down in New Orleans by the names of Jamison and Swenson, and they told me about having their ranches taken from them by some guy by the name of Oscar Thorndale. It sounds like he's the local Baron that runs everything."

"It was then I knew where I was headed. The reason why is a little hard to explain, so I'll skip that. It's a long story Jo. It's my destiny however and I'm going to follow through with it."

"I bought their ranches and livestock and gave them a fair price for it all. They had the original papers they recorded in Helena. I now have them with a proper Deed and Bill of Sale that I'll take to Helena and record it on my way to Northland."

Jo just looked at him in amazement, and shook her head. "Wolf, you're walking through the Gates of Hell if you plan on doing what I think you are. Those people are dangerous. Deadly dangerous. They have no morals at all and kill people without even thinking about it. It's a way of life for them and they get by with it in Northland. They're not just bad, bad people Wolf. They're flat evil."

"I know Jo and that's why I'm destined to go."

It was all quiet in the room now as everyone had been listening and stared at Wolf.

Wolf, Thorndale runs that whole country with gunslingers. He's gotten rich by killing and stealing. They are completely ruthless and have no moral fiber whatsoever."

"The only reason he puts up with Northland at all is he needs

Northland. He needs the bank, he needs the Saloon and brothel, and he needs the town merchants for his supplies."

"He can't do that and he knows it. He needs us so he puts up with us and everyone toes the line."

"If anyone, and I mean anyone, gets out of line they disappear. No one asks a question about it. They're just gone. Their store is closed up and their merchandise disappears. They're history."

"He had a problem with the man that owned the Hotel and some adjacent buildings because Thorndale wouldn't pay his bill and the man just disappeared while hunting. Thorndale's daughter now owns the properties and she's letting it go to hell. They take, they don't give."

"What's the law say?"

Jo laughed and said, "He is the law, Wolf. He owns the Sheriff and the deputies."

"Well it'll be interesting to say the least. I'm on my way and I'm not turning back. I've faced trouble all along the way. It was meant to be I think."

"Well I hope you survive, Wolf. That's going to be the challenge, just to survive."

"Well the day you see me walk into your Saloon you'll know that I've been to both of the ranches and things have been put in order."

"It'll sure be interesting then I bet," he said with a grin.

"You'll know that at least I've made it that far. I hope you'll keep me informed as much as possible about how things are going so at least I have a bit of a heads up on matters that may affect me."

"Rest assured I will. It may not be direct, but you'll know."

Clem butt in and said, "Sounds like you may be in for another shoot out Wolf. Carl and Lucas told us about that Indian mess you were in down in the Kiowa country. Sounds like you killed a bunch of Indians down there. Sure would like to hear about that."

"Well that's history Clem. What Carl and Lukas told you was probably how it was. I just don't like to think in the past about those things. I just press on to the future and what challenges lie ahead."

"Here's the mail I was telling you about, Jo. There's a letter to you and one to Billy your bartender, the pastor of the church, the banker and a mister Klein who runs the dry goods store."

"There's also one to a Mexican by the name of Jimmie Rodriguez who has a restaurant and a Chinaman, a Charlie Foo who has a laundry, bath, and runs some Chinese labor in the area."

"The Jamisons told me they were all good people and would be a help to me along the way. I'm looking forward to meeting them when I get to town."

"Speaking of the banker, would you tell him I'm having the reward money sent to his bank to deposit in my account I'll be opening when I get there?"

Clem said, "You mean "if" you get there?"

"No Clem, I'll get to town, one way or another."

"I just need you to tell them that I'm not a new gunslinger as you call them. I'm going to be an honest rancher."

Jo had been reading her letter while Wolf was talking, and when she finished she just stared at Wolf and shaking her head said, "Well Wolf, I hope you make it."

"Well I better leave you folks alone. I need to get something to eat and some rest. We've a long way to go tomorrow with our detour and all. You folks have a nice evening and a safe, blessed journey."

★ ★ ★

When Wolf was gone Jo looked at the others who were anxiously awaiting her comments, and said, "I can't believe it. This Wolf guy is a wealthy man from New Orleans. He has it all down there. What in hell possessed him to go to Northland, an outlaw headquarters run by a damn immoral criminal? I just can't figure it out."

Everyone in the room knew something about Northland and not much of it was good. They just shook their heads in wonderment.

★ ★ ★

Wolf went to the fire, where Betz, Irma and Willie were eating.

Betz saw him coming and filled a plate for him and a mug of cool water.

Wolf thanked her and looked over at Jake who hadn't missed a thing and said, "Good boy Jake."

That brought on a wagging tail.

CHAPTER 41

The ladies had breakfast going before the Stage group put their skillet on the fire.

There was a lot of fun conversation around the cooking fire while Willie and Wolf got the horses ready to travel and discussed the plan for the day.

The men were well tied without boots, and their horses were being led by Wolf and Willie. Betz and Irma had the rest in tow.

Wolf followed Willie as he was concerned the two in front of him may try and make a break for it. He could watch them and if there was a problem he'd be on it in a heartbeat.

He had the dead robber and the injured Tompkins on his tether. Neither one of them were going anywhere.

The going was slow but it was going to be worth it in the long run.

★ ★ ★

They made it into town by mid-morning and finding the Sheriff's office wasn't difficult as a group of boys saw the dead man across the saddle and came running. They were full of directions and suggestions.

Wolf tied the captive's horses securely to the hitching rail and sent Willie inside to get the sheriff.

The Sherriff wasn't too interested in Willie when he walked in the door. They didn't want any slaves in this town creating trouble.

"What can I do for you, boy?" the Sheriff barked in a nasty tone.

"Well sir we'd like you to come outside, sir."

"What the hell for, boy?" I'm not going anywhere with you."

"I'm riding with the Wolf sir and he's got some stage robbers to turn in for the rewards, sir."

"The Wolf, you mean that Kiowa guy?" He's got Stage robbers?"

"Yes sir, that's what I'm telling you."

"Well why didn't you say so in the first place?" he said as he took his feet off the desk and hustled to the front door.

The sheriff threw the door open and his mouth dropped. There was Tompkins, Bloom and the two Grant brothers.

"Well I'll be damned. You must be that Wolf guy huh? Heard about you."

"How'd you catch these guys Wolf? What makes you think there's a reward for them or if they are even wanted?"

"Well sir I caught them when they were robbing the Stage and Carl and Lucas gave me these fliers," he said handing them to the Sheriff. "They say there may be a new flier out with a higher price on their heads. That's why I know who they are and what they are Sheriff," he said looking the Sheriff in the eye.

The sheriff was obviously caught off guard. He cleared his throat and said. "Yes sir, you got em all right. Bring them inside and we'll see what we can do about this," he said as he turned around and walked back into the Sheriff's office reading the fliers leaving the door open.

Willie and Wolf just looked at each other and smiled.

Betz said, "Sounds like that guy's a real asshole to me."

Irma laughed and said, "I guess so."

★ ★ ★

Wolf and Willie got the men off their horses and shoved the barefoot men into the office.

The Sheriff was sitting in his chair still reading the fliers when they came in.

Wolf said, "Hey Sheriff if you got a minute you think you could open the jail up for us? Unless of course you're planning on taking these guys home with you."

The Sheriff looked up, cleared his throat and said, "Oh sure got the keys right here," as he dug in the drawer of the desk and threw the keys on the top.

They led the three men into the jail and Wolf untied each of them while they were cussing him out.

The sheriff went back to his desk and was reading the fliers again.

Wolf said, "What do you want me to do with the rest of this?"

"Put it right here on my desk," he said without looking up.

Wolf and Willie looked at each other. Willie was confused and Wolf winked at him.

"Come on Willie" he said as he walked out the door.

Willie said, "I don't think that man can read Wolf. He's been looking at those fliers for a long time and hasn't said a word."

"I know Willie. We're going to have some fun now. Get Betz to help you with all the boots and I'll get the Grant boy out of the saddle. Then we'll go in and dump the whole mess on his desk just like he asked."

Willie laughed as he walked off and said, "Boy I can hardly wait to see the look on his face."

Wolf had the Grant boy over his shoulder and Willie and Betz had the three pairs of boots.

The door was still open and the sheriff was still reading the fliers.

Wolf walked up to the desk and threw Grant on the desk so he would slide off onto the sheriff, who tipped over with the chair and landed on the floor under Grant. Willie and Betz threw the boots on the pile.

The sheriff started screaming and pushing Grant off of him, rolling across the floor as the boots came crashing down.

The three men in the jail were laughing hysterically at the sheriff's antics as he was trying to get up and wipe himself off.

"Are you crazy you son of a bitch?"

"Look sheriff, we asked you what you wanted us to do and you told us to put everything on your desk. We were just following instructions."

"What am I supposed to do with him? He's dead for Christ sake."

"What do you usually do with dead bodies in your town sheriff?"

"I gotta go find the Sheriff. Oh my God, things have gone to shit," he mumbled as he ran out the door.

"I guess he isn't the sheriff after all," said Betz.

"That sure scared the shit out of him for sure," she added with a chuckle.

She looked around the empty office and said to the three men in the jail cell, "No one's here gentlemen. How much will you pay to be let loose?"

They all started talking at once and telling about the great amounts of money they would pay.

"You got that money with you," Betz said.

"No but we'll get it for you."

"Sure you will. Well no deal gentlemen. We'll just collect the reward instead."

They were all yelling at Betz when a tall, serious looking man walked into the office looking everyone over.

The man that was here earlier followed close behind the big man looking around the man like a bird dog.

"Morning folks. Emmit here tells me you brought in some Stage robbers," he said as he pointed with his thumb over his shoulder.

Wolf walked up to the man extending his hand and said, "I'm Wolf and these men here are the ones on the fliers your man here has been trying to read" he said nodding to the jail cell.

"I heard about you Wolf. Name's Jon McGrath. I'm the Sheriff in these parts. Emmit here is a part time deputy. I can't be in the office all the time so it's necessary to have Emmit cover the square."

"What in hell is that guy doing on the floor over there with all those boots?" he said, as he saw the dead man on the floor.

"Well sir, Emmit told us to put everything on his desk as he was busy reading the fliers so we did just that," Wolf said with a shrug.

Jon looked around at the others and they all shrugged.

Emmit started to talk and Jon just raised his hand for silence, shook his head and walked around the desk looking at the dead man on the floor and said, "Wolf give me a hand with this guy would you?"

CHAPTER 42

Emmit was sent for the local burial man and Jon read through the fliers and made arrangements to send a telegraph message to the state for payment. The money would be sent to the Northland Bank in Northland Montana sooner or later.

"Sheriff I have four horses and tack that I'd like to sell to someone. Do you know of anyone that might be interested?"

"As a matter of fact you're looking at him. I need some decent horses for the town deputies and yours look like pretty good stock to me. I haven't looked them over, but from what I've seen their pretty decent. I can make arrangements through the local bank to get you paid. What do you think you have to have for them?"

★ ★ ★

A price was struck and the paperwork for the reward was completed. The Sheriff took Wolf to the bank for payment of the horses and tack.

★ ★ ★

Wolf got back to the Sheriff's office where Betz, Willie and Irma were waiting for him.

"They have a pretty good place to eat over there," he said pointing across the street. "Let's go get a real meal and I want to talk to you about some things."

Willie spoke up and said, "Wolf I don't think Irma and I can get in there. Folks are pretty fussy about that you know?"

"I know Willie. I talked to the Sheriff about that and they have a room in the back where we can all eat, so let's go. You're working for me now remember?"

★ ★ ★

During the meal Wolf outlined his plans for the day. First they would go to the local dry-goods store and buy some jeans, shirts, socks and boots for them all.

Willie and Irma had one pair of jeans and shirts and Betz was still in her buckskin cover. It was time to get them into some new clothes.

The first thing Betz said was, "I need a bra. You have any idea what it's like with your tits bouncing up and down all day in the saddle? They'll be down to my waist pretty soon. I need a bra. How about you, Irma?"

"I never had a bra. I don't know, but I guess it's a good idea. I know what you're talking about."

"Okay it's settled then," said Wolf. "We get whatever we need plus a couple of bras. Don't want any tits down to the waist line for sure."

Everyone laughed, and Betz punched Wolf on the arm.

CHAPTER 43

Wolf got Betz aside the next evening, and they went for a walk along the stream they were camped by.

Betz we need to talk about where you're getting off. You said you were going to go see some uncle in Wyoming and we're here. Where're you headed Betz and what can I do for you?"

Betz walked along with her head down in silence. She finally reached over and took Wolf's hand and said, "Sit with me Wolf. We need to talk about that."

The sun was low in the sky and the night was going to be crystal clear and warm.

Betz lied down in the grass and pulled a green shaft of grass and put it in her mouth, chewing gently.

Lay with me Wolf. Let's talk about this. This has been bothering me for days and we need to talk about it."

"Go ahead Betz. What have you go on your mind?"

"You enjoy my company Wolf? Are you happy that I've been along? Do you like lying with me at night or whenever we feel like it? Do you like the way I treat you?"

"Hell yes Betz. You know that. What's that got to do with your plans?"

"Well it's like this. I don't even know this uncle of mine that I was going to go and live with. I've never seen him and don't know a damn thing about him. I'm not even sure where he lives."

"I'm asking you if I can just hang with you. I mean, I won't interfere with any woman you may decide to take for a wife or whatever, but I'll be there until that day comes. I'm not asking for a commitment of any kind Wolf. Hell I know you can't even make a commitment until this damn quest of yours is over with. I just want to continue being your woman until that time comes. What do you think of that?"

Wolf rolled over and plucked the grass out of her mouth and said, "I think that's a great idea Betz. I've grown accustomed to you now and the way you are. You've become an important part of my life with all that's been going on."

"I've been concerned about you leaving and wondering when you were just going to ride off into the sunset."

"You think you can continue to put up with me huh?" Betz said as she rolled up on top of him with a big smile. She kissed him and snuggled down into him.

Wolf said, "Well let me think about it."

CHAPTER 44

They hit the Big Horn River in a day and a half. The terrain was hillier but the trails were well used.

They arrived at Fort Smith and Wolf went in to check on the Indian situation in the area they were going to travel.

He found he was never going to talk to anyone in charge as they were too important to talk to strangers that were traveling through but a sergeant was more than cooperative.

"There were still skirmishes in the area, but after all the Indian wars of 1886 and 1887 things had quieted down in this area substantially," the man said.

★ ★ ★

They would follow the Yellowstone River until it hit the Missouri River and follow it into Helena where Wolf would register his Deeds and Bills of Sale.

They would be crossing a large Crow Indian reservation and were cautioned to avoid any trouble. The 1886–1887 wars with the Crow were not forgotten.

CHAPTER 45

They were all surprised at the bustling town of Helena, the new Capital of Montana.

The mix of people was amazing. There were ranchers, farmers, people going to and from the gold mining districts and businessmen of all types making a living off the thriving town.

Violence was not unheard of and they kept their business as brief as possible.

The offices of the Capital directed Wolf to the land section where he recorded his Deeds and Bill of Sale for the livestock of all three locations.

He had the young man check to confirm there were no other filings of any kind after the Jamisons' and Swensons' filed their claims.

They were on their way to Northland.

CHAPTER 46

The going was slower in this country. Not as flat and easy as it was down south but they got to where Wolf wanted to be in three days. They had to skirt the south side of the Belt Mountains and go north through the central break in the mountains.

When they hit the town of Barnes they broke off through the hills to the Swenson's ranch which was the nearest and adjacent to the town of Northland.

Wolf was well in the lead now with Jake. He didn't want his troop to be spotted by any ranch hand at the Swensons J/M ranch.

★ ★ ★

He found a place where he could sit in the trees and see the layout of the ranch. He looked the place over with his brass scope and surprisingly there was no activity at all. There was some smoke coming from a small building which Swenson had identified as the cook house where the "cookie" George lived but the main house, which was finely built by Jamison and Swenson, showed no activity.

The buildings seemed to be in a reasonable state of repair and the winter poll barns were clean and cared for. Someone was doing something.

In front of the ranch there was a large lake that must be over a hundred acres Wolf estimated. There were cattle spread all over the place working on the lush grass. The lake had wild ducks as well as a horde of tame ducks that were followed by a gang of ducklings.

He remembered Swenson telling him how they ate a lot of roast duck on the ranch. He could now see the source.

There was a large overgrown fenced-in garden that was greatly in need of attention.

This was a beautiful, successful ranch. No wonder Thorndale wanted it.

Wolf retraced his entry and bent a sapling across the trail which was the signal that this was the place for Betz to stop and wait until he called for them.

Jake stayed and calmly waited for their arrival as Wolf went off alone.

★ ★ ★

It was late in the afternoon that a lone rider came in from the fields where the cattle were grazing.

He wasn't armed which surprised Wolf.

The man tended to his horse and went into the big house.

About an hour later four men came out of the house and headed over to the cook house. The man he'd seen earlier was still unarmed but the other three carried pistols on their hips. Wolf noted that the holsters were tied down to each man's leg. These were probably the gunslingers the Swensons talked about.

Now that he knew what he was up against he could plan ahead. Make a plan and follow the plan.

★ ★ ★

The men made a few trips outside to urinate and two of them went to the outhouse in the trees north of the big house.

It was deep dark now and Wolf started to move.

He was wearing dark jeans, a black shirt and no hat. He was going to blend in with the night as much as possible.

The Swensons' said the gunslingers killed their dogs when they took over and Wolf had not seen any during his observation so he didn't have to worry about their alarm.

He moved well out of sight of the big house and closed in on the cook shed which housed the "cookie".

Wolf eased up to the window on the porch and could see an older man sitting at a lantern lit table smoking and looking at a catalog.

The man appeared to be exactly as the Swensons described him so he opened the door and moved in quickly and quietly putting his finger to his lips to signal to the man to remain quiet.

"Hi, you're George. Is that right?"

"Who the hell are you mister?"

Wolf moved so that he was out of sight of the window that faced the house and sat on one of the chairs used by the men at mealtime.

"George, I'm Wolf. I'm a friend of the Swensons and I bought this ranch and all the livestock, fixtures, you name it. Lock stock and barrel so to speak."

"The Swensons' and the Jamison's' told me what happened here and I bought their ranches and am about to run these gunslingers, as Swensons' call them, off the property one way or another."

"I saw three men with revolvers and one man without when I looked through the window. What can you tell me about them?"

George had been staring at him in amazement and hadn't said a word.

He looked at Wolf a long time after Wolf stopped talking and finally shaking his head a little a smile crept across his face and he said, "Well I'll be damned".

"I got a letter here for you George from the Swensons'. You want to read it or do you want me to read it for you?"

"No I can read just fine. You say your name is Wolf?"

"That's it, Wolf said as he handed the man the envelope with George's name printed on it.

George took his time reading. He then looked up at Wolf smiling and said, "Well I'll be damned."

"Well I hope not George. What can you tell me about the guys in the house?"

"Well Bobby, that's the guy with no guns. He worked for the Swensons'. He's a good boy. They kept him on to do the work. The others just sit in the house and smoke, drink and play cards all day. Once in a while they go out in the fields to check on the cattle but damn seldom. They don't do a damn thing," he continued.

"We had another hand that hung around but the bastards shot him because he would argue with them about what needed to be done around here. Bobby just keeps his mouth shut and goes about his business. I'm surprised he's still here. They treat him like shit. I thought he would just ride off one day and not come back for dinner."

"Okay George. Here's my plan. I'm going to in there and try and run them off. I'm sure that may not work and there's gonna be shooting. I want you to go get Bobby and tell him you need some help or something. We'll fill him in on what's going on and he stays out of the gunfire. That sound okay to you?"

"Ah Wolf, you a little crazy or something? There're three crazy assed killers in that house that will shoot anyone, anytime. You don't stand a chanch man."

"I'll work on that assumption George. Now go get Bobby, okay?"

★ ★ ★

Bobby came into the cook house and closed the door behind him. He then he saw Wolf sitting in the corner out of sight.

"What's this shit, Cookie? Who's he?"

"I'll let him tell you, Bobby. Sit down and listen."

★ ★ ★

Wolf walked up on the porch of the main house not trying to be quiet. He was just Bobby returning.

Wolf studied the three men through a window and had decided on his plan when he went through the door.

He would try and talk to them and get them to leave. If they started to get up that meant they are going for their guns and the target would rise with the men. He had to keep that in mind.

Concentrate. Targets left to right. They'll be rising.

Two men were sitting at the large table near the kitchen part of the house and the other was sitting on a couch with his boots up on a heavy wooden table staring off into space. All three men were smoking. There was a lot of laughing and cursing going on over the card game. There was money and a whiskey bottle on the table. Cards were being studied with a lot of mumbling.

Wolf opened the door and casually walked in and moved to within ten feet of the card game before anyone noticed it wasn't Bobby.

The two men at the card table moved as one reaching for their guns and cursing Wolf without asking any questions.

They both went down with their revolvers and chairs, clattering to the floor.

The man on the couch was slower in getting up. He saw what happened and didn't try to reach for his gun.

"Who the hell are you, mister. What ya doing shooting my friends?"

"Well they were trying to shoot me, mister. Who're you?"

Wolf had his Colt back in its holster now but not jammed down tight as he faced the man.

"I don't tell you shit, mister. This is my boss's ranch. You just bust in here and shoot it up. You're dead meat, mister."

The man ranked on getting himself more worked up the more he yelled. He was reaching a point of being dangerous. He was going to be impossible to talk too.

Wolf concentrated on his target and let the man carry on.

The man kept glancing at the two men on the floor shaking his head.

It finally came to a crisis. The man had worked himself up to frenzy where he thought he had to act, and fast.

He waved his hands around which Wolf knew was an effort to distract him. Wolf waited for the man to move.

The screaming man had just touched his gun when he toppled over on the floor with a bullet hole in the center of his forehead.

★ ★ ★

Wolf went outside and called for Bobby and George.

He didn't have to wait long as they were already outside the cook house.

"Bobby, give me a hand will you to get these guys out of the house. They've fouled it up enough without them bleeding all over the place.

"Jesus Christ," Cookie mumbled.

"How'd you do that Wolf?"

"Well I wanted to talk to them about leaving but they had other ideas and---well you know the results. Now let's get to work.

★ ★ ★

They hauled the three men out into the back yard and Wolf whistled loudly. He knew Jake would hear him and come running with the rest of the troop.

Wolf was in the house when he heard a yell from the yard.

Bobby and George were looking the men over when a huge wolf raced into the yard snarling and snapping his teeth.

"God damned wolf, cookie. Run for it."

Wolf laughed and called, "Jake" and the dog raced into the house.

Cookie said. "Did I just see a big God damned wolf run into the house when that Wolf guy called him. Christ, I think I shit my pants."

Bobby was just standing there shaking with his mouth open. "Holly shit, Cookie," he mumbled.

"I'm sorry guys. I forgot to tell you about my dog. This is Jake. He's really a friendly dog. Not really a Wolf. Only part Wolf but he's a good friend. Come over here Jake and meet these guys."

Both Bobby and George backed up as Jake approached them wagging his tail.

"Don't be fearful boys. You need to know Jake. He'll be around here with us. You'll find him great protection for the ranch, believe me."

"Shit I believe you mister. That's the scariest damn critter I've ever seen. You say he's tame?"

"Oh sure, go ahead and pet him. He'll love you guys."

"Is the damn thing gonna eat me," said George staring at Jake.

"No, not unless I tell him too," Wolf chuckled. "Go on and pet him. Call him by his name so he knows that you know him. He'll be a good friend when you need him."

Betz was the next to arrive and looked at them men on the ground.

"Well so much for conversation and convincing them to move on Wolf. Looks like that didn't work."

"No. It was just like Jo and George said. They just shoot people. They don't talk."

CHAPTER 47

Wolf knew he had to move on to the Jamison place before someone found out what had happened here. It was just a matter of time that someone would come by.

★ ★ ★

They all pitched in for the evening cleaning up what they could.

The next day Bobby would take Wolf to the Jamison ranch and show him how to get there unseen. He would talk to the "Cookie" Mike, and keep him out of the way. There were three more gunslingers at that ranch that had to be dealt with.

They wanted to arrive just after dusk when they could look the ranch over from afar then make their way to the cook house and to get a look in the window of the big house to get a lay of the place.

This ranch was more opulent. The main house was two stories and had a porch that went all the way around the house under a sturdy overhang.

The cook house was large and had what appeared to be a couple of sleeping quarters attached to it.

Like the Jamison's ranch there was a large elongated building that was probably the quarters for cowboys as they needed them. All the buildings, like Jamison's, had steel stacks through the roofs for heating stoves.

These people knew how to ranch and live. These ranches were real cherries for Thorndale.

★ ★ ★

After the men had returned to the main house after dinner bobby made his way to the cook house unseen from the main building. He was inside about a half hour when he came outside and waived in Wolf's direction.

The cookie was out of trouble.

Bobby was armed now, but hopefully he would not have to get involved.

The men were much like the first bunch at Jamison's.

Wolf watched them through a window and all three were playing cards at a large table with a bottle of whiskey and three glasses. One man was chewing tobacco and every once in a while he would spit on the floor.

When Wolf walked in this time they would not be expecting anyone like at the Jamison's. They would be on alert immediately. If he couldn't talk to them, which he knew now was highly doubtful, there will probably be shooting. Prepare---concentrate.

The only thing he had going for him was his faith in what he was doing and the daily practice that had served him so well.

Targets, left to right. Concentrate, he thought as he pushed the door open.

All three men looked up from their cards in surprise, and for a moment froze in place.

"Evening boys. It's time to leave."

They looked at each other in confusion and all three started to rise and draw.

Targets one and two went down immediately and three had his gun out now but too late. He was faster than Wolf could imagine. That was close. Too close.

The three of them bowled over on the floor taking their chairs with them.

Wolf waited to see if anyone was going to move but he saw his shots were true and each was hit in the head.

They weren't going anywhere. It was time to clean up the place and plan the next move.

CHAPTER 48

Early the next morning they arrived back at the Jamison ranch and found everyone happily cleaning up the mess the former occupants had left. It was starting to look like the pristine ranch it had once been.

Bobby and Wolf sat on the back porch and talked about what to expect and how Wolf should move next. It was Thursday, and Friday was the big day for Thorndale to hit town. He never wanted to be there on Saturday when his crew would raise hell in Northland. It was important to confront him before he was aware of what happened at the two ranches he had confiscated from the Jamisons' and the Swensons'.

★ ★ ★

The plan was worked out.

It was the middle of the afternoon on the day that Bobby knew Thorndale would be in town playing cards. It was a Friday ritual. He always came with a few of his boys to look after him, but they drank and played while Thorndale cheated at cards.

Bobby would slip into the saloon and see who was there and compare them to the horses out front. He knew the riders and the horses and they wanted them all accounted for.

★ ★ ★

Wolf was unknown in town so could move around freely.

His first stop was the bank.

He walked into the bank and asked for Mister Montgomery, the president of the bank.

"Sure, can I tell him whose calling?"

"Yes ma'am. Just tell him Wolf is here. Thank you."

A large man came out of a back office with a surprised look on his face.

"Mister Wolf?"

"Yes sir, it's I. I believe you received a letter of introduction for me. Can we talk in your office?

"Absolutely mister Wolf. Come on in. Can I get you a cup of coffee or anything?"

"No thank you sir. Just a little of your time if I may?"

Small talk and the preliminaries were finally done and the banker said, "From what I've been told, and you being in town, means that you have secured your ranches. Is that correct?"

"Yes sir. It's all been taken care of and I'm now in town to make my appearance. I believe you received a notice of the funds that I have coming for the reward down south?"

"Yes we have, and I expect the funds to be here momentarily. It usually takes a couple of weeks I understand from the stagecoach driver that comes to Northland."

I'd like to open an account now and make a deposit if I may so you'll have a place to deposit the money when it comes in."

"I'm going to be in need of funds from time to time so I hope you have funds on hand that I can withdraw to pay for help and ranch expenses."

"I also have a letter of credit from my bank so you will know where to draw funds from as I may need them from time to time. I don't know what the procedure is up here so I have to leave that up to you," he said as he handed Montgomery the letter from his New Orleans banker.

While Montgomery was reading Wolf pulled his money belt

from under his shirt and laid it on the man's desk which didn't go unnoticed by Montgomery.

"Well yes everything seems to be in order, Mister Wolf. I'm amazed why you are in this God forsaken town when it's quite obvious from your banker that you're a wealthy man with many properties there."

"Well sir that's pretty hard to explain. I just trust in the All mighty that I can make a success as a rancher in this neck of the woods."

"Today is the day I've chosen to make my appearance in town and hopefully get acquainted. As far as I know no one has checked on the two ranches I bought to see if there is anything out of line. I thought this was a good time to hit town before they found out."

"My God man," he said shaking his head. "I hope you know what you're doing."

★ ★ ★

The next stop was the EL CHARRO CAFÉ.

When he walked in the door he was assailed by the wonderful cooking aroma of a fine Mexican restaurant.

He found a table and sat down to wait for Bobby. This was going to be their meeting place.

I nice young lady came up to him with a menu and said, "Can I get you something to eat?"

"I plan on eating here later miss but I could use a glass of water and if it's possible to talk to Jimmie? I would like to meet him. I think he's waiting for me."

A quizzical look came over the young lady and she said, "Sure I'll get him for you."

Jimmie arrived with a pleasant smile on his face as Wolf stood up to greet him.

"Hello Jimmie. I've heard a lot of good things about you and your family. I'm Wolf. I believe you got a letter of introduction from Jo for me."

A big smile jumped across his face and he turned to the window at the kitchen and yelled, "Margie he's here."

"Sit. Please sit, Mister Wolf. I never thought this day would come. I guess you must have cleaned up the mess at the ranches huh?"

"The Jamisons' and the Swensons' were good friends of ours. We had a big garden at the Jamison place until those gunslingers kicked them off the place. I can't believe anyone can get away with that now days."

"Those guys are just plain evil. Can I get you anything? It's on the house. Damn I'm glad to see you," he babbled on in his enthusiasm as a portly lady came to the table in an apron wiping her hands on a towel.

As Wolf rose Jimmie said, "Margie this is the Wolf Jo was telling us about. He's in town. He's cleaned up the Jamison and Swenson ranches and he says he's here to stay." "Well feed him Jimmie before the man starves to death," she said looking at her husband.

"No ma'am. I'll eat here later on. I have some things I have to do first and then I'm coming in for dinner with Bobby. He works for me now. Then I want to go next door and meet Mister Wong. I hear he's an important man in town like you folks and I think I'll try his bath house. I could sure use a nice hot soaking bath for a change and you folks can start your gardening again any time you want."

"Thank you. I'll tell Wong your coming, Wolf. I know he'll be glad to see you too. We've talked about the possibility of you showing up one day and this is amazing. Really great," Jimmie said enthusiastically.

★ ★ ★

Bobby showed up and the Hernandez folks went back to their work.

The count was five of Thorndale's gang that's with him. There are four in the bar and Thorndale himself was playing his usual game of cards with the sheriff, one deputy and a local man.

The brown hat was there. This is the man that Bobby said just shoots people for no purpose. He's feared by everyone including the men he works with. He's the one to watch. If he reached for his gun he was going to use it. He's not fast but he's deadly.

★ ★ ★

Bobby returned to the bar and hung back by the front door when Wolf walked inside.

Heads turned to see the stranger in the strange looking hat and a loose fitting shirt as he headed to the bar.

The big man at the bar had to be Big Al. He fit the description Jo had given him to a tee.

"You must be Big Al. I'm Wolf. Jo told me about you," he said as he extended his hand to the bartender.

"Well I'll be. I thought you were a myth. Jo talked about you but said you wouldn't be here until you cleaned up the mess at the ranches you bought. Has that happened yet?"

"All done Al. that's why I'm here," he said as Jo walked up behind the bar with a big smile on her face.

"Well welcome to Northland and "The Place," Wolf. I often wondered if I'd ever get to see you again, she said with a happy face.

"Well I made it this far, I'm---".

Wolf was pushed aside by a tall man that resembled the one Bobby had told him about. They called him "Spike" as he stuck people with the dagger that was on his gun belt.

"Oh sorry there, Mister. I didn't know this was your position at the bar. I'll just move down a little," Wolf said as he glanced at a worried Jo and Al.

"No problems here Spike," said Jo.

"Hey stranger what kind of a stupid hat is that your wearing?"

There was laughter all over the bar now and everyone was watching Spike do his intimidation act.

Wolf glanced at Jo and gave her a quick wink. This confused her but she quit talking to Spike.

"What kind of boots ya got on there boy? You a damn sod buster? This is cattle country not sod buster country.""

Wolf looked down at his boots. Yes they were different alright. They weren't the sharp toed cowboy boots but they were a hell of a lot more comfortable and a hell of a lot sturdier.

The laughter was moving through the crowd as Wolf backed away from the big man to stay out of his reach and started a little jig with his boots stomping on the floor.

"Well sir these are my stomping boots," he said, looking the man in the eye.

"Stomping boots. What in hell is a stomping boot?"

"Well sir there for stomping the shit out of assholes like you," Wolf responded as he jigged a little further away watching the man.

There was dead silence now as the lanky man looked at Wolf in shock. No one had ever talked to him like that---ever.

"I'm gonna cut your gizzard out you crazy bastard," he said as he pulled his knife waiving it around for all to see.

"Now if I have to take that knife away from you mister I'm going to take the belt it came on and your horse. That's the way it's done where I come from.

"Over my dead body."

"Well that's why I get the horse and belt. You won't be needing them anymore."

It was a double edged blade of about eight inches. Wolf had seen them before. They were primarily thrusting knives so he planned accordingly as the man approached him flashing the dagger around.

Concentrate. Remember your training. Slow things down to your level. Pay attention to the important things. Concentrate he thought as the man moved forward.

There it came. Just like the Kiowa. Thank you Wong Tu. *"It's an armature move Wolf and easy to defend against and turn into your favor,"* he remembered him saying, with that little smile of his.

Wolf moved back and swept the knife away with his left hand grabbing the wrist in a vice-like grip and pulling the man through with the momentum.

Spike was obviously surprised. His eyes were wide open as Wolf kicked him behind the knee of his right leg, lifting it high in the air.

The man was airborne now and Wolf cupped the heal of the knife in his right hand and rode the blade and man down to the floor.

The man screamed as they went down. He knew he was finished.

The weight of Wolf on the dagger crushed ribs and drove the blade into the planking on the floor of the Saloon.

Wolf got up unbuckling the man's gun belt and said. "Mister Bartender look here. This man done stabbed himself. Look at that," he said indicating the lanky man's hand still gripping the dagger.

Wolf put the gun belt on the bar and said, "Can I put my things up here for a moment sir?" as he pulled the man's gun out of the holster and laid it on the bar to reach easily.

Big Al had looked over the bar without a word. His mouth was open and his eyes were glazed.

Jo was leaning against the back bar with her hand over her nose and mouth with tears running down her face.

The bar started to come alive now. There were comments from every corner of the room and fleeting glances at Thorndale's table. Wolf watched Thorndale's table with his peripheral vision to make sure no trouble started from there.

No need to worry about them. Trouble was walking straight for him.

'Evil will find you.'

CHAPTER 49

hree men were walking straight toward Wolf. Brown hat was in the middle with a sneer on his face.

People were scattering all over the bar running to the corners away from the shooting that was to come.

This told Wolf what to expect. These people knew what was going to happen.

Concentrate! Left to right. Target one has his gun out but not cocked. Target two brown hat, hasn't reached for his gun yet. Target three was a tall lanky man with his left eye looking off to the man's left. He had a big smile on his face showing many missing teeth and the remaining ones were brown. He was twirling his revolver around his trigger finger.

Showing everyone how clever he is. He said, "we're gonna shoot your ass full of holes."

Concentrate! They were in a good position now. They were about nine feet away and coming to a stop.

Target one's thumb had touched the hammer. Target two was reaching for his gun. Remember he's not fast. He just shoots to kill. Target three was still twirling away.

Wolf had been pointing his finger at the three men for a little distraction as it moved toward his fanning position saying, "You boys have your guns pointed at me"---and he moved.

One and two went down almost simultaneously and three was

still twirling but with wide eyes. He hit the floor an instant after one and two.

At first there was complete silence in the Saloon. Then the comments started. They were in shock. Four big killers had just been eliminated. They couldn't believe it as they watched Wolf waive his Colt around the room.

"Listen up everybody. You saw these three men had their guns out and said they were going to shoot me full of holes. Did you see that? Did you hear that? Speak up now.

Mister Bartender did you see and hear that."

"Hell yes, I saw it and I heard it."

"I did too," said Jo.

Everyone started getting in on it and they all admitted seeing what happened.

"You same folks saw that man that ended up stabbing himself say he was going to cut my gizzard out and tried to stab me. You all saw that, right?"

Everyone was in agreement with many comments of disbelief.

Wolf looked over to Thorndale's table and said, "You see sheriff everything was done in self-defense. There's a whole saloon full of witnesses."

"Deputy you put your hand back up on the table real slow like or you'll be joining these men on the floor."

The Sheriff barked, "Are you threatening my deputy, mister?"

"No Sheriff. I'm just telling him how it is. I just came into this town and this fine establishment and everyone has been trying to kill me since I walked through the door. I get a little upset when that happens."

The deputy slowly moved his hand back up on the table and Wolf eased his Colt back in his holster and once again turned to the bartender.

"Shit, these guys were shot right in the forehead. Each one of them," a small man said that was kneeling by the three bodies.

Wolf looked at him and said, "Well yes I find that's a good place to shoot somebody if they're trying to kill me. That way they're not flopping around on the floor groaning, making a mess and trying to get a shot off at me. I find the shot between the eyes just blows out the candle."

"Would you collect those guns and gun belts for me, friend?" he said with a smile.

He had turned back to the bar where Big Al was still in shock and Jo was still leaning against the back bar with both hands over her nose and mouth and tears in her eyes.

Several of the working girls were sitting at tables in the back of the saloon looking at Wolf and chatting like magpies.

A ruckus was heard and Wolf looked across the Saloon to the balcony where there were two hallways apparently leading to cribs for the girls. A man had pulled a curtain aside and got up to the railing with a revolver in his hand.

Wolf's revolver was in his hand automatically and he raised it in a two hand stance. The shot was going to be about fifty feet and with the bobbing head that shot was out of the question at this distance. It had to be a chest shot.

He was a big husky guy in a one-piece Union Suit that covered his whole body except for one arm that didn't make it back into the sleeve of the underwear.

The man surveyed the scene below as people were now again running for the corners of the room.

Wolf aimed at the man's chest just as the man was preparing to shoot at Wolf.

Wolf squeezed the trigger. He cocked the gun with the thumb of his left hand which he had practiced at great length and squeezed off a second round immediately after the first.

The big man's gun fired and the round went somewhere into the wall or the ceiling as he toppled over against the wall at the back of the balcony.

Another man showed up on the balcony.

He was an older man, thin as a rail with a weather worn grizzled face and had a carbine in his hands.

He took one look at the big man and shoved the barrel over the balcony railing looking for a target.

Wolf's sixth, and last shot, knocked the old man over with a clatter as the carbine bounced off the floor.

Wolf holstered his gun and simultaneously reached for the knife fighter's gun that he laid on the bar.

"Mister Bartender there's gunslingers coming out of the woodwork around here," Wolf said.

Wolf could see in his peripheral vision that Thorndale started to rise.

"I'll teach you, you son of a bitch to gun my boys down," he barked as he got up and started to pull his gun.

"Don't move a muscle old man," said Wolf with the cocked knife fighter's revolver in his left hand pointed at Thorndale.

Thorndale was in shock. *Where did that man get that gun?* He wondered.

"Well old man. I see you're a bushwhacker. You knew I was out of bullets and you were going to be a hero and shoot an unarmed man. Oh yes. A real hero."

"I noticed you didn't try to stop him, sheriff."

In his peripheral vision he caught the deputy, who was a slight narrow faced young man probably in his early twenties move his right hand off the table again as he stared at Wolf.

"Deputy Dimwit. I won't be telling you again. You put your hand up on the table real slow," he said without taking his eyes off Thorndale.

"Mister now you know what the situation is you can go ahead with your bushwhacking draw anytime you want.

"I'm sure the souls of all your boys are floating around in this room looking down to see what you're going to do. Are you going to join them or not?" he said as he waived his hand through the air indicating the souls drifting around.

People were looking around the room to see if they could see the souls and Thorndale was starting to sweat.

"Now Deputy Dimwit I want you to take your pointy finger on your right hand and stick it out like this," as he demonstrated, still watching Thorndale.

"No deputy. The other right hand."

"That's it. Now put that pointy finger right in the center of your forehead---now."

"What am I doing that for?"

"That finger is covering the hole that's going to be in your forehead if you move your finger. That finger stays there until I tell you to move it. If you move it on your own there will be a hole right there."

"You understand that Deputy? See I don't trust you at all," he said as he started walking around the card table behind the players always keeping his gun on Thorndale.

"You see Deputy you're just not to be trusted," he said as he reached down and pulled the man's gun out of its holster with the last three fingers on his right hand.

He straightened up and said, "If all these gunslingers are yours and the Sherriff and the Deputy are yours you must be a really big rancher in these parts, huh?"

"The biggest, asshole."

As he started to walk back around the table he reached down and snatched the Sheriff's gun out of his holster with his thumb and forefinger. The sheriff flinched as it happened. Now he had both their guns in his right hand.

"Don't worry sheriff. You'll get your gun back."

Wolf slowly walked back to the bar with the barrel of the knife fighter's gun never leaving the sweating Thorndale.

"Oh wow, look here. Look what the Sheriff's shooting. A silver gun. Last time I saw one of these was a cheap gambler on a riverboat had one," he said as he waived it around.

"That's the gun I want to shoot this old fart with. Yes his own sheriff's gun. Damn right.

"What do you think of that old man?"

"Good idea huh?" he said as he laid the knife fighter's and the deputies guns on the bar.

"You know since you're such a big rancher and all maybe you'd like to make a deal and you could ride your own horse home from here today. What do you say?"

Thorndale started to straighten up and Wolf barked at him, "Don't move a muscle. The next time you move I shoot. I don't know what you're going to do. If the gun wiggles, goes up or down, I squeeze the trigger. You got that old timer? You can go on with your draw anytime you want however. Don't let me stop you. The boys are all watching," he said, waving his arm around again.

"What kind of a deal?"

"Well you being a big rancher and all and me just starting out I could buy some cattle from you."

"What you got in mind?"

"Well sir the calving season is over so I buy one hundred mother cows with calf. That means no little heifers or old dried up cows. Each one has a calf. That's one hundred cows and one hundred calves---and let's see," he said stroking his chin while looking at Thorndale. "I think five mature bulls. That's no calves and no old bulls that can't get up on their hind legs. Mature bulls about two to four years old."

"Now I'll pay you the total sum of fifty dollars in gold and you can ride your own horse home today. How does that sound?"

"You're crazier than a shithouse rat mister."

"Well let me think about this." Wolf said stroking his chin again.

"Well sir you're the only one that knows what your life is worth. It doesn't mean a damn thing to me but I think your right. I'll give you paper money instead. I got the ratios all wrong too. You'll make a good neighbor."

"We'll make it one hundred mother cows with calf and eight bulls. Yes sir that's a better ratio and I appreciate you calling me on that."

"Of course we can't sit around and argue all night so we settle it the way we do down my way."

"It goes like this. I count to three, like one hundred and one, one hundred and two, one hundred and three."

When I get to the word three we draw. No more delays. Of course you can continue on with your bushwhacking draw anytime you want. That's okay."

"Now I've made an offer and if you want to make the deal you just yell out DEAL. I'm going to be counting so you need to speak up real loud so I can hear it. Okay?

"Now I want you to know I'm a fair man so I'm going to put my gun in the same position as yours so I won't have an advantage even though you were going to shoot me when I was unarmed.

No one had returned to their tables so Wolf said, "gentlemen return to your seats. There's not going to be a lot of shooting going on. There's only going to be one shot fired and it's already found a home so sit down and enjoy your beer. Go ahead."

Wolf slowly lowered his revolver to the same position as Thorndale's who was sweating profusely now and said, "Okay is D O D time now."

"Sorry, do you know what that means?"

"Never heard of it before."

"That comes from my country. D O D stands for Deal or Dead."

"See if we don't make a deal then one of us is going to be dead. Understand how that goes. Pretty straight forward when you think about it."

"Okay here we go---, One hundred and one---, One hundred and two---, one hundred and---.

"DEAL"

"Okay, we have a deal folks. Ma'am would be so kind as to get me a pen and ink. We'll need paper and something to write on so we can have this all legal like. Mister take off that gun belt and give it to my friend over there please," he said indicating the small man that had collected the guns and gun belts for him.

The little man was all grins when he put Thorndale's revolver on the bar.

"What's you name friend?" Wolf asked.

"They call me Tim because I'm so short."

"Well Tim would you go get that fancy brown hat for me please?"

Tim scurried over and picked up the hat giving it a close up look.

"Yes sir that seems like a real fine hat Tim. What do you think?"

"Yes sir, a real fine hat."

Wolf reached over and took off the crumpled hat Tim had on and put the brown hat on the man's head saying, "Mister Bartender look at that. I think that hat looks real good on Tim. What do you think?"

Tim was in grinning from ear to ear when Big Al said, "Looks damn fine to me, Wolf."

"Yep Tim I think you've earned that hat and that guy doesn't need it anymore. I think it's perfect for you. What do you think?"

"You really think it looks good on me?" he said smiling but doubtful.

"I think it looks great Tim. If anyone gives you any trouble about it you tell them that the Wolf gave it to you and it's yours."

"You're the Wolf?"

"That's what people call me Tim."

★ ★ ★

The Bill of Sale was worked out, signed and witnessed by a Mister John Higgins, the card player at the Thorndale table who signed with his mark.

"It seems to me that a week should be enough time for you to get the herd together mister Thorndale so why don't you have your boys deliver them over to the old Jamison ranch next Thursday in the morning sometime. That sound okay to you?

"Jamison ranch?" Thorndale said, wide eyed.

"Yes sir. I bought the ranch from Jamison. I have a deed to the property all recorded in Helena and a bill of sale for the livestock and everything else. Does that sound okay to you?"

Jamison ranch is one of my ranches. What's this bullshit anyway?"

"Do you have a deed for the ranch?"

"Do you have it recorded in Helena?"

"Do you have a Bill of Sale for any of the livestock, or anything else for that matter?"

Thorndale was red as a beat and silent.

"Oh I get it. Those gunslingers that were living there that turned it into a pig pen. They were more of your guys?"

"Well they left. I own the ranch and have the paperwork to prove it unless you have something I don't know about."

Thorndale was silent.

"Bobby here," Wolf said pointing at Bobby, "Will have a crew set up and we'll make a catch area so we can count the animals as they move through. We want it to be accurate and I'm sure you do too."

Thorndale spoke up for the first time. "Bobby works for you?"

"Oh yes. You see I bought the Swenson ranch too. Oh wow, were those three ugly slobs that were living there your gunslingers too?"

"Mister Thorndale you've got a hell of a lot of no-account gunslingers around. What do you need all them for?"

"Where are my men that were working those ranches?"

"God only knows Thorndale. I sure don't. They're not there anymore. They moved on. Good riddance. I can't see that they did much accept trash the houses. Those guys were real pigs."

We'll set up a catch area Mister Thorndale and we'll see your cowboys Thursday morning.

★ ★ ★

Wolf got up and walked back to the bar and said in a loud voice.

"I'm hiring cowboys and handymen with tools. I don't want gunslingers. I pay an honest wage, good quarters and great food. If you're interested or know anyone who wants honest work ride out to the old Swenson ranch just out of town and we'll work it out. You can talk to Bobby over there too if you want," he said pointing at Bobby who had now settled into a chair at a table full of local men.

★ ★ ★

It wasn't long before Thorndale got up and rode out of town. No one wished him well as he left. He'd lost face and stature he knew he could never recover without a war.

Wolf had unloaded both the sheriff's and the deputy's guns. He's pulled the pin that held the cylinders and dropped the pins and cylinders in the large spittoon by the bar. The guns were now ready to return at some point.

"Wolf you headed out of town now?" asked Jo.

"Hell no Jo. I'm going to hang around. I want people to know that I'm here to stay and not hit and run. This town has to change and that's why I was sent here. Don't ask me why or how, just accept that."

"I'm going over to El Charro and get dinner take a bath and maybe see the preacher man.

CHAPTER 50

Bobby came into the El Charro café about the time Wolf was trying a combination plate of Margie's cooking. Jimmie was sitting with him and he said he was at the door of "The Place" looking in when all the shooting occurred. He had never seen anything like that in his life. "Hell I never seen anyone shot before and you dumped a whole bunch of them. God almighty, things are going to change. I can feel it. The words getting around and people are going over to the church. Hell man this is Friday, not Sunday."

"Well let's hope they're giving thanks Jimmie, and not the opposite."

"Oh no, the ladies were smiling."

"Sit down Bobby. Glad you could make it," he said as Bobby reached the table. "You need to try some of this cooking. It's really good."

★ ★ ★

He had to stop Margie from bringing food and she wouldn't accept any money.

She was thrilled with the fact the garden would be available again. Tomorrow she would go out to the ranch with some help to see what kind of shape it was in and pick some fresh vegetables.

★ ★ ★

Wolf made it into Mr. Wong's laundry and bath house. He was expected and greeted with a smile and a slight nod of the old man's head.

Wolf nodded to the man in return and extended his hand saying, "I've heard a lot about you Mister Wong and it's all been good. The Jamisons' and Swensons' spoke very highly of you and what you've done with your people that have moved into this country. There're a lot of Chinese people down where I come from and I've made some great friends with many of them. I had an instructor, a mister Wong Tu who taught me a lot. He's helped me survive, and taught me a lot about life in general. A fine man."

"Yes I've heard of him. I think he's in New Orleans. We Chinese have a network of our own so we can keep in touch with what's going on. It mostly comes out of San Francisco. They keep track of many things in this country."

"I understand that you would like to take a bath so I had my niece make up a clean bath for you. She will assist you in anything you need. Let me show you the way," Wong said as he led Wolf down a short hallway.

The niece was a pretty girl. She could have passed for a teenager with her satin-smooth skin but upon closer examination her body was mature. She was very pretty and talked with intelligence far above her presumed station in life.

Mister Wolf, I'm Maddie and I'm here to see that you get everything you want. I've heard so much about you I was beginning to think it was all a myth. But from what I've heard about today I realize you're for real. Give me your clothes and I'll see if they need any washing while you're in the bath. I'll be back in a moment."

Wolf was soaking in the huge tub of very hot water that smelled of fragrant oils but still had bubbles on the top when Maddie walked through the door.

Wolfs hand had made it to the Colt sitting on the chair by the tub when he realized it was Maddie.

She now had a fairly snug slipover dress on as she approached the tub.

"Lean forward Wolf and I'll start on your back. You could use a good scrub which you can't give yourself."

She was amazingly strong and the scrubbing with the coarse towel left the skin tingling. She showed him the results of the scrubbing as she went on and the results amazed Wolf.

When she leaned Wolf back against the tub she handed him the towel and said, "do that to the rest of your body and I'll be back shortly," she said as she walked out of the steaming room. "The bathing you've been doing with cold water or very little hot water cleans the top of the skin but doesn't get down into the pours. That's what soaking in the hot water does. It opens the pours and then the towel scrubs them out."

When Maddie returned with Wolf's clothes she said, okay, Wolf, I'll do your hair now and then you can rinse off with this fresh hot water," as she set down a shining bucket of water near the tub.

"Here are a few clean towels to dry off with. I hope we get to see you again soon."

"Maddie you can count on it. This is wonderful believe me. I don't know why I never tried this before."

CHAPTER 51

He made it to the church and went around to the back door as people were going in and out of the front door. He was trying to be inconspicuous.

Wolf quietly rapped on the door and waited.

The door opened and Wolf looked the grey haired man over that was standing tall in the doorway.

"Are you Pastor McLeod?"

"Yes sir I am," said a booming voice. "If I'm not mistaken I'd take you for Wolf?" he said looking Wolf over.

"You'd be right sir. I'm happy to meet you at last," Wolf said extending his hand that was grasped in a huge mitt.

"Come on in Wolf. It seems like you've stirred up some trouble today that has people coming to the church in droves."

"I hope that's a positive sign sir."

"It seems to be. Why not tell me just what's going on. I've only heard part of it from Miss Jo."

They sat for a long time and Wolf told him about his harrowing journey and the continued conflict along the way.

McLeod sat silent and listened to it all and finally asked, "What prompted you on this journey to start with. It sure seems like a God awful crazy thing to do."

"Well I can't explain it too well but like I said in the beginning something came over me and I knew I had to do it."

"What came over you do you think?"

Wolf told the pastor about his past and his near death experience.

He tried to explain that when he was looking down at his body on the bed that he was talking with someone who he couldn't really identify at this time and that he was given the opportunity to go on with life and be prepared to fight evil.

"I prepared as much as I could. All I remember is that I didn't have to look for evil it would find me and I had to be prepared. That seems to be the way it's been all along my journey. Thank God I've survived but I've worked hard at surviving every day and it hasn't been an easy task. I just know that I have to finish this. Where it ends I'm not really sure but I'm going to see it through."

McLeod leaned back in his chair staring at Wolf in contemplation, and finally said, "It sounds like a familiar story Wolf."

"What's familiar about it?"

"The Lord sent the archangel Michael to slew the evil dragon and it sounds like that's what you've been sent to do. I think your dragon is here."

"Well I don't think I fit into that category. All I know is what I have to do and God willing I'll get it done. I'm amazed how this town has been taken over by this Thorndale guy. There's no freedom here. Everyone's a captive. I'm surprised he hasn't burned the church down," Wolf said with a chuckle.

"He needs the people of Northland Wolf. It's his support system."

"I've taken enough of your time pastor. Thank you for hearing me out. I'm not too sure if it makes a lot of sense but it's something I'm destined to do. Somehow I feel it is my redemption, and for what I'm not really sure."

The pastor's hand shake was long and firm as he stared into Wolf's eyes.

"Go with God Wolf," is all he said.

★ ★ ★

Bobby was still in town when Wolf got back to the ranch. Everyone was waiting on the porch for him as they saw him approach from a half mile away.

No one said a word. Betz slowly walked up to him looking him in the eye to see if he was all right.

"Well Wolf we see you survived what ever happened in town. Come on in and tell us about it. My you smell good. You fool with some of those Saloon girls?"

Wolf laughed and said, "No I had a bath, and I mean a real bath. I'm clean as a whistle right now, and they put some oils or something in the water that smells good. I can't believe how my skin feels."

"Well come on inside. We want to hear all about it."

★ ★ ★

Bobby showed up about two hours later and was filled with enthusiasm.

"I bet I had ten guys come up to me and ask about a job and they know a lot of other men that would like a job as well. It sounds like there's a lot of guys wanting work or wanting to change work. We need to figure out what you want to get done and what help you need to get it done so you'll know who to hire.

"Rumor has it that Thorndale will try to get even fast so you better be careful. He's not a guy you can trust. He'll send someone after you for sure and the word is that he'll send out for some more help. That's gunslinger help I'm talking about. It sounds like he's down about a dozen men right now and that makes him real uncomfortable."

"The delivery of the cattle could be the start of something," Bobby said.

"Well Bobby with the Lord's help I've been very lucky so far. I practice and work on things that I think will keep me alive to accomplish what I'm doing. How many of those gunslingers do that? I have no idea but I know I have to keep at it to survive."

★ ★ ★

Two days later a rider came out to the ranch looking for work and said someone in town told him to pass the word to Wolf that the banker wanted to see him.

He sat down with the man and found he was a skilled carpenter and knew how to build pole barns as well. They struck an agreement for the man to start work and bring his tools and helpers to the ranch the following week.

They rode back into town together with Jake close on their heels. Wolf didn't go anywhere without Jake now and he somehow had the suspicion that Jake knew there was more at stake as he was keeping near Wolf all the time.

The two men said their goodbyes and Wolf headed to the Bank.

★ ★ ★

"Afternoon ma'am, is Mister Montgomery available?"

"I think so mister Wolf. Just a minute please," she said as she walked into Montgomery's office.

Montgomery came out of his office with a smile on his face and said, "Wolf, good to see you. To what do we owe this nice surprise?"

Wolf was amazed at the comment and immediate worry took over. "Can we go into your office sir?"

"Of course come on in," he said as he turned and led the way.

Wolf closed the man's door which Montgomery looked at with some concern.

"Mister Montgomery you didn't ask me to come to town to talk to me about something?"

"No I didn't, Wolf," he said with some surprise.

"That's pretty disturbing. I just had a man come out to the ranch that I hired and he told me that someone told him to tell me that you wanted to see me right away."

Montgomery looked around the room and through the glass to the front area and said, "What's happened in the last couple of days Wolf I would say that someone's trying to set you up. Be very careful. I wouldn't hang around town if I were you. I'd suspicion that someone is lying for you in town. You better watch your back. I don't know who we could call to help as the Sheriff's office is owned by Thorndale. They'd probably be the first to shoot you."

"I think you're right sir. I'm going to get on back to the ranch where I can see what's going on. If you hear anything I'd appreciate it if you'd let me know about it."

"I'll do better than that. I'll see what the talk is around town. I have a lot of connection I'm sure you know as being the only banker in town," he said with a grin.

★ ★ ★

Wolf and Jake headed back to the ranch. There were several areas that were thick with trees that they would have to pass through so he sent Jake well ahead on his return trip and watched his every move. Jake somehow sensed what this was about.

It was when they crossed a small stream coming out of Jamison Lake that Wolf saw Jake stop and lift his nose into the air. He immediately rode Blondie into the nearby trees watching Jake's every move.

Jake made his way across the stream and worked his way around a hill where the creek flowed. It was then Wolf clicked his tongue to get Jakes attention.

His signaled for Jake to come and the dog obeyed immediately but kept looking in the direction he was following before he was called.

"What do you have boy?" Wolf whispered as he stroked the dog looking all around.

Jake's muscled were trembling excitedly with that wild beast breeding that set him aside from regular dogs. He was ready to hunt and kill. "Let's go have a look boy. You stay with me okay?" he whispered.

Wolf kept Jake close to him so Jake wouldn't be spotted if he ran into someone on his search.

Jake stopped dead in his tracks and Wolf clicked again to get his attention and called him to his side.

Wolf crept ahead, Colt ready to see what Jake had seen.

There was an unarmed man with three horses tied alongside the stream. He was alone which meant there were two unaccounted for.

The trail back to his ranch would pass below the hill the man was sitting behind and Wolf guessed the other two were on the hill to bushwhack him as he passed by.

The man was casually sitting on a log looking at the stream smoking a stogie of some type. Wolf made his way into the sparse trees along the stream where he could move forward out of the man's line of vision.

He could smell the cigar now. The aroma was maybe what Jake picked up on but Jake was also looking up on the hill when Wolf left him.

The ground was soft with pine needles and ferns and made for quiet stalking.

★ ★ ★

Wolf slowly crept up to the man and put the end of the barrel of his revolver on the edge of the man's eye and whispered, "don't say a word or make a sound."

The man stiffened as he was touched on the eye and slowly turned his head.

He was an elderly man and certainly not one of Thorndale's gunslingers.

Wolf whispered to him and asked, "Where're the other two?"

The man just pointed with his thumb up the hill he was sitting behind.

"Who are you and what are you doing on my ranch," he whispered in a low growl.

In a whisper the man responded, "Look mister, I'm just taking care of the horses. I'm the cook for the hands. The old man told me to come out here and watch the horses. There're two guys up on the hill waiting for you to return to your place. I've got nothing to do with all this bullshit that's going on. I'm just the cook."

"You want to live through the day?"

"Hell yes. You plan on killing me? That's the reason I don't want to have anything to do with this crap and I told Thorndale that. He's a real asshole to work for believe me. I wouldn't be here if I wasn't forced into it. What're you planning to do?"

"I'll decide that. What's your name?"

"Erik."

"Well Erik here's how it's going to work if you want to live. I'm pretty damn tired of Thorndale trying to kill me every time I turn around."

"I'm going to tie you up and then I'm going to up the hill to see where these guys are. If something happens to me you can explain that I tied you up and you couldn't warn them. You understand that?"

"Hell yes. I appreciate it mister. The two guys up on the hill are a couple of the assholes that Thorndale's hired. They don't know from sickem about cattle or ranching. That whole gang he has is just plan damn bad. The cowboys are okay but they don't have anything to do with the shooters he's got."

"You the guy they're supposed to be collecting the cattle for?"

"I'm the guy. Are they doing it?"

"I think a lot depends on what happens here today mister. If you're out of the game they won't be collecting any cattle, that's for damn sure."

"You know where those guys are up there?" he said pointing to the hill.

"I got no idea but I'm sure they are in a position to see you approach the ranch house. You'd better be damn careful going up there."

* * *

The man was tied up and gagged with the bandana he had around his neck.

Wolf clicked for Jake who came around the corner of the stream at full tilt.

Wolf signaled for the dog to be quiet and slow down and Jake immediately obeyed as he approached the fearful cook.

"Don't worry Eric. If you don't make any noise or sudden movements he won't tear your throat out. Just sit nice and quiet. Got it?"

Eric's eyes were wide open and he just nodded. Wolf slowly and quietly started up the side of the hill.

The hill was only about thirty feet high and the approach was gradual. He only had to cover about thirty yards or so to the top. The ground was soft with pine needles, and the moving was quiet.

He could finally hear the men talking and laughing in hushed tones.

He cocked the long Colt he'd taken off Blondie and moved in slowly.

He eased under a Spruce evergreen tree on his stomach and could see the two men were sitting about ten feet apart and talking to each another in low hushed voices. It sounded like they were talking about everything but the job at hand. They were obviously confident they could, and would, accomplish what they were sent to do.

Wolf made his way up behind the men so that they were both in line with his vision and line of fire. He didn't want to get between them as it would be more difficult to defend his position. This way they were both within easy shooting sight if it came to that.

He slowly drew out his other Colt and pointed each of them at their respective targets.

He cocked the Colt and with the SNICK of cocking, he said, "You boys looking for something?"

They didn't even attempt to talk or find out what was going on. They both had carbines in their hands and the revolvers were snug in their holsters making their moves slower and more difficult. They obviously were planning on the long shot with the carbines.

There was not going to be any conversation.

The both swung the long guns at Wolf.

There was no choice but to shoot or die.

The men were moving so a head shot would be difficult. Go for body mass he told himself and aimed at the moving chests.

Both Colts roared as one.

★ ★ ★

He collected the carbines and gun belts and headed down the slope to the cook who was quietly waiting at the bottom staring at Jake.

Wolf put the carbines in the saddle scabbards and removed the scabbards from the horses and whistled for Blondie who came on the run.

He untied the man and said, "Come on we've got some work to do."

★ ★ ★

The two bushwhackers were laid across their saddles with their belts looped over the pommel and Erik had them in tow.

"Erik you know what to tell Thorndale, right?"

"Hell yes. I imagine the cattle collecting will speed up some now. You seem like a pretty regular guy, Wolf and I'll pass the word to the boys that you're looking to hire real cowboys."

"I appreciate going home sitting on a horse rather than lying on him and. I'll tell Thorndale not to try you again for sure."

"You're not part of the problem Erik. Stay out of trouble and don't get involved in any of this if you can help it. I understand you may be forced into doing something like this again but don't raise a hand against me or what I'm doing or the rules will change."

Erik laughed and said, "Hell I'm never going to get involved in what that damn Thorndale does. You can bet your horse on that."

★ ★ ★

As Wolf watched the man work his way back to the Thorndale ranch he wondered who had tried to set him up.

The new carpenter? Or did someone really tell him to go to town to see the banker.

I guess I'd better find out, he thought.

CHAPTER 52

Eric slowly made his way back to the Thorndale ranch. He wasn't in any hurry as he didn't know what old Thorndale would say about the cargo he was leading.

When he slowly walked his mare through the big upright posts that marked the main road to the ranch buildings his stomach was a tight as a knot.

"I'm not going to say a damn thing," he thought. "To hell with it," he mumbled as he removed his hat and wiped his brow with his bandana.

★ ★ ★

Eric just rode his horse past the main house as two men got up out the chairs sitting on the porch and just dropped the reins of the horses he was leading. He didn't look at the men and he didn't say anything.

"Where the hell you think you're going," barked one of the men.

Eric just gave him the finger and kept on riding to the corral to unsaddle his horse.

The men were yelling up at the main house now and men were coming from everywhere. He was fearful that there was going to be hell to pay. Thorndale had been meaner than shit since the bar incident. He was impossible to be around. He had to show everyone how tough he was. His ego got shot in the ass and he's trying to make up for it.

"*Maybe it's time to move on,*" he thought as he unsaddled his mare and stroked her neck and head.

He just got his saddle hung up when one of the regular cowboys came running into the tack shed and said, "Hey cookie the boss wants to see you pronto."

"How is he George?"

"Mean as a fucking rattlesnake so tread careful Eric. He's a smoking stick of dynamite. I'm thinking of leaving. I hear that Wolf guy is hiring real cattle-men. That's me. This place is getting too damn dangerous. I just gotta figure out how to leave without getting myself killed."

"I hear ya George. I'm thinking the same thing. That Wolf guy aint half bad. He could have killed me easy but it wasn't even in his mind. He's got a big fucking Wolf that travels with him and both the wolf and the horse mind him real well."

"He told me what to say to Thorndale so I guess I'll just quote him and leave it at that."

"What did he tell you to tell Thorndale?"

"He said for Thorndale to stop trying to get even if he wants to stay alive. He said Thorndale's days of grabbing ranches and killing people is over. Get on with life and be a rancher."

"Shit. Thorndale won't like to hear that."

"That's what I'm afraid of."

★ ★ ★

The walk to the house was a slow one. George said he would go with him for moral support.

"Get your ass in her Eric, you for shit cook, I wanna talk to you."

"Yes sir, Mister Thorndale. I'm on my way," he said as he looked at George who had a fearful look on his face.

"Eric what the fuck happened out there? How come you got off Scott free? Can you tell me that? You bag of shit."

"You know Mister Thorndale I didn't have to come back at all you know. I could have just moved on but I told that Wolf guy I would bring the bodies back here for you to bury."

"Ya, well why weren't you shot too? Can you tell me that?"

"I wasn't armed. He just slipped up like a quiet breeze and put the barrel of his pistol in my eye," he said as he put his finger in his right eye. "Then he gagged me and tied me up. He slipped up the hill like a snake in the grass and killed your two gunslingers. Hell I don't even know their names. They didn't do fuck all around this ranch."

"That guy travels with the biggest damn wolf I've ever seen. He damn near bit my face off but that Wolf guy just called him off."

"Wolf told me to bring them back to you and sent you a message."

"Ya, well what's the message?"

Eric repeated it the best he could, and he could see that Thorndale was getting madder all the time.

"So that's it mister Thorndale. That's what he told me to tell you and you know it might be good advice," he said as Thorndale walked back and forth in front of him.

★ ★ ★

Eric hit the floor with a thud. He didn't expect Thorndale to pistol whip him but the bastard just turned and slapped him with his revolver. The side of his head was bleeding and things were just spinning around. He thought he was going to throw up but he figured Thorndale would probably shoot him if he puked in his house.

George wasn't around so Eric figured he left out of self-preservation.

"Get your ass out of my house you bag of shit and get cooking. See if you can get that right and it better be damn good to boot."

★ ★ ★

Eric staggered his way back to his bunk house and dropped on the bed holding his head.

George came in and said, "Jesus Christ what happened to you Eric?"

"The bastard pistol whipped me. I'm through George. Fuck that old bastard. I'm out the door."

"Do me last favor would you George?"

"Hell yes anything. What ya need?"

"Go get my mare and saddle her and bring her around the back of the bunkhouse. I'm going to slip off into the trees out of sight of the main house. I'm out of here."

"Where in hell do you think you're gonna go?"

"Between you and me I'm gonna slip over to Jamison's old place. The cook over there and I are pretty good friends. I'll hide out there a few days and then find something. Somebody always needs a cook."

"Damn we're gonna miss you Eric. Sam will really be upset. Hell that kid you got helping you isn't for shit. Damn man we'll probably all starve to death," George said with a grin.

"I'll go get your horse and sneak him around back. You get your gear together."

"Not much gathering to do George. Don't have shit," he said with a smile.

CHAPTER 53

The delivery of the cattle was set for tomorrow and Wolf was getting his people ready to go and count heads.

They'd spent three days making a chute that would neck the herd down so they could count them as they passed through. Some people would only count calves and others all animals. Two men were assigned to spot the bulls. They all had pads to make their scratches on to count when the herd was finally through the chute.

They used the dry river bed and its bushy bank to make one side of the chute so it was an easier job. The final neck of the chute was the hard part as it had to be sturdy.

The herd would leave Thorndale's at first light so should start straggling in fairly early.

The only person that wouldn't be there was Wolf. He had his own plan.

★ ★ ★

At one o'clock in the morning Bobby and Wolf quietly rode out of the ranch.

Wolf was dressed in buckskins, moccasins, and a tan pull over knit cap. Today he was being an Indian. He would be practicing what he had done all his life---stalking.

★ ★ ★

They quietly worked their way well away from the ranch and the gathering chute completely out of sight.

When they were about a half mile from the chute Wolf got off Blondie and gave the reins to Bobby to take her back to the corral.

When Bobby disappeared into the dark Wolf just sat and listened for a while.

When he was satisfied it was quiet he made his way through the trees to the dry river bed up to the end of the chute.

He then climbed out of the dry river bed and walked about fifty yards away from the chute.

There he started picking grass as he walked north in the direction the herd would be coming from and tucked grass into his tan woolen skull cap until it was in itself a grassy bush sticking straight up.

He stopped frequently to listen. After he had covered about a hundred yards he slowly crept neared the river bed and laid down in the grass. His buckskins and grassy mop would blend in.

He was on the eastern side of the river and chute now. All he had to do was wait and see if his prediction would come true.

★ ★ ★

He used his time to give thanks for keeping him alive and support of his quest against evil.

These conversations always made him feel better and felt an absolution each and every time.

It was about an hour before first light that he heard the first sound. It was a hoof sliding off a rock and could only come from one place, the river bed.

He waited to hear more and finally heard horse noises as they worked their way down the dark river bed passing directly in front of Wolf. He was too far away for the horses to smell and slightly down wind. He was deadly still.

He waited until they had passed then crept parallel to their travels in the river bed. He could hear whisper talk so there had to be more than one person.

The horses finally came to a stop in the wash and he could hear people clearly as he crept forward. They tied the horses up and made their way on foot in the direction of the end of the chute.

Wolf let them get out of hearing and then slowly crept up to the river bank. There were three horses.

He made his way back away from the wash without disturbing the horses and slowly paralleled the stalkers. He knew where they were going.

He could hear them clearly. They had determined that no one had arrived yet and were openly talking about the job ahead. There was a woman with them and she appeared to be giving the orders.

★ ★ ★

Wolf waited and listened. Then he crawled on his stomach very slowly toward the talking threesome that had stopped in the wash.

He wormed his way up to within five feet of the river bed and had a clear view of all three individuals. They all had carbines and the two men each carried a side arm.

He was low in the grass which was a good foot over his head and body. He would be almost impossible to see but he could see them and had a perfect shooting stance. All he had to do was wait.

He knew that when they looked in his direction they would be looking for someone standing and he being tight to the ground would be almost invisible.

Their plan was simple. Shoot everybody. There was some concern that none of the three had seen Wolf and couldn't recognize him so the best thing was to shoot everyone.

★ ★ ★

The sun came up behind Wolf and up for almost an hour when the first of his tally team started to arrive.

The two men were on each side and the woman in the middle.

They were lying in the wash with their carbines on the berm of the wash facing the approaching riders ready to fire.

They were discussing the group as they approached and talked about the order of shooting to get the best effect.

The men had their holsters on their right hip so that meant they would roll to their left to get at the gun when Wolf announced himself. They were just waiting for as close a shot as possible to get the job done fast and accurately.

"That woman is mine," said the lady in the middle. "You work your way in from your side and I'll start in the middle with the bitch. Only about thirty yards now boys. Time to go to work."

The SNICK of Wolf's two revolvers being cocked was a clear warning. He was only fifteen feet from his targets and the sound was crystal clear in the early morning air.

"Good morning folks---," was all he got to say.

The two men rolled over to their left as predicted and dug for their revolvers looking well above where Wolf was. He was nowhere in sight.

Two shots crashed together as the men were searching for a target as they pulled their guns. Chest shots were clean and both men only had a moment to glance at where the rounds came from before they were gone.

Wolf could hear the woman's bowels let loose and a moan came from her throat. She was only half turned over looking well over where Wolf lie. She couldn't see him.

All three carbines were still on the edge of the riverbank.

"Well ma'am you going to get your carbine and give it a try?"

"If you're going to die in this wash you might as well give it a try huh?"

Her bowels moved again and a huge wet spot had appeared in the front of her tan riding britches.

"What's it going to be?" he said as he stood up in plain sight. The morning sun had been directly in their eyes and she just hadn't seen Wolf until now.

"You going to kill me you bastard?"

"I'm unarmed as you can see. You know who in hell I am?"

"Gosh ma'am, I don't know who you are. Don't you know who you are?"

"I'm Trish Thorndale you pile of shit. That's who I am."

"Well ma'am, you're a chip off the old block for sure. Your old man is a bushwhacker and so are you. I generally kill bushwhackers right off. That seems to be the best remedy."

"Oh Jesus mister don't shoot me, please don't. I'll never do it again. I promise."

"Well I went through this with you father ma'am and the first thing he did was to send out two bushwhackers to kill me on my own ranch. You think for an instant that I believe you."

Some of the tally takers that had come on the job were now riding over to see what the shooting was about.

Wolf waived them off and said, "Everything is okay here folks. Get back to work. No problem."

"Wait. You let my dad buy his way out. I'll do the same."

"Well I'm sure your dad isn't going to let you give away anymore cattle ma'am and I sure don't know of anything you have I would be interested in. That's for sure."

"Look I own property in town. I'll trade you that for my life and for not shooting me up. I'll do anything."

"Look lady I don't know what you have to offer and I'm not really sure if I'm interested. The law here isn't worth a damn and you won't go to jail so there's not much of an alternative is there?"

"I own that whole corner where the hotel is. There's that Mexican restaurant, the Chinese laundry and the three buildings down North Street."

"Where's North Street?"

"It's the buildings adjacent to the hotel around the corner from the restaurant. You can have em. I don't know what to do with them anyway."

"Yes I heard they were all going to shit as there's been no upkeep on anything."

"Well I tell you what. I won't shoot you up and when we're done with this cattle count you ride into town with Bobby and see your lawyer and have him draw up the papers all legal like. Then you're off the hook."

"I can't go like this. I shit my pants and pissed all over myself."

"You think I'm going to let you go home lady to change clothes you're crazy for sure. The Thorndale's as far as I know haven't done anything trustworthy. You obviously think I'm stupid but that's ok. You probably think everyone but you folks are stupid."

"Get your ass out of the wash and walk over to that wagon over there," he said pointing.

"It's either that or go for your rifle. Your choice ma'am."

She groaned as she crawled up the river bank. It was obvious her riding britches were full, and she was wet to the knees.

Wolf sat her on the ground with a squish and tied her arms behind the wagon wheel. Not too tight but enough to keep her in place. She had considered herself lucky and accepted her fate.

★ ★ ★

The herd was nearing when a man broke out of the group of cowboys and headed over to where Wolf's people were standing, waiting their arrival.

"Howdy. I'm Sam Jackson the foreman. You folks ready for us?"

Wolf walked up to the man's horse and extended his hand and said, "Hi Sam, I'm Wolf. We're ready. Are they all accounted for?"

"Best as I can tell Wolf," he said looking over at the wagon with the woman tied to it.

"What the hell is that all about," he said, spurring his horse to the wagon and dismounting.

Wolf walked up to the man as he was trying to talk to the crying woman.

"Wolf what the hell is this all about? What's Missy doing here?"

Wolf turned and started to walk to the river bed and waived his hand at Sam and said, "Come on Sam I'll show you."

★ ★ ★

Sam just stood on the bank where the three rifles were still all lined up ready to shoot without saying a word. He then looked off in the distance at the lush countryside and the slow moving green grass.

Wolf didn't say a thing until he knew Sam was ready.

Sam turned to Wolf without saying anything and just stared at him.

"Well this is how it came about Sam. Your Missy here and these two guys came long before dawn and got ready to bushwhack my whole team. They were going to kill everybody. No survivors."

"I was lying in the grass not fifteen feet away," he said as he pointed, "and heard all their talk and planning. Missy here was giving shooting orders to the other two. They planned on killing my whole bunch."

"It seems like the Thorndale's are a bushwhacking family. Not very honorable I'd say, but I'm not passing judgment on your boss Sam. I'm just telling you my thoughts. I'd think it rather difficult to work for someone like that but that's your business."

"I've heard good things about you Sam and if you're ever looking to make a change I could use a good foreman. That's just a suggestion Sam," he said as Sam continued to stare at the ground.

"Let's get those cattle through the trough. You got anymore gunslingers with you Sam? I'd hate to have to face off with them. That's not my way. I don't go picking fights. I just try and stop them."

"No Wolf, they're all cowboys. Got one that's a "wanna-be" gunslinger. He likes the image but he's not too smart and doesn't really understand that lifestyle. If you see him he's wearing all black and rides a black horse. He's really playing the role. Please stay away from him, okay?"

"No problem. Let's get with it," he said as he saw the first of the cattle going through the control zone.

★ ★ ★

It went smoothly and the counters were busy comparing tabs to make sure their count was right. There was enough overlap to hopefully eliminate too many errors. A head or two one way or the other wasn't important in this case.

"That looks like that's it Wolf. How's the count look?" Sam said as he rode up to Wolf who was with the counters now tallying on the tailgate of the wagon Missy Thorndale was tied to. Sam's cowboys were starting to return to their ranch.

"They're getting a tally on it now. I think it's good. I saw the bulls go through and they looked pretty fair to me. We should have a count in a minute.

Sam said, "what are you going to do with Missy here Wolf?"

"She made the same deal her bushwhacking father did. She bought her way out. Bobby is going to take her to town for her lawyer to work out the paperwork, and then she can go home as far as I'm concerned."

"I just hope I don't see any more of the Thorndale clan. None of it's been a good experience."

"I think I'll be taking her back to the ranch," a voice said behind Sam and Wolf.

They both turned and here was the cowboy that Sam had told him about. He was a lean six footer with a curved mustache. He was standing with his legs apart ready for a fight. His hand was hovering over his revolver that was hung at a dramatic angle.

"Damned Willie, get back on your horse before you get yourself killed. What in hells the matter with you?" Sam barked.

"I'm staying for my Missy Sam, and no one's going to stop me."

"Trish Thorndale spoke up for the first time and said, "Willie don't do this. Just go back to the ranch. I'll be there shortly hon. Believe me."

Wolf and Sam looked at each other. Wolf could see that this as the first he'd heard of the Willie-Trish relationship.

"Get on your horse Willie. That's an order. Get out of here right now. You don't know what you're doing boy."

Wolf said in a low voice to Sam. Let me talk to him and slowly walked up to Willie so they were now just three feet apart. Wolf never took his eyes off Willie's eyes. He could see Willie was sweating now. Wolf didn't know if it was because of what he was about to do, or the herding of the cattle.

"You pretty fast Willie? You a gunslinger now like those lowlifes that hang out at the Thorndale place. Go for your gun Willie. Let's see how fast you really are. Let's see if you're ready to gamble your life on a quick draw. Go ahead Willie. Go for it while you can.

Willie was pushed into the corner now and to save face in front of Trish he had to try.

He grabbed for his gun.

He'd barely touched the handle of the revolver when he heard wolfs gun cock and saw it pointing at his chest.

Wolf could hear Sam grunt and Missy screamed.

"You're dead Willie. See how easy that was? Your time on earth has ended and you threw it all away on some damn fool fantasy that being a big gunslinger is something special. They all die Willie," he said as he reached over and took the man's gun out of its holster.

"Be a cowboy Willie. Learn how it's really done. Do something with your life while you still can."

With that Wolf walked back to Sam who was shocked at what just happened. He gave him Willie's revolver saying in a low voice, "You'll know when to give it to him Sam. Let's check the tally."

Trish was weeping openly and said, "Thanks mister."

★ ★ ★

The tally was good and it seemed that they had an extra calf. Perhaps one of the cows had twins.

Bobby had arranged to get the horses in the wash and retrieve the firearms and load the two dead men on their horses.

Wolf noticed three men on horseback calmly waiting as he and Sam walked to their horses. The other herders wandered back to the Thorndale ranch.

Sam said, "What's up boys?"

"We'd like to talk to Mister Wolf, Sam."

"What can I do for you boys?" Wolf said as he and Sam walked up to them.

"We hear you're hiring riders, Mister Wolf. Is that true? We'd like to see if you got a place for us. We know you got a hell of a lot of ground to cover with these two ranches and we've been working cows a hell of a long time. No offence Sam. We're just damn afraid of what's going on back there" the man said pointing over his shoulder with his thumb.

"You boys can do what you want George. You know that. I understand your feelings."

George said, "Hell with Cookie gone the foods not up to par. I know you're doing your best Sam but I don't know anyone that will work for Thorndale once they find out what he did to the last cook."

"Yes we're looking for good cowboys, not gunslingers. We rely on honesty and loyalty. We have good bunks and good food. What are you guys getting paid now?" asked Wolf.

George answered, "Forty a month," "Gosh I'm paying fifty a month if that's okay, and if your good workers you'll get a raise. Does that sound fair?"

The men were grinning from ear to ear and nodding their heads. Yes sir that sounds pretty damn good. We'll go get our bed rolls and slip on over. Where do you want us to go?"

"Why don't you boys start here on this ranch and move these new cattle around a little bit so they don't clean up all the grass in one area."

"I'll be back over here in a day or two and we can talk some more. Welcome to the M C R boys."

"I'm George this big guy is Earl, and the red head is Dan. We sure appreciate it Mister Wolf. I got a question, and you don't have to answer if you don't want to but that damn Wolf you got hanging around, is he dangerous?"

Wolf laughed and said, "Only when I want him to be. When you get here I'll introduce you to him and he'll know you're one of the family around here."

The men nodded and galloped off with a hoop.

"Sam I hope that doesn't hurt our relationship. I want to be on friendly terms with you folks but I can sure use good cowboys."

Sam smiled and shook his head, "Hell no Wolf. I can't say I blame em. Things aren't real good over there now that you killed off a bunch of his hired guns. You gotta know Wolf rumor is that he's out looking for more."

"Thorndale pistol whipped our cook when he came back with the two bushwhackers you shot. That's why he bailed out."

"Ya I know. He showed up over here on this ranch. I guess the two cooks know each other pretty well. I hear they've been cooking up a storm around here. My offer is still open to you Sam. Give it some thought," he said as he shook Sam's hand, "and I'd sure appreciate it if someone would tell me about the new killers he's hiring."

Sam just stared off toward home and muttered, "That's a good possibility Wolf. You've sure been square with me and my boys, and Willie will turn the corner for sure. Damn I didn't know about the Willie and Missy thing. Shit. That's a surprise, but hell, I'm only the foreman," he said with a grin.

CHAPTER 54

Bobby took Trish Thorndale back to the Jamison ranch so she could clean up and get a change of clothes before he took her into town.

She was openly talking now about how happy she was to get rid of the property in town as it was going downhill and she had no idea what to do about it as she couldn't find workers to work for her.

"They were all too busy they claimed," but she knew no one was going to work for her if they had a choice.

She knew her dad would be mad as hell about it but she was home safe and that was what was most important. Hell he gave away 100 head of cattle to save his skin and she would remind him of that if he got too damn furious.

She had mixed emotions now about that Wolf guy. He seemed like a pretty straight person and damn he was fast on the draw. She'd never seen anything like it before.

The gunslingers her dad hired were all a bunch of misfits and thought they were big stuff. She'd seen them shoot and draw and they weren't even in the same league as that Wolf guy, and that fucking wolf that traveled with him was a damn nightmare.

★ ★ ★

Bobby left her in town after she met with the lawyer who drew up a quit-claim deed to the property to some damn corporation. She was glad it was over with.

Now it was going to be 'show time' when she got back to the ranch and damn it could be bad.

★ ★ ★

The cowboys were back out in the field and the few remaining "shooters" as her dad called them were on the front porch of the house waiting to see if she was really going to return. Dead or alive.

They didn't say a word when she got off her horse throwing the reins to one of the men to put her horse up and stamped into the house.

The men all looked at one another and thought this may be a good time to take a walk somewhere, anywhere but here.

★ ★ ★

Her dad was sitting in the big room, with a drink in his hand which was a bad sign, and smoking a cigar when she walked in.

He looked at her over the rim of his glass from the big leather couch he was slumped in and didn't say a word.

"Well I got rid of that damn property in town that you gave me when you ran old Smithers out of town. Thank God for that. I didn't know what in hell to do with it anyway and it's going to shit. That was a win-win situation for sure."

Her dad just took another drink, belched and laid his head back on the heavy couch.

"So the stock got delivered and your idea of shooting everyone backfired dad. Maybe---just maybe we should back off a little because things sure as hell aren't going our way and that's for damn sure."

"I don't need any advice from a fucked up daughter, Trish. I'm going to get some real help and finish this thing up like it should be."

"Well it sure hasn't worked out so far and it seems to me that Wolf guy aint half bad. It could have been a lot worse. You could be digging a hole for me now. Hell some of your boys got hired over there when we delivered the stock."

"What," he screamed, "Who in hell moved over there?"

"Damned if I know. I just heard about it that's all. It seems that Wolf guy is hiring cowboys, not shooters. Got a hell of a spread now."

She was a little amazed at herself that she didn't name off the cowboys that quit and went to work for Wolf but there's no sense in getting them killed if she could help it.

Trish walked over and poured herself a hefty glass of bourbon and headed out of the room.

"I'm going to get cleaned up a bit. I'll see you later."

CHAPTER 55

Wolf sent Bobby to town to talk to the new carpenter and have him point out the man that told him the banker wanted to see Wolf.

Wolf had other things to do and decided it was time to see the other Jamison ranch in the high country where they ran sheep and cows. It was called *"Far Away Ranch."*

It was run by a family of Italians that had been in the sheep business for two or three generations before they arrived in America.

Wolf had received word that Thorndale had taken over that ranch too but didn't get rid of the family because Thorndale didn't know how to handle the sheep and the old sheep herder that lived there was vital to the ranches success.

Cowboys didn't like sheep or sheep herders but it was a known profitable business and he didn't want to destroy it.

Wolf knew that by now the sheep ranch people would probably know about Wolf so he had to be careful as the shooters Thorndale had out there would undoubtedly be waiting for him and there was no way to get word to the resident family.

★ ★ ★

Wolf had the map the Jamison's had given him of the ranch location and Bobby knew it fairly well so Bobby filled Wolf in on the best approach to the ranch. Wolf would be going alone with Jake.

Wolf wanted to make his appearance unannounced sometime during the evening mealtime when everyone would be busy doing something, even the shooters.

He was about a quarter mile from the ranch house and well into the trees with Blondie well out of sight.

He scanned the property below him with his brass telescope and could see the old sheepherders' camp well up the side of the mountain behind the ranch where white specks moved among the trees and grass.

People were settling in for the evening and the family had all gone into the main house. The evening fire was started and Wolf could smell the smoke working its way through the trees below him.

The second building closer to the barns was now spouting a column of smoke where someone was preparing an evening meal. This had to be the helps quarters and probably occupied by Thorndale's men. No one had come or gone out of that building since Wolf started his observation but there was a lot of activity around the family ranch house.

It looked like the family was made up of all women. A man never did appear while he watched.

It was time to move.

★ ★ ★

Wolf and Jake quietly made their way down through the trees behind the main house out of sight of the helps quarters. Jake was tight to his side and constantly glanced at Wolf to see if there were any instructions.

His intellect is incredible, Wolf thought.

Wolf worked his way around the house below the window line and when he got to the front porch area he stopped and glassed the helps quarters which was only about fifty yards from the main house. There was no movement in the windows, so he made his move.

He and Jake barged into the main house and closed the door behind them.

The family looked up from the dinner table startled, and were about to start yelling at Wolf when he put his finger to his lips and said SHHHHH as loud as he could.

This took the family by surprise who were now looking at the huge Wolf that came into their house with the stranger and who now had his nose in the air taking in the aroma of the evening meal.

Please be quiet folks. I'm not here to harm you. I'm Wolf, the new owner of the ranch. I bought it from the Jamison's and they told me all about you folks. Where's mister Bartallo? I don't see him around. I must say you certainly have a beautiful family, ma'am. You must be very proud. Where's mister Bartallo? I must speak to him please."

The youngest of the four girls whom appeared to be about eight years old said, "Is that Wolf going to kill us mister?"

Wolf laughed and said, "No he's my dog. He's real friendly when you get to know him and I want each of you to get to know him. When he's around you've got some super protection if you're his friend. His name is Jake."

With this Jake's ears perked up and he looked at Wolf waging his tail. Wolf reached down and stroked the side of Jake's big head and pointed to the family around the table and said to Jake, "these people are our friends Jake. He didn't know if Jake understood that but it was a plus for the strangers sitting at the table for their evening meal.

"Mister Bartallo?"

"I'm sorry mister Wolf. We've been very impolite. Would you join us for dinner please? Maria set a place for Mister Wolf and bring some fresh water for the dog."

A beautiful girl of about eighteen got up from the table, glanced openly at Wolf with some interest and went into the kitchen area for supplies.

"Pat-- mister Bartallo has come down with a stroke of some kind Mister Wolf. He's been mostly bedridden since those robbers came and took over our ranch and beat him half to death. I'm surprised they didn't kill him."

"I'll take you into his room to see him. Follow me, she said as she headed down a hallway flanked by open doors.

They entered a large bedroom in the rear of the house where a middle aged man was propped up on pillows against the back of his bed with a vague look about his face. The man was obviously damaged. To what degree it was impossible to know.

"Mister Bartallo, I'm Wolf. I'm the new owner of this ranch. I understand you've had some difficulties with the gunslingers that came out here and took over the place. I aim to clear that up today. Do you understand me sir?"

A grin passed fleetingly over the man's face and he nodded his head.

"I'm afraid Pat doesn't talk too much right now Mister Wolf, but Holy Mary I think he understood what you said. You think you can do that? I mean cleaning out those bastards that moved onto our ranch? It's been hell around here and I'm scared to death about the girls. They have to stay far away from those two men."

"They look at the girls like they're special for them. Why they haven't attacked them I don't know."

"Don't you have any guns in the house? I mean you live way out here and I'm sure you all must hunt."

"The first thing they did when they broke into our house and knocked us all about was to take all our guns. We had three rifles and two six-shooters and two shotguns."

"We had to sneak in and out of the house each time. We each keep a kitchen knife within reach at all times and those guys know it. I don't think they're supposed to shoot us. Why? I don't really know."

"I'd like to pay a little visit to them while they're eating dinner. I'd like one of the girls to come with me. She doesn't have to go in or anything. I just need her to give me the lay out when we're there."

"Any suggestions?" wolf asked.

"Maria is the oldest and a damn good hand and a great shot. She knows how to handle herself and I think those two guys know that and don't fool with her."

"Perfect," he said as he looked at Mister Bartallo. "Mister Bartallo I'll see you a little later sir. I hope your recovery is very rapid. I'll get the Doc out here if you think it will help but I don't see any cuts or bruises he can work with."

"I'll be right back sir," he said as he left the room and signaled for Misses Bartallo to follow.

Ma'am, just call me Wolf. No Mister stuff ok. We'll get to know one another shortly I'm sure."

"You really think you're going to run those two out of here?"

"Yes ma'am that's what I came here to do, now who's Maria?"

aria was the prettiest one of the bunch. They were all beautiful girls. She was strong and straight forward in what she said and did. The perfect guide.

The plan was that Wolf would stay out of sight of the windows and Maria would hang outside when Wolf barged into the quarters.

Maria would come in as soon as the situation was clear that there wasn't going to be any shooting and would be able to tell Wolf the layout of the living quarters for him to look over with her help.

Wolf worked his way around the house well below the window line and Maria was close on his heels.

The porch on the building was pretty rickety, so Wolf told Maria to stay off the porch as he quietly worked his way to the front door.

When he was ready he turned and winked at Maria. This brought a big smile to her face.

Wolf pushed the door open and stepped into the large room with his hand on his gun.

Both men were sitting at the table eating.

One man had his shirt and pants off and was sitting in his long johns. The other man was fully dressed but neither of them were armed. They just stared in shock at the man that just barged into their domain.

"Evening gents. Sorry to interrupt your dinner but we have some things to discuss.

"Step outside if you would and sit on the porch so we can have a talk."

The man in his underwear found his voice.

"Who the hell are you mister? What the fuck you think you're doing? You know who we are, and who you're talking too?"

"Oh yes, I know you two guys. I'm the owner of this ranch and I'm throwing your ass off of it right now. Thorndale doesn't have anything to do with this, boys so stand up and walk out the door."

Both men were looking over to where their side arms were hanging on the bunk beds.

"Hey if you boys want to make a try for your shooters go for it. I'll wait."

The men looked at each other and then back at Wolf. Underwear then said, "You the guy from the bar?"

"You mean am I the guy that had the small disagreement with Thorndale? Then I guess I'm the guy."

Both men looked at each other and slowly stood up and started walking out the door.

"Maria go inside and collect all the guns and ammunition you can find would you, and get a couple of your sisters to help you haul it back over to your place."

Maria put two fingers in her mouth and let loose with a tremendous whistle that brought everyone to the door of the main house.

She yelled at a couple of her sisters and they came running with big smiles on their faces as Maria vanished into the men's quarters.

★ ★ ★

Have a seat on the edge of the porch boys. We need to have a talk."

"Nothing to talk about asshole. You're in deep shit now."

"Ya that's the same thing the guys said at the Swenson and Jamison ranches. I never did know what they meant. That's why I went to town to find out what was going on. "Old Thorndale sure use to have a bunch of gunslingers around. He doesn't have too many now boys. You guys are right down to almost the last. This is the time you decide what you're going to do with your future. Now take your boots off, and if I see a boot gun, you're dead."

The girls came giggling out of the building with several guns and ran to the main house.

Maria was going through everything in the men's quarters, even looking under the mattresses. She was a thorough lady for sure.

The men grumbled as the girls ran past, back and forth. They knew their days at this ranch were over.

"You gonna kill us now asshole?"

"Not planning on it unless you want killing. I can sure oblige you for certain.

"Your days as gunslinger are over now and you can make a decision whether you want to live or die."

"If you want I'll let you head on out of here but if I see you with any of the Thorndale gang you're dead meat. You understand that?"

"Piss off asshole. Where do you think we could go? Huh? You think there's any place for us but Thorndale's. Our kind of work is pretty limited you know."

The men were both laughing now. They thought it was a great joke.

"Okay if that's the way you want it you can go back to Thorndale's ranch. Now take off your shirt and pants."

The men were swearing up a storm and refused to do it until they were looking down the barrel of a Colt revolver that seemed to appear from nowhere.

"You can take em off or start digging a grave, your choice."

"Okay, okay asshole, give us a break huh?"

"Like the break you gave Mister Bartallo? Sure I can give you a break just like you gave him and leave you in a lump right here on the porch. You---fat boy," he said pointing at the heaviest set man. "Get up. You'll be first to get a break. Let's see now, you broke the man's head didn't you? I guess it's only fair then that I break your head huh? So get up and I'll pistol whip you around a bit until you can't talk anymore and can't stand on your own. Then I'll pick the next guy. So let's get at it, okay? Everybody gets a break."

"Hold on mister we're gettin our clothes off right now. Come on take it easy huh? Hey we're sorry about that old man but he was giving us a bunch of shit and needed a little straightening out, that's all."

"Oh well if that's all it was I'll just give you a little straightening out, okay? I guess that's fair. I'm glad you clarified that for me. Come on fat boy you're first," he said, as he whipped him across the side of his head just hard enough to knock him down.

The men were shouting now to stop. They would do whatever Wolf wanted.

"I want your clothes off and I'll let you walk out of here. You're not going back to Thorndale's place. You're headed over the hill to Barnes. If I see you again anywhere in this country you're dead where you stand. You understand that?"

"Hell mister that's a long way off and without our boots and clothes we may not make it."

"Well that's the choice you're getting, so get up and get moving."

The men were limping by the time they got to the tree line and they had to climb up and over the large hill to get to Barnes. They could make it if they were smart

★ ★ ★

Everyone made it back to the house and Wolf went into the barracks where Maria was still going through everything, throwing clothes and junk into the center of the room.

"What are you doing Maria?"

"I'm throwing everything out that even reminds me of those bastards, Mister Wolf," she said, without looking up and tearing things off the heavy boarded walls.

"I'm going to burn the whole damn mess. You have no idea what we went through these last months. We're damn lucky they didn't rape us. I guess they get that in town."

"You mean these guys actually went to town?"

"Yes but only when a few of Thorndale's gang would show up to relieve them. Hell half the time we had to hide in the damn woods."

"We cut some lances and spears and they knew it so they didn't come after us. They tried one time and we sent the bastard limping back to this damn shack with a shaft through his leg. They had to take him to town for the Doc to look after him. Don't know what happened to him and don't give a damn. They never saw us. This is our country and we know it and they sure as hell don't."

Wolf smiled and said, "Well I guess that explains why you girls were left pretty much alone. They have to see a target to shoot at it."

★ ★ ★

The girls were all well-armed and Mister Bartallo was smiling from ear to ear. It was probably the best medicine he could have received when he heard the story.

Jake had been instructed to follow and guard the two men working their way up the mountain and they knew he was close behind. Jake would never let them stop to rest when he was on guard. They would either "buck up" on the trail or die.

Dinner was a happy time and all were relieved of the dangers they had been living under. They wanted to stay up all night and talk but Wolf was tired after his long day on the trail and stalking the ranch and said he was going to the bunk house to sleep.

"Mister Wolf you're not going to the bunk house. You can sleep on the couch over there if you want but your part of this family and you're staying in this house. We'll all hit the sack and you can get a good-night's sleep. Come on girls clean up and get to bed. This is going to be a wonderful night for sleeping."

"Look ladies please don't call me Mister Wolf. It's just plain Wolf, and that's really a "Nick name."

Thank you Wolf. I'm Georgiana, they call me Anna, you've

already met Maria she said with a smile, as she nodded to Maria, and then went on to name off all the girls.

"My husband's name is Pat."

★ ★ ★

Wolf went outside with a bucket of water and washed. He sat on the porch looking at the stars while the ladies were finishing up in the kitchen and going to bed.

The stars up here were as crystal clear as diamonds in the sky. The three-quarter moon lit up the whole country side.

When things quieted down in the house and Wolf was about ready to go in the door opened slowly and Maria came out in a long night gown and sat down on the porch alongside of him.

Wolf was shocked at the unpredictable attitude. She was as casual as could be. He was afraid to look directly at her.

In a low voice Maria said, "I come out here every night to look at the stars, and started pointing and naming them off."

Wolf was amazed at her knowledge of the heavens and said, "Is this for real or for pretends?"

Maria laughed and said, "no. I have a book about the stars that I sent away for several years ago. It's amazing what's out there don't you think?"

Wolf was well educated and knew a little about the stars but had little knowledge about their names.

Wolf said in a low voice, "What amazes me is that each one is a sun just like ours except for the planets that ride across the sky each night. I wonder how long it will take to understand what's out there."

Maria laughed and covered her mouth, "Not in our lifetime, Wolf. That's for sure.

"I'm going to go in now, Wolf. You can sit out here as long as you want. Good night and thanks for today."

Wolf watched as she got up. She was all woman.

★ ★ ★

Wolf was sound asleep under the blanket when he felt some one move onto the couch with him.

Without even thinking he moved to make room and then realizing what he had done he opened his eyes to see Maria curled up alongside of him.

She was facing away from him now and skootching up to him like she was going to spend the night.

Wolf looked down the hall towards the bedrooms to see if there was anyone watching and whispered, "Maria, do you know what you're doing?"

Without saying a word she took his hand and put it on her firm full breast, holding it there and nodded her head.

CHAPTER 57

Wolf heard the stirring before he was awake and opened his eyes. It was still dark but the couch was empty.

A lantern was lit in the kitchen area and Anna was starting the fire in the big cast iron stove.

"You get up early around here, Anna," he said as he dug for his watch on its rawhide lanyard.

"I like to get an early start so the girls can have breakfast as soon as they get up in the morning. It's just how I was brought up that's all."

She turned to Wolf and with a smile on her face said, "You get a good night's sleep?"

"Yes ma'am I did, thank you."

"Remember no ma'am stuff around here okay? You're part of the family now. We'd like to see a lot of you around here."

"Well they keep me really busy right now. Old Thorndale has been raising hell and doesn't like what I've been doing. He can't accept the fact that I bought these ranches and plan on running them. He thinks he can just take what he wants and he's been able to get away with that so far. The townsfolk have got to get together and do something about it."

"Not a chance, Wolf. The preacher man has tried to get the folks attention without raising too much trouble. You never know who's on Thorndale's side and you gotta be careful."

"Ya, I figured that out. He sure collected a bunch of Low-lifers for sure. I can't imagine what it's like having them around all the time."

"I've got some warm water now Wolf. You can go outside and clean up and shave with it if you want."

"That's great, thank you," he said, as he pulled on his jeans and headed into the kitchen area.

"Looks like you got a mark or two Wolf. Been a hard life so far?"

Wolf forgot to put his shirt on before he went for the water and his marked up body was obvious.

"I apologize, Anna. I should have put my shirt on."

"No apologies needed Wolf. We all bear our scars. Go get cleaned up. Maria will ride with you up to the sheep holdings and introduce you to Albert the sheepherder. He's a fine man and knows his animals and can sheer like you can't believe."

★ ★ ★

They were saddled and working their way through the tall grass and Maria was pointing out the cattle and giving a little history on most of them.

Wolf was looking around for Jake who hadn't returned as yet. He knew the dog was safe but he worried about him anyway.

★ ★ ★

Albert was camped about eight miles up the grassland canyon against a thick stand of trees.

Wolf could finally make out the man and his dogs. They were with a group of sheep that were working the grass among the trees.

Maria hadn't said a thing about last night. Just like it didn't happen so Wolf thought he'd better bring it up.

"About last night Maria. I was somewhat shocked that you showed up like you did. I mean---it was great and all, but I'm flabbergasted that you would be so bold."

Maria laughed and said, "I guess that's the Italian in me, Wolf.

We go after what we want and it's accepted by everyone. I won't come back if you don't want me to but I know what I wanted and it was a simple as that. Didn't you enjoy yourself? You certainly seemed like you did," she said with a smile looking at Wolf.

"Hell yes I enjoyed being with you. I think it's great, but what about your family? What if they catch on to what you're doing?"

"Remember what I said? I'm sure they all know where I was last night and they accept it as my choice. Hey---I'm a big girl. I can do what I want within reason, and that's within reason."

"You think your mother knows?"

"Heavens yes. I told you. She even asked me how my evening was. She knows damn well where I was. Its accepted and your accepted Wolf. It's a simple as that. If you were one of those gunslingers as you call them it would not be acceptable and it would not be allowed."

"My mother caught me looking at you right off and gave a nod of approval. You're part of the family now Wolf. Enjoy my company. When we leave Albert I'll take you to my favorite swimming hole and we can take a dip. How does that sound?" she said with a smile as she stared at Wolf.

"Damn, that sounds great Maria."

lbert turned out to be a man of few words. His eyes constantly wandered over his flock and occasionally he would whistle and motion for one of the dogs to move some sheep to another area. He was a devoted sheepherder and it was his life.

He was just the kind of man Wolf would want for the job.

Albert was happy the shooters were gone. They didn't wander out to bother him but he feared for the family and he knew old Pat was struggling.

Wolf asked in detail what was needed for the winter to protect the herd. Wolf told Albert that he expected a hard winter this year.

Albert looked Wolf in the eye at great length while Wolf was talking about it and finally said, "yes I think you may be right, Mister Wolf. I think you have that message right."

Maria was looking back and forth between the two men wondering what was going on. There was a message of some kind that passed between them and she missed it.

"Hey what's going on? What am I missing? What's all this about a bad winter coming on?"

"It's a little hard to explain Maria," Wolf responded. "I just think there's gonna be a tough winter this year. I know it's a long ways off but I just wanted to know what was necessary for a bad winter."

"You know---are the sheep sheds adequate? How much hay has to be put up? That sort of thing."

"We always have a bad winter up here Wolf."

"Not like this one I'm thinking," said Albert, as he looked up the side of the mountain.

"Grainger pass is still snowed in up there Miss Maria. It should be pretty clear by now. Not gonna be any folks going west through that pass this year I'm thinking. Yep---I think Mister Wolf got the message right."

★ ★ ★

They talked about what would be necessary and Albert said he would start working on it.

They discussed the possibilities of expanding the sheep herd and what kind of sheep Albert thought would be the best if they expanded the flock. The old man was a wizard when it came to talking sheep.

★ ★ ★

The ride into the hills to the mountain stream that they were going to swim in was nothing short of magnificent. Coming from New Orleans and traveling through deserts and plains the mountains were unbelievable and he couldn't say enough.

Maria grilled him somewhat on the bad winter thing, but Wolf didn't have a logical explanation as to why he thought it would be that way. He explained "it was just a feeling I have." He just suggested that they start cutting fire wood, to a chuckling Maria who quit laughing when she looked at Wolf and knew he was serious.

"Damn let's go swimming," she said as she got down off her gelding and tied him to a tree where he could nibble grass.

Feeling and mounting Maria in the dark was one thing but when she was completely naked she was spectacular, which brought an immediate reaction to wolf.

She looked at him and laughed and dove into the cold pool of water popping to the surface and yelled, "Come on in, Wolf".

* * *

They worked out a plan to patch up the sheep sheds and cut as much hay as possible and get it down to the winter sheep sheds. They would cut and stack as much firewood as they could.

Wolf would send a couple of men up to the "Far Away Ranch" with axes, saws and the necessary tools to work on the sheds, put up wood, and cut grass alongside the competent ladies of this ranch.

The time came when Wolf had to leave and head back to his headquarters. He had learned not to be away too long at one time.

Anything could happen.

CHAPTER 59

Wolf had been at the Swenson ranch for almost a week. His trips into town were careful and unannounced.

The carpenter he hired who had told him to go see the banker, said, "The gambling man" had passed the word.

Who the gambling man was Wolf had no clue but he was going to find out.

He was not about to step foot in the Northland bar on, or near the weekend as some of Thorndale's shooters may be there and he didn't want a conflict at this time.

He'd stepped up his practice now and got Willie to work with him on a plan he had in mind for the next, sure to come, shootout.

When he was in town he managed a regular hot bath and a visit to pastor McLeod. McLeod understood Wolf's quest and prayed for him.

It was when he was eating at the El Charro that a Wong boy came into the restaurant looking for him and said, in a low voice close to Wolf's ear, "My dad wanted me to tell you that there are some strangers coming into town and they look like real bad people, mister Wolf."

The young man was Charlie Wong and about fifteen years old and smart as a whip. He could slap his abacus board back and forth at an alarming rate and figure out the cost of things for his dad and for the Garcia's. He was friendly and sounded well educated. Far beyond what wolf had seen in other children and young people in Northland.

"Thank you Charlie. I've been meaning to ask you---do you think you could teach me how to use the abacus?"

Charlie smiled from ear to ear and said, "Sure can, Mister Wolf. Be mighty happy to. Anytime you want to start I'm ready."

"Thank you Charlie, we'll get to it pretty soon. I've got a few things I need to take care of first and thanks for the tip about the men. Tell your father also."

★ ★ ★

He made his way back to the ranch with Jake well in the lead all the way. Jake seemed to know exactly what this was all about after the last conflict.

The first thing he did was go to see Willie who had been working on the project Wolf set him on.

"How's things coming, Willie?" he asked as he entered the tool shed that had everything a horseman would need.

"I've got it pretty well figured out, Wolf but I need you to test it to see how much protection is needed."

"Ok. No time like the present. Get your stuff loaded in a buggy and I'll get a gun and ammo to test it out."

★ ★ ★

They moved well away from the ranch to a place in the trees that Wolf had set up to practice shooting "We need to see what the penetration is going to be at different distances Willie so we know how to proceed. I heard today that shooters are arriving in town so things are going to come to a head real soon. We need to finish this up. We're running out of time."

Wolf said, "We'll start at fifty feet and then back up fifty feet for each test. I'll shoot the ammo I think they'll be using and then we'll test my high-loads and see what that does."

Wolf and Willie had been working on a make-shift armor system that Wolf could wear when the time came.

They had worked out the shooting position Wolf planned on using and what armor was needed to cover vital areas. He didn't need to be completely protected, only the areas that would be exposed to the shooters.

The head couldn't be covered of course so if he got shot in the head it was all over anyway and Thorndale was back in business.

Wolf just had to choose the time and place to seek every advantage he could. He practiced daily and was very good at what he did. He just needed to control the circumstances to fit his requirements.

He'd been wearing a pull over serape kind of cover the last several times in town. It wasn't a fashion statement and was really unusual in this area but it was an attempt at getting people to see him in this outfit so when he showed up with his hidden armor trappings and arsenal, it wouldn't be so obvious.

Willie had cut and hammered old stove pipes they found into the forms they had agreed on. Now they needed to know how well it worked.

★ ★ ★

They started shooting at fifty feet using scrap metal in different assemblies. The regular .40 caliber bullet went through a single layer with no difficulty and buried itself in the tree. It was the same for two layers, but interesting enough when they added a sheepskin that had been sheered down to about one inch of wool, the penetration of the second metal later was much weaker. The sheepskin acted as a pad absorbing the force.

They worked most of the afternoon and found that at one hundred and fifty feet two layers of metal with sheepskin between and on the inside were complete protection. The bullet never got through the second layer of stove pipe. Now they just had to get it all together and maybe beef up certain areas.

Willie had hammered out some old buggy scrap metal and wove

them together like shingles that would hang around his neck against his chest on top of the regular armor.

★ ★ ★

The Swenson and Jamison ranches were getting squared away. The vegetable garden was doing well under the care of the El Charro employees who came almost every day for fresh vegetables for the restaurant.

The Swenson crew had fresh vegetables on their table every day and George was busy canning tomatoes and everything he could as they came ripe to store for winter.

There was a timber crew on each ranch cutting timber and sawing it into pieces to use in building a pole barn and the small pieces were cut for use in the iron stoves.

Wolf had rigged up a huge two man saw which he suspended one end from a rafter in the large shed and had a cutting table that he could move the logs down and cut the log to length by swinging the large saw with one hand while holding the log with the other. It was fast and clean. The saw dust that piled up was hauled to the ice house.

It was hard work but Wolf loved it. He could feel it in his chest and shoulders when he went to bed at night after a few hours of sawing wood. Willie kept the blade razor sharp and the wood was piling up in the big shed.

For some reason he had a real concern for the next winter. He didn't know the pass near the "Far Away Ranch" even existed but when the sheepherder pointed out the snow problem his concern increased and confirmed his prediction.

★ ★ ★

The three ranches were all on the alert for any unusual activity and had worked out an escape system to warn the other ranches if it came to that.

The interesting part of the new cowboys was that now that they were settled in and enjoying their work. They too were concerned about Thorndale's threats and had voiced opinions to Bobby and Wolf that they could be counted on to defend the ranch but they all hoped it wouldn't come to that.

★ ★ ★

It was a hot muggy late July day when three riders came up to the Swenson ranch where Wolf was staying.

They didn't appear to be a threat and waived their hats when they saw someone. They all had packs on their back and rolls behind their saddles. These were men on the move.

When Wolf went out on the porch as the men were closing in on the ranch house ne noticed a few of his new cowboys had moved closer to the building.

"Damn---these boys are serious," Wolf thought. He had added protection without asking for it.

The three men rode up to the porch and kept their hands on their reins or pommel at all times.

"You're Mister Wolf?" one of the boys asked.

"Yes sir, and who might you be?"

"They call me Ron, and this is Jessep and Steven. We just left the Thorndale ranch Mister Wolf and were wondering if you are still looking for cowboys?"

"We talked to Sam and he knew we were leaving and coming over here to see you and he wanted me to tell you that Thorndale has eight new men at the ranch that aren't cowboys. I don't know what you call those guys but their bad news shooters and we don't want anything to do with that outfit anymore. Hell they don't have enough cowboys to run the place and there sure as hell isn't any coming out looking for work. I think everyone knows about that place."

"Hell Missy doesn't even go out riding anymore. I think she's scared of those guys too and old Thorndale just doesn't give a shit."

"How's Willie holding up?"

Ron laughed and said, "Willie gave up being a gunslinger. I

think you taught him that lesson. Sam keeps him damn busy. Hell we're all busy now and it's gonna be worse with us gone."

"Sam said he understands and don't blame us none. He's a good man. Make you one hell of a Forman Mister Wolf."

Wolf laughed and looked the men over. "Well he knows the job is available." I've offered it to him but he's the only one that can make that decision."

"Okay boys, here's the deal if you're interested in working on my spreads."

CHAPTER 60

They were under the gun. Thorndale was serious about getting rid of Wolf and getting the ranches back. The man was obsessed.

"Bobby, I want you to go into town and talk to Tim. He knows everything that's going on in town and everything that's going to happen."

"I want to know what he knows about the new batch of shooters Thorndale has and when they go into town. We need to know the number of men. Is the town under threat etcetera, you know what I'm talking about. Check with Wong and Rodriquez. We need all the information we can get, and also talk to the banker and see what he knows. Tell them all to get word to us about any changes.

Billy and Joanna can gather a lot of info. Hell everyone talks in there. We need a pipeline to this ranch as to what's going on. I'm thinking that the Wong boy might be a good one to pass the information if he'd do it. No one would expect him to be our pipeline that's for sure, and besides he's damn smart."

"He could come out here any day to work on the garden and no one would think anything about it. I think he's a natural. Get Tim to pass the bar information to him and the others can talk to his dad or something. We need to know Bobby. Our lives depend on it."

★ ★ ★

It didn't take long for the information to start trickling back to the ranch. Charlie was a godsend. He was smart and didn't have to write things down to remember them. He was a fountain of information.

The town was in fear of Thorndale like never before. There were rumors of a couple of rapes and several beatings. People were staying home on the weekends when the men were in town and only ventured out during the week when the shooters were back at the ranch.

Thorndale was back to his old habits. Friday was his time in town and all eight of the new shooters would accompany him. They'd drink until some got sloppy drunk and then they'd raise hell with Jo's girls who mostly stayed out of sight when the men were in town as a couple of the girls were injured by the drunken shooters.

Some were even talking of leaving.

The plan was put in place for next Friday. Charlie would inform the necessary people their role to play, if any, and the time to expect wolfs arrival.

CHAPTER 61

The day arrived and Wolf didn't sleep much the night before he was going into town for hopefully the final showdown.

He knew Thorndale's shooters would be in town celebrating their arrival and their conquest of Northland. It was their town now and everyone knew it. They just had to eliminate that damn Wolf guy and that would be easy. One day they would just ride out to his ranch and shoot the whole damn mess of them.

Pastor McLeod named them properly. He called them "the devils disciples" from the pulpit, and he was probably right, Wolf thought.

What ever happened today hinged on his belief that this was what he was sent back to accomplish. This was the culmination of his quest and the redemption he felt he had been told about.

He remembered all too well the message that remained in his mind, "Only your faith and belief can protect you".

The Lord is my fortress he thought, and the homemade armor shield was going to be his fortress in the streets of Northland. He had to believe he could and would survive the day.

Willie had hammered out all the pieces and the girls had tied them to the sheepskins with heavy rawhide like shingles on a house. They moved freely as the body moved.

Everyone knew the preparation was for hope and determination. It had to work. Too much was depending on the single act.

Willie helped him dress in his new armor. He practiced kneeling like he would in the street to make sure it all fit and moved properly.

He would drop down on his left knee so his right shin and left thigh were armored. The body armor overlapped the thigh and crotch and hang to the ground.

He would put his right elbow on his right knee for stability and that hand would aim and hold the trigger down. The left hand would solidly grip over the right and the thumb of the left hand would be working the hammer. Hours of practice made it a fast, smooth and accurate combination.

He could slam six shots into a ten inch target at fifty yards in less than five seconds.

CHAPTER 62

They awaited the proper time to slip into town. The "devils disciples" would be drinking and hopefully the overabundance offered by Big Al and Jo, who would make sure they always had a bottle on their table would give Wolf an edge.

The men were impressed with their importance and accepted the liquor as a token offering of the bar to keep them as honored customers.

★ ★ ★

The time arrived and Wolf rode Blondie and Bobby drove the small freight wagon with Betz and Willie into town via a route where they would not be seen.

Blondie and the wagon were stashed behind the Chinese row houses.

Charlie Wong, who knew the plan, had his people move the wagon and horses between two of the houses where they covered them up. Blondie was taken out of sight into a tree grove behind the houses.

It was 4 o'clock in the afternoon and Wolf would start by the Chinese homes. He had paced off the distance to the bar and it was perfect for his shooting capabilities. This was his practiced distance and hopefully it would make it very difficult for the average shooter to hit the small target he was going to make and the sun was at his back.

Most of the buildings in town were between himself and the bar entrance. He was on the west side of North Street facing east. They would be a long way apart but that was to Wolf's liking.

Bobby was in place on North Street looking down the alley behind the bar as they were sure McGrath would send someone to bushwhack Wolf from behind.

Willie was at the corner by the dry goods store next to the bank where he could see the buildings across the street from where he was stationed. He wasn't a very good shot but if he fired it would sure distract whomever was trying to shoot Wolf in the street.

Betz who was now an excellent shot was on the north side of North Street against the wall of the saddle and leather shop. She would cover the buildings across the street from her which included the sheriff's office, a potential hot spot.

The signal was given to Tim to tell Thorndale Wolf would meet him in the street.

CHAPTER 63

Tim walked up to the table that Thorndale was busy cheating at cards and said, "Mister Thorndale, that Wolf guy is out in the street and said if you guys have any balls at all you come out in the street and meet him."

Tim immediately backed away from Thorndale as he knew he'd probably get hit for his announcement.

Thorndale stood up knocking his chair over and said in loud voice, "Okay boys it's time to earn your pay. That bastard is waiting for us out in the street. Let's go. Let's shoot his ass right now."

The men got to their feet and some not too steadily. They all laughed at the chance to finally meet that Wolf guy everyone was talking about.

Joanna crossed herself and signaled for the girls to get to back of the saloon.

★ ★ ★

Wolf waited in the center of the street. He had his arm under his serape with one of the long colts firmly gripped in his right hand. It was now or never.

The men straggled out of the saloon and some not too sure footed Wolf noticed.

"Lord make my fortress strong," he muttered as the men spread out across Main Street.

★ ★ ★

Thorndale was in the center of the street with his arms crossed over his chest like a baron staring at Wolf, who seemed a half mile away.

Three men had walked past Thorndale and all of them were now focusing on Wolf. The sun was in their eyes and they were all adjusting their hats. They knew the consequences of shooting into the sun. This was their business after all and they had to do the best they could.

The men mostly laughing at the ridiculous shoot out that was about to take place. Eight proven deadly shooters against one ranch hand.

"Piece of cake boys," one of the men laughed.

"One hundred dollars in gold for the first man that shoots that bastard," shouted Thorndale.

★ ★ ★

They were still moving when bobby's carbine barked.

Wolf glanced over at Bobby who was jacking in a new round.

Bobby looked over to Wolf and said, "Deputy down."

Their prediction had proven out. They probably won't be sending anymore down the alley.

When Bobby's gun barked, all the men went for their handguns and were looking all over the street to see where the shot had come from. It was a good distraction for Wolf.

The time had come.

Wolf dropped to his left knee with the long revolver in place and his elbow braced on his right leg. He'd just cut their target in half.

Bullets were whizzing through the air in a wild pattern as Wolf started his work.

Left to right.

Concentrate. Both hands were working in unison.

The third man had just dropped when Wolf thought he'd been kicked in the chest. It was then he noticed the plume of dust where the bullet had ricochet off Main Street.

The shooting had slowed considerably. The five closest to the Saloon that were all bunched up were now on the ground.

Thorndale was looking at them in absolute shock. His arms were no longer crossed on his chest but wide from his sides like he didn't know what to do.

Six went down and Wolf lowered the empty revolver to the ground with his left hand as the right pulled the other long colt out and cocked it.

Seven was reloading and eight was trying to take a two-handed well placed shot so he was the first to go down and eight's shot went well over Wolf's head.

Seven was now in a panic and just started fanning his revolver hoping to hit a live round which he found as he was toppling over.

The street was deadly quiet.

Wolf just stayed where he was with his long colt moving up and down the men that were on the ground. Thorndale hadn't moved his arms. He was looking back and forth at the eight men on the ground.

★ ★ ★

Tim, who had been watching the whole matter by peeking out over the window-sill in the saloon shouted, "Holy shit, Wolf's killed that whole damn bunch. Thorndale's the only one standing. Mother of God. That whole gang is gone. Damn. I can't believe it," he said as he turned to everyone hiding in the rear of the saloon.

Some of the patrons and several of the girls were visibly in shock.

Jo wiped her face off with a bar towel and looked at Al without saying a word.

"Sheriff, Deputy Dimwit is down in the alley and Thorndale's whole gang is down out in the street. I guess it's up to you to get the job done now, huh?" Tim said with a smile on his face looking at the Sheriff who was staring at his drink on the card table in front of him.

★ ★ ★

Wolf was not in a hurry. He knew that body shots sometimes took time to actually kill the person. There could be some still alive even though he thought he'd scored all chest shots.

He was looking up and down the street for any activity whatsoever and saw that Betz and Willie were doing the same thing.

Bobby was checking the alley behind the bar but also looking behind Wolf for anybody making an appearance there.

Wolf was in safe country in the Chinese sector so he wasn't worried about them.

He saw Wong and Rodriquez looking up and down the street as well.

They both looked at Wolf and gave a slight nod with a grin.

One of the Rodriquez kids came up and handed Jimmie a carbine and Jimmie said, "I got your back, Wolf."

★ ★ ★

Wolf to Jimmie and slowly got to his feet and stretched to get the nervous tension out.

He scanned the buildings on both sides of the street for any activity and slowly started walking to the silent Thorndale.

"Betz and Willie, keep your eyes open now. This is the time when anything can happen. Thorndale's just too complacent for some reason," Wolf said in a low voice.

Wolf slowly walked down the center of the street scanning from side to side but paying close attention to the Sheriff's office that was coming up on his right.

"Betz watch the Sheriff's office. Not all the deputies are accounted for.

"I got it," she said, with her carbine at her shoulder and pointed at the Sheriff's office.

He was adjacent to the Sheriff's office now. He was directly in front of the office when he heard Betz's carbine roar.

There was only one place to look and he saw two men on the roof of the building behind the façade. One was obviously hit and staggering when Wolf knocked down the other man who was aiming at Betz. The distraction had worked.

His second round hit the staggering man who was trying to raise his rifle and they both went rolling off the roof and hit the ground with a thud.

"Good shooting Betz," he said as she jacked in another shell.

Thorndale was anxious now and started yelling at the Sheriff to get out there and shoot this bastard, and do it now.

Thorndale was a coward and he wasn't going to take a chance of pulling his gun. He did that once so Wolf's attention was on the saloon door which was wide open.

He pulled another colt from his left side and aimed it at the left door jamb of the saloon.

McGrath was right handed he remembered when he took the man's revolver so he was going to shoot right handed.

He couldn't make it across the big open door to shoot from his left side as he'd probably be shot. He had to shoot from his right side and would expose part of his body to do so.

Wolfs revolver was cocked and aimed at the left doorjamb chest high waiting for the man to appear.

The continued taunts from Thorndale weren't helping things as far as the Sheriff was concerned.

★ ★ ★

The Sheriff got up from his table, polished off his last drink of whiskey and with a worried look on his face slowly walked to the door pulling his gun from its holster.

Thorndale made a mistake. He was looking at the open door of the saloon and quit yelling.

That meant only one thing. The Sheriff was on his way.

CHAPTER 64

Wolf now had both revolvers pointed at the left door jam. Thorndale wasn't going to do anything. He was counting on the Sheriff to get the job done.

The barrel of the Sheriff's revolver was the first thing Wolf saw. It was up against the frame of the door when Wolf pulled the trigger.

Splinters tore off the doorjamb just where the barrel appeared and the round caught the Sheriff in the left shoulder pushing him into the open doorway.

Two more rounds barked and the Sheriff was slammed back and toppled over onto the saloon floor.

Wolf swung both revolvers back to Thorndale who was in shock.

He holstered the now empty long Colt and put the other Colt in his right hand and slowly walked to within six feet of Thorndale looking the man directly in the eye.

His peripheral vision caught movement off to his left and he glanced over and saw number four trying to sit up.

Without a word he shot the man who flopped back on the ground and continued looking at Thorndale.

"You're not going to shoot a man who's not drawn his gun are you," said Thorndale grinning.

"Yes sir, I am. First I'm going to shoot your crotch off. Cock and balls gone. Then I'm going to shoot out both of your knees.

And when you're falling down I'm going to shoot out your right shoulder."

"Now if you live through that, which I hope you do, You'll live in pain every day sitting in a chair with a diaper on and eating whatever you can hold with you left hand."

"You're going to lead a miserable life. Just like that you imposed on everyone else."

"If you ever try me again or if you ever send anyone after me again I'll burn all your buildings to the ground with you in them, and scatter your livestock. The Thorndale Empire will cease to exist. You'll only be remembered as an evil old man who went to hell."

Thorndale's face was white as a sheet. He knew that what he heard was true. He was a doomed man.

★ ★ ★

People were coming out on the street now so Thorndale spoke very quietly.

I'll give you anything you want Wolf. Please, just don't do that to me."

"You're hardly worth saving Thorndale, what've you got?"

"Land, lots of it."

Wolf shook his head in wonderment and said, "I'll take everything south of the road. That's all that high country from the Jamisons' east to the Ridge Mountains. You can keep everything to the north. You don't use that country anyway and it's adjacent to my property." "Done."

"First you drop your gun belt in the street. Then you get over there to the land office right now and have the man start drawing up the papers. If you need your lawyer there you send someone for him. It's going to be done today---right now."

"I'm going to tell these people this war is over and if you hire anymore gunslingers you and your buildings are ashes. You understand that?" "Yes, I've got it."

Wolf noticed a slight shake to the man as he walked to the land office.

Charlie Wong came running up to Wolf and said, "You okay, Mister Wolf?"

I'm fine Charlie get Tim and help him round up all the gun belts and guns. Put the men's name on a piece of paper and jam it in the holster when you put the gun in there, will you?"

"Sure, but what do you want all the guns for, Mister Wolf?"

"I'm not really sure, Charlie. I just know it's important somehow.

Pastor McLeod got the message. The church bells were ringing and the people were coming out of their houses in droves.

Many were heading to the church but a lot of folks were coming out on Main Street to see the holocaust.

Wolf started shouting as loud as he could.

"People of Northland, This war is over. This town is yours. This town and you have been redeemed. Go to Church and give thanks. Get honest people to run your town and an honest Sheriff."

"This town is yours. Make the very best of it."

Wolf walked into the bar where the Sheriff was lying on the floor. He stared at the last of the "disciples of the devil" lying in a pool of blood.

The sheriff's badge had a notch knocked out by one of Wolf's bullets and he reached down and tore it off the man's shirt.

He stood up and looked at Jo who was staring at him with tears in her eyes.

"Jo, get some honest people to run this town. You know everyone. You ought to call this town Redemption I think," he said as he walked out of the saloon into a crowded street.

CPSIA information can be obtained
at www.ICGtesting.com
Printed in the USA
BVHW031046120419
545356BV00005B/41/P

9 781728 305776